My Time Again

Ian Cummins

Prologue

It's surprising just how mundane the last few hours of a person's life can be.

"I'm feeling tired, I think I'll go to bed early," Ron said, getting up from his chair and putting the newspaper into the wastepaper basket.

"Oh yes, you had that experiment today, didn't you?" Sheila replied, remembering that these events at work always made him weary. "How did it go?"

"It didn't work at all the first couple of times, but it went well enough the third time. Going through it multiple times was very tiring."

Ever since he had attended the presentation entitled Secrecy and Security, he was careful to have only the briefest of chats with his wife about his work. She respected that and did not press him any further.

"OK, I'll be up later, good night," was all she said.

It was far too early for her to even think about going to bed, but she checked up on him half an hour later, using only the light from her mobile phone in the darkened bedroom to be sure not to wake him. He was fast asleep.

When she finally went to bed a couple of hours later, she was immediately worried when seeing him in exactly the same position he had been earlier on – and decided to run the risk of waking him by touching his cheek. It was unnaturally cold. Using the training her father had given her, she felt his wrist and realised there was no pulse. But a doctor's daughter does not panic. She performed CPR whilst using her mobile phone to call first her father, and then the emergency services.

She had worried whether her and Ron moving so close to her parents would bring problems, but it never had done – and now she was only too grateful for their proximity.

Her father reached her in record time – well before the ambulance, and he immediately examined Ron. He hesitated briefly before telling her that her efforts were wasted. Ron was dead.

The only difference that resulted from her father being a qualified doctor and responding so quickly, was that the official date on Ron's death certificate was recorded as October 7th.

For all the others it was recorded as October 8th.

Chapter One – The First Term

Graham was familiar with the strange feeling that persisted for those few seconds while you passed from dream to waking. He had experienced it more frequently in the last five years than during his entire working life. Maybe it was due to the reduced stress now he had retired. Or maybe it was because he now woke when his body was ready, not when an alarm clock told him to.

But this was nothing like that. It was more like a feeling of waking from reality into a dream, and he was sure of one thing: the room in which he was waking was not his bedroom.

At the age of seventy, when you wake up in a place you do not recognise, your first thoughts are likely to be health-related. 'Have I had a heart attack or a stroke?' Graham wondered, before quickly realising that this was unlikely. There was no equipment attached to him, no medical smells, and although the room was bland and had only a chair as furniture, he was sure this was not a hospital.

Next, he wondered if he had done something stupid and ended up in a police cell. Although the room was small enough to be a prison cell, it was far too clean and comfortable. Could he possibly have had a memory lapse, wandered somewhere, and been met by strangers? He replayed his movements of the previous day. A trip up to London to meet his financial adviser for a review of his pension. Followed by a pub lunch, a couple of beers, a train ride, and a walk home from the station.

Once home, he'd pottered around for a couple of hours, made a sandwich, and watched the football on TV. After that, feeling surprisingly tired, he had gone to bed, deciding it would be a good idea to have an early night in anticipation of the big day to follow.

He was sure that was all that had happened before he went to bed and fell asleep almost immediately.

He looked around the room again – trying to make sense of things before making the big step of getting up. A distant memory stirred. The room was uncannily like his room at university all that time ago. A single room in the college halls of residence where he had lived for the first year. But the walls were bare – none of the posters he had put up to brighten and personalise the room was in evidence. Not even a timetable on the wall next to the work surface. He could see this clearly because the window above the worksurface spanned the width of the room, and the cheap unlined curtains were letting in plenty of light.

His final check before getting up was his bedside table. A slightly crumpled, half-empty Embassy cigarette packet – white with a broad red strip and not even a printed health warning – a cigarette lighter, a keyring with two keys on it, some coins, a wallet, and a watch.

The watch was not the Rolex with the chrome strap that he had left at his bedside last night. This was a Timex with a leather strap. And the coins were pre-decimal ones. The UK had decimalised its currency in February 1971, so this day that he was dreaming, or experiencing, must be before that.

He checked the contents of the wallet – an old five-pound note, three old one-pound notes, a student union membership card, and a London Underground season ticket. Its expiry date was December 31st, 1970. This, with the coins on his bedside table and the lack of decoration in the room, told him that this was very early in his first term.

He swung his legs around and sat up. This was definitely his college room – or one identical to it. For the first time, he noticed that he felt different. He could not say exactly how - but certainly different. Looking down, there was no longer a paunch above his waistline.

He walked around the unit at the head of his bed. The face that looked back at him from the mirror above the sink was his – just as it had looked fifty years ago. Thinner, younger, and with hair that was slightly longer and considerably darker.

Graham splashed some water on his face and dressed. Jeans, a T-shirt, and a jacket – the same way he had dressed for all his student life and his retired life, but never on a weekday between those two periods.

He needed to step outside the bubble of this room and confirm where – and more importantly when – he was.

He turned left, walked to the end of the corridor, and descended the three floors to the entrance of the residence hall. The clock in the lobby confirmed the time on his watch – seven-thirty.

6

Very few students were to be seen this early as he made his way up the driveway to the main road and received more confirmation that he was back in the nineteen-seventies. Every car he saw was built in the 1970s or earlier. And he thought that he had driven along this road in the 1980s and seen the parade of shops opposite the halls had been demolished to make way for the widening of London's North Circular Road. But here they all were. A dozen small shops, in plain sight.

Crossing the road, he entered the newsagent and picked up a newspaper. He was about to take one of the pound notes out of his wallet but quickly remembered that if this was the nineteen seventies, only a few pence would be needed for a newspaper.

Having paid, he walked out into the daylight and looked at the date on the top of the paper: Thursday, October 8th, 1970. The penultimate day of Freshers' Week – the introduction to university life for first-year students - and Graham's eighteenth birthday. Exactly fifty-two years earlier than the day he had expected to wake up on.

Graham walked back to his room with thoughts flooding his mind. Chiefly, how did this happen? Why? And, most important of all, what the hell am I supposed to do about it?

"If you've sent me back to stop the pandemic, you'd have done better picking a biologist. What bloody use is a mathematician?" he called out, but thankfully there was nobody to hear.

He returned to his room and put the newspaper on his work-surface unread. 'I can read about economic woe, labour unrest, and political turmoil later,' he thought. Some things did not change in fifty years and the front page of the Daily Mail was one of them.

One of his many mixed emotions and confusing feelings, he recognised as hunger. Maybe things might seem clearer, and he might even be able to fashion a plan of action after some breakfast.

He descended the stairs once more and followed the other students heading for the dining area, watching so that he could be reminded of the procedure to be followed. He picked up a tray and helped himself to some cereal and toast, then filled a cup at the coffee dispenser. The food went down well, but the coffee was as terrible as he remembered it.

Sitting alone, munching his Weetabix, there seemed to be only one immediate course of action – to go with the flow. If he really had been transplanted in time, he needed to act as if this was all normal.

He returned to his room and looked through the papers in his bag to determine his agenda for the day. The morning was filled with an overview of the Mathematics Department, and the afternoon with a (shorter) overview of the Computer Science sub-department.

He remembered that the journey from halls to the college campus took just under an hour - a ten-minute walk to the station followed by a twenty-minute ride on the London Underground, then another fifteen minutes walk to campus.

The first session was due to start at ten a.m., so, allowing that the journey might take him a little longer than normal, he set off at eight-thirty. The route was ingrained from having taken it every day for a year – a long time ago. Left outside the halls, cross the road, then take the first left down the hill to the tube station.

As he walked, he was constantly reminded that this was a different time. People were dressed more smartly – dowdier maybe, but more collars and ties were in evidence on the men and more dresses rather than trousers on the women. So many were smoking – men, mostly, but some women too – and very few people of colour were visible.

He briefly wondered if they were 'people of colour' back then (or back now). Or coloured people? Once upon a time, 'coloured' was the polite thing to say, but by 2022 it had become a racist slur. When did it change? And were black people proud to be called black or insulted by the term? He was not sure when that had changed. This would be one of many challenges in the use of his mother tongue that he would have to face.

He boarded the tube train – noticing it was the old, rounded shape – and was lucky to remember at the last moment to get into one of the two non-smoking carriages. Being stuck in a smoking carriage must have been the norm back then, but the thought revolted him now.

He passed the journey reading the adverts in the train carriage and wondering what was going to happen to him. He tried to concentrate on the here and now, making his way to the Maths department for the meeting in the main lecture theatre, attended by every first-year student.

He took copious notes during the session. Topics included the college two-semester / three-term calendar and the course unit system, which allowed students to select courses from other departments in their second year. Year one had already been planned according to the chosen course – his being combined Maths and Computer Science.

'So don't be surprised to see second-year students from other departments attending your courses,' they were told. 'They are there to improve their knowledge of maths for the betterment of mankind - and to help them pad out their degree'.

A range of other topics was covered – the building layout, lecture etiquette (being on time, keeping quiet, paying attention, and not eating, drinking, or smoking), and the tutorial system. Each student was allocated an individual staff member who would schedule a meeting with them each term to address any welfare issues.

Time was also spent on the huge importance of the 'pigeonhole' for each student, located behind the main reception. All correspondence from departmental staff – and any other department or student in the university – would be placed here. It was vital to check it at least once a day. For someone from the internet age, this method of communication seemed positively medieval – 'but it must have worked,' he thought.

By lunchtime, he was ready for a break, having been talked at for almost three hours (with only a fifteen-minute pause for another awful cup of coffee). Graham followed the crowd to the Student Union Bar and partook of the standard student lunch of a sandwich and a pint of beer.

The afternoon was more of the same. Computer Science at this university at this time meant learning how to program. And in contrast to the maths courses, passing the computer courses would depend not only on exam results but also on a final programming project.

They were told how to submit programs – which were to be input on punched cards. Students could do it themselves by booking time on the punch card machines on the top floor of the building. Or they could submit completed input sheets to the office to be converted into a stack of punched cards by the college's data entry staff. The cards and the results of the program would be returned to the student's pigeonhole.

After the lecture – interrupted for another dreadful cup of coffee – Graham returned to the halls of residence quite exhausted. He was grateful that he had an eighteen-year-old brain. His seventy-year-old one would probably have suffered an information overload long before now.

He then had to face a unique challenge. For the first time since reading the date of the newspaper that morning, he remembered that today was his birthday. He was unwinding in his room when his name was called over the PA system, announcing a phone call for him. A phone call on his birthday from his mother.

Why was this a unique challenge? Imagine being seventy years old and taking a call from someone who treats you like a child – someone who happens to have died twenty years earlier.

As he would be away at university for his birthday, his parents had taken him for a meal the week before, and the cards and presents from his relatives had been opened before he left home. So, the phone call was mostly about his mum checking he was OK. He assured her he was safe, the food was OK, his room was nice and clean and comfortable, and he had met some nice people but had not yet made any friends. He told her he would be having a beer with a couple of lads on the same corridor as himself, and that he was getting on with things. The call lasted only a few minutes.

All of which led to a train of thought about how this might all have started.

He remembered he had spoken the previous day (in his first life) with Steve, who occupied the room opposite him. Going down to the dining room together they had talked about how good the week had been with entertainment every night so far. With nothing being organised for Thursday evening, Steve had asked what his plans were, which had led to Graham revealing that it was his eighteenth birthday.

"I'd offer to buy you a beer, but my grant cheque hasn't appeared yet," Steve had replied, "so I'm afraid I'm skint."

"Let's have a beer together anyway," Graham had replied, "My treat. You can return the favour when your money arrives."

This might have been an innocuous conversation, but on the eve of Graham's seventieth birthday, Colin, his financial adviser, had asked him what his best birthday had been. Graham couldn't think of which had been his best birthday but told him that he was pretty sure that his worst birthday was his eighteenth.

"I spent the evening in the company of a guy called Steve that I hardly knew, and on top of that, I had to buy all the drinks because he had no money," had been how he'd explained it.

And now, here he was, reliving exactly that experience! He briefly wondered, while his mind was still in two places at once, so to speak, if there could be any possible connection between what he had said to Colin in his last conversation in his first life, and his recent arrival in what he was beginning to think of as a second life. But the evening meal was about to be served, and he had no further time to sit alone and idly speculate.

Having bought a few rounds of drinks, he was back to his room by eleven, still half expecting the appearance of some version of the Ghost of Christmas Past at any minute. Either that or expecting to wake up back in 2022 with the memory of an amazingly detailed dream.

He went to sleep nursing a single, worrying thought. 'How often have I said, "If I had my time again I would …"?' Well, it looks like I might have the chance to convert some of those thoughts into deeds.'

But he slept like the proverbial log and woke early the next day in the same room and same time.

Friday's agenda was a morning series of talks about the College, its history, structure, and facilities (library, bookshop, chapel, medical facilities, etc.), its place within the larger London University, and the additional opportunities and facilities this offered.

In the afternoon he was to learn all about the Students Union and to attend the "Societies Fair". This was where the various social, sporting, and political, groups within the college pitched their exciting plans to the new intake and tried to recruit new members. Graham collected all the handouts but did not sign up for any of them – even a decision about joining a society seemed to be beyond him at present.

Tired out once again, he returned to his room after the evening meal and summoned enough strength to arrange the paperwork gathered during the week and assess his situation.

Seemingly he had completed all the tasks needed: he had registered, joined the student union, collected his grant cheque, and deposited it in his bank account. Once again, he gave a silent prayer of thanks for being part of the generation that not only did not pay tuition fees but actually received a grant from the state to cover living expenses. Enough to pay for his term's fees at the halls of residence which assured him of a roof over his head for the term, two square meals a day on weekdays and three on weekends. It even stretched far enough to buy books, lunches, and other essentials.

He filed his paperwork and drew up his timetable. He then went to the Halls bar for a couple of pints and a brief chat with some fellow first-year students. It was enough to complete the day and he fell asleep minutes after turning in for the night.

He had a plan for Saturday. After breakfast, he walked to the local shops and took the opportunity to look around. Having got over the 'old-fashioned' look of all the cars, he noticed they were so much more colourful than the palette of the first part of the twenty-first century; not just pastel shades but bright reds, greens, blues, and yellows. Not a metallic grey in sight. And they were British. Hillmans, Austins, real Minis, Rovers, and Triumphs. Hardly a German, Japanese or French marque in sight – and certainly no Spanish or Korean.

His quest was for a means of making a decent cup of coffee in his room. He had no thoughts of finding a domestic coffee machine. Even the cafetiere was not yet available, at least not in a small shopping street in suburban London. He bought an electric percolator, a pound (not half a kilo) of ground coffee, and two mugs (he lived in hope of companionship). In acknowledgement of his mind being that of a septuagenarian, he also bought some plastic bags to dispose of waste coffee grounds – his eighteen-year-old self would probably have just tipped them down the sink.

He thoroughly enjoyed his first mug of coffee back in his room after lunch as he set about his 'project plan'.

He was well-equipped for the task. In his 'first life' Graham had joined the management trainee programme of a large engineering and construction company when he left University. This was comprised of a month in each of six different departments to get a good overview of the company and to arrive at a career choice that suited both him and the employer. Having enjoyed his time in the project planning department and feeling that this might prove to be an interesting and rewarding area of work, he settled there at the end of his induction.

After working in this department for ten years, reaching a junior management position, the company implemented a computerised project management system and Graham was given the role of liaison with the software company providing it. After a successful rollout of the system across the company's offices in the UK, he was then seconded to the project of implementing it in their subsidiaries in France, Germany, and Benelux.

The system had promised greater efficiency for the company and Graham helped to contribute to this at the end of his secondment. He reduced the department's headcount by one by leaving the company and becoming Installations Manager for the computer company.

He spent the next ten years installing the system at customer sites – travelling throughout the UK, Europe, and the Middle East. Eventually, the company was bought by a global computer company, where Graham worked for ten more years. He took early retirement on his sixtieth birthday and passed the last five years of his working life as admin manager for a charity – doing every task imaginable for a paltry salary but a huge sense of well-being.

Now he was creating a small project plan for a large project – the rest of his life. And his only tools were a pencil, a rubber, and a blank A4 pad. He drew a line down the centre of the paper and labelled the two columns: WORK and OTHER. He then drew three horizontal lines and labelled the sections FIRST TERM, FIRST YEAR, NEXT 2 YEARS, and BEYOND.

This would force him to plan for his unique situation– and help ensure that if there was anything he needed to do he should be aware of it.

His first entry was in the WORK column in the third horizontal section. Get Degree. This had to be a goal.

If he was to spend his life in this new plane of time, he could afford to invest the first three years in getting a degree. This was essential to reward his parents for the sacrifices they had made to get him this far. He could remember even now the pride they had shown when he got his degree the first time around and there was no way he could deprive them of that. Besides, he would need to get a job – and it would be a whole lot easier if he had the letters B. Sc. (Hons) after his name.

His mind wandered a little as he thought about how he had spent his time at university the first time around. As far as he could remember there had been a lot of sitting around talking, playing cards, drinking coffee, and listening to music. That would change now for several reasons.

He was very wary of joining in any conversations. He had noticed, overhearing conversations in the dining hall, that the whole pattern of speech seemed different from what he was accustomed to before his jump back in time. He could not quite put his finger on the difference, but it was definitely there. At first, this surprised him, but then he considered that if he took another backward step in time equal to the one that he had just taken, then he would be back at the end of the first world war. It would be natural to expect a very different style of conversation back then – so it was reasonable to expect that the everyday language of 1970 and 2022 would also be significantly different from each other.

And there were many other pitfalls in speaking with his fellow students. Apart from using unknown vocabulary – Google, Alexa, internet, cell phone, and probably several hundred other words – there was also the risk that the conversation might refer to recent events or cultural phenomena. These would be fresh in everyone else's memory, but the same memories could easily be either missing from his mind or, at best, viewed through the binoculars of fifty years. And if his vocabulary did not betray him, then his viewpoint might. After all, what eighteen-year-old wants to hear his colleague speak with the experience and attitudes of someone over fifty years older?

He realised that he was painting himself into a corner but was not too worried. He'd lived alone for the last five years since his wife had been so tragically killed. So, he was not too worried about spending time in his own company. He felt confident that the problems would shrink over time, and he would rejoin society soon enough.

Taking this train of thought a little further, he knew he would have more time on his hands. He would need some of that time to catch up with those courses which built on knowledge from the syllabus of the last years of school. He would have to re-learn stuff he'd not used in the last fifty years. But even allowing for that – he would have to find other activities to fill the time.

It was not just concern that the devil might find work for idle hands. It was more a case of too much thinking time might lead him into areas he did not want to dwell on – like the things (and people) that he had lost and would never recover. And there would be a whole string of things he might feel he had to do something about: mass murderers, preventable disasters, and so forth. He would have to think about whether he could or should change some of the bad things that were going to happen.

For now, he would just make a note in his plan 'Fill Time' in all six boxes of his project plan covering his time at university.

He also considered the degree he had achieved the first time. He had worked just hard enough to get a lower second-class honours degree (or a 2:2 – long before it got the nickname of 'a Desmond'). The minimum expected. Good enough to comfortably get the satisfactory job offer he had received – but if he had higher aspirations this time around, he should invest more of his time into studying – it might even be interesting.

So, under his previous entry of 'Get Degree,' he added '2:1 or Better'.

He refilled his coffee cup – and this prompted another chain of thought. He was likely to be tempted by other creature comforts in the coming months. His grant had been sufficient to get by on – buying books, eating lunch in the college bar, the occasional night out, and attending one or two football matches. But he was now more aware of what he might be missing – and even the act of studying more might necessitate the occasional extra book purchase.

This led him to the next entry on the plan. On the line labelled FIRST TERM line in the column headed OTHER he wrote Earn Money.

Again, his mind wandered. Surely there must be some way he could use his knowledge of the future to make money. Betting was the obvious way – but what could he bet on? He knew very little about horseracing – the main area for betting in the UK in 1970. He might remember the winner of big races like the Derby and The Grand National. But they were only two events, so this was unlikely to produce a significant income.

He knew much more about football. That would be a better avenue to pursue. Arsenal had 'done the double' – winning both the First Division and the FA Cup - in his first year at uni., hadn't they? He remembered going to a couple of their games. And he'd watched the Cup Final on TV in the residence hall with his girlfriend. He particularly remembered because it was the first live football match he had ever seen on a colour TV. Arsenal had beaten Liverpool by two goals to one.

A bet on Arsenal to win the double would certainly be a big odds bet since it had only happened once in the previous century. The odds would probably be at least fifty to one. But there were two problems. The bet would not pay out until May of the following year – and he did not have any money to bet with. And placing a large bet on a high-odds event might attract unwanted attention.

However – if they were to win the league, then they would have to win most of their games – and there were still more than thirty games to go. A bet every week would not always win but should show a clear profit. And several smaller bets would not arouse any attention. (He had already noticed that there were three betting shops in the local area and no doubt there would be a similar number at most stops on the tube line), And both Arsenal and Liverpool would win every round in the cup before the final so he could bet on that too.

So, the next entry on his plan, under the words Earn Money was Bet – Arsenal - League, Arsenal/Liverpool - Cup.

But how to raise his stake money? And the money for those little extras. He was already feeling that the silence in his room was a little oppressive. He would need to buy himself a small radio. Perhaps tomorrow, no – this was the nineteen seventies. No shops would be open on a Sunday - it would have to wait until his free afternoon on Wednesday. Another entry in the FIRST TERM box. Radio.

How to raise the money? He thought for a few minutes. He could get a job at the college bar! He had not done this in the first year of his first life because he had no previous experience. But now he could honestly state that he had many hours of bartending experience. If asked how he had acquired this experience before his eighteenth birthday (which would be illegal) he would reply that his hometown was a seaside resort and that holiday camps did not check up on employees' ages (which he knew to be true).

Another entry in the plan. Line one column one – 'College Bar Job'.

Satisfied that he had made significant progress on his plan – and having used up almost all the afternoon, Graham's Saturday was completed with an evening meal and a trip back to campus for the 'Freshers Ball' – a rock concert featuring a heavy metal band. At last, something he could really enjoy. His liking for live rock music was undimmed and he was able to unwind for the first time.

Sunday was taken up with two activities – a visit to the laundry facilities in the basement of his hall, and more importantly, buying two Sunday papers. The Sunday Times for the news, and the News of The World for an update on popular culture. He spent the rest of the day reading both from cover to cover - a habit he continued for the next few weeks to make it less likely that he would be caught out in conversation. He equipped himself with so much knowledge of current affairs and popular culture that his knowledge was more up-to-date than it had ever been. But there was another reason, hidden in the back of his mind. He was hoping to read a novelty story about someone who had found himself transported back in time.

But no such story was to be found. He appeared to be alone. 'I'm certainly having my time again!' he thought.

-

The first week of the term flew past. Graham got a job in the college bar and learned that the Wednesday and Friday lunchtime sessions were the easiest to sign up for. And Saturday evening sessions lasted six hours and were always short-staffed. So much so that the hourly rate of pay was increased by fifty percent.

By working these three unpopular shifts he could amass a staggering total of nearly four pounds a week.

Adjusting to the difference in the value of money between 1970 and 2022 was one of many difficulties Graham faced. Using the comparison of the price of a pint of beer, he was able to create a simple multiplier. Think 'times thirty' he kept telling himself. And if this did not provide enough motivation to sign up for a six-hour Saturday session he added 'remember this is for stake money – money to make more money,' to his mantra.

He found some lectures tough, particularly those which extended the A-level syllabus he had studied at school. But thankfully most lectures were on entirely new subjects, and in these modules, he was at no disadvantage to fellow students.

He bought a small radio, worked hard at his subjects, and slept well every night. He was certain that this change of life was permanent - and his fears of a visitation from the Ghost of Christmas Past receded to nil.

He visited five different betting shops on Saturday morning, placing a one-pound win bet on Arsenal in each. He recognized that this was quite a significant size of bet – using his 'times thirty' rule – significant but not so high as to raise any suspicion. But the progress he intended to make needed his bets to be this high. And frankly, he felt that betting a lesser sum – ten shillings or even five shillings like many fellow punters - was just silly.

On Saturday afternoon, he settled in his room with a pot of coffee, turned on his radio, and revisited his project plan. Although he had very little spare time in the previous week, he was sure that as time progressed, he would complete everything more quickly and have several hours spare.

He also dared to think about the general direction he was to follow in his new life. Confident that he could better his previous 2:2 degree, he planned to follow a similar strategy on his subject selection that he had followed the first time around. He would go into commerce. And to assist in this aim he intended to broaden his subject choice even more than last time. To his previous extension into Economics, he would also add some modules on Law to create as close to a Business Studies course as he could, under the cloak of a Maths degree.

But employment in a general engineering company would not be his destination in this second life. With a better degree and a lifetime of experience that should help him in interviews, he was sure that employment in the financial area of London, 'The City' as it was known, should be his destination. Where better to use his knowledge of the future to place bets than in the biggest casinos in the world – the Stock Exchanges! The financial institutions' recruitment strategy would aim to pick the best of the best - as they always did. But could he use his spare time to add any more value to his offering to them?

He tried to remember how things were when he left college the last time around. Times were pretty awful, economically. The world was reeling from recent troubles in the Middle East, petrol prices had gone through the roof and disputes between the government and the trade unions had led to the implementation of a three-day week. A great time to enter the workforce! But sarcasm apart, it could be just that. The only way that things would move from that situation was up - and he felt sure that the stock market had continued upwards almost uninterrupted from the low point of the early nineteen seventies.

But what could he offer to a potential employer to enable him to get on the first rung of that elusive ladder? He considered where the money for new investment would be coming from. Petro-dollars of course. The governments and institutions of the OPEC countries located in the middle east would be keen to invest all the extra money they were now gaining from their oil and gas deposits, wouldn't they? And the London Stock Exchange – and the companies that gave access to it would be queuing up to get their business. What if he was able to offer some relevant skills? He had visited the middle east a few times in his first life, but that was not of much value, and it would be very difficult to get that onto his CV.

'Could I use my spare time over the next three years to get some more usable skill?' he wondered, and a thought crossed his mind. Maybe I could acquire a skill that would be highly usable and marketable to companies seeking to do business with the middle east.

He opened his desk drawer and pulled out the file containing the details of the different societies that had pitched their wares the previous week. There it was: 'The Arabian Society.' Its write-up made it clear that it was open to both Arabic and non-Arabic students and aimed to improve the knowledge and awareness of the Arab World to any interested students. The name and department of the membership secretary were printed on the flyer.

He would put a note in the appropriate pigeonhole on Monday morning and seek to join and attend meetings as soon as possible. He could acquire an understanding of the area and culture. And even more importantly, the language. Surely there would be a student somewhere prepared to get paid for a couple of hours a week to teach him. Yes – that was a plan. And in the appropriate box on his project plan, he entered 'Learn Arabic?'

Hopefully, he could attend a meeting and then erase the question mark against this item. He wrote a note to the secretary and placed it in his bag to deliver on Monday morning.

The first meeting of the society took place on Monday evening, and luckily, he checked his pigeonhole before leaving college that day, or else he would have missed it. He found a note from Soraya, membership secretary of Arabsoc as it liked to be known. The first meeting would be an introduction to the group and include a presentation about the city of Petra from a visiting speaker who had visited there during the recent summer.

He attended the meeting and was fascinated by the talk on Petra – a place he had heard little about, but which was brought to life by an interesting speaker. A presentation of her visit was illustrated by slides and included coverage of the city's unique history.

After the talk, Soraya made sure to introduce herself to him and express how pleased she was to see new members. He estimated that about twenty percent of the attendees were, like himself, non-Arabic – and was not surprised when she brought the conversation around to ask his reasons for attending. He stuck with the story of being generally fascinated with the Middle East and his intention to use the unique opportunity that having so much free time at university gave him to learn about something well outside his experience.

Learning that he was a first-year student in the Maths department, she introduced him to Tariq, a fellow Maths first-year member, who had been standing on his own until she fetched him over.

"Salaam alaikum," Tariq said, extending a hand. Graham shook it - but felt that the greeting might not have been made purely as a standard opening to a conversation. He was reasonably sure that the greeting was supposed to express peace, but it seemed to be more an expression of superiority. He felt that Tariq was signifying that he was comfortable in both English and Arabic, knowing that Graham would not be. But he put the thought to the back of his mind and concentrated on his objective.

Soraya continued circulating, leaving Graham and Tariq to talk over a plastic glass of orange squash and some small curling sandwiches. Having heard his explanation of his interest to Soraya, Tariq asked him if he found it difficult to follow the parts of the talk that contained a lot of Arab names.

"Yes, I'll admit that was difficult," Graham answered. "Hopefully if I can learn a bit of the language, I'll understand a bit more of future talks."

Tariq wished him luck, "I think you'll find it difficult to pick up the language from a few talks."

"Oh, I'm hoping to go further than that. One of the things I'm hoping for is a chance to meet someone who might be willing to act as a tutor and teach me some basic Arabic."

Tariq was interested, and they continued their conversation for several more minutes. Graham expressed his idea that if someone was willing to spend a couple of hours a week teaching him – paid for at the same rate as he received for two hours of work behind the Union bar, he might make some progress. Whether it was sheer fascination, shortage of cash, or the discovery that Graham had a coffee percolator in his room that finally persuaded him – Tariq agreed to give it a try.

As neither of them participated in organised sport, the obvious time to get together was Wednesday afternoon. This was when the timetable was left empty to allow students to develop a healthy body to go with the healthy mind that the rest of the week was intended to develop.

Two days later, Tariq sat with his mug of coffee in Graham's room and expressed his total lack of any idea of how to go about this.

"Well, I've read a bit about language learning," Graham lied. He had some experience of language learning as an adult from his first life when he attended an intensive two-week German language course during his employment. He remembered the room in an office in West London, kitted out like a kindergarten with lots of objects, shapes, and colours. And the teacher pointing repeatedly at each, getting him to repeat blau, gruen, rot, gelb, and scores of other simple German words. But he could not explain that experience to his new tutor, so had invented the book-learning explanation.

"The suggestion is that you teach it in the same way that babies learn. Lots of nouns for everyday objects, body parts, and so on; colours and numbers – counting by rote; and then simple sentences. Make sense?"

Tariq agreed and they began an extensive session of Graham learning how to say nose, hands, eyes, teeth, cup, bed, book, etc. in Arabic. The only variation on the method used for babies was that Graham wrote a list of the words and their translations. He would need to revisit this list often since he was not going to receive the continual stimulation that a baby gets from its parents.

Graham broke the session into two with the serving of the second cup of coffee and asked if he could have a few minutes rest – it was a new challenge to his brain to take in so much so quickly, but he was determined to give it a good try.

He tried to engage Tariq in a little conversation but found this very difficult. They had very little in common – even the universal bonding method of football seemed to draw a blank – and moments later they resumed the session.

At the end of the two hours, Graham had a headache and several pages of common English words and their translations – some of which he could even remember.

-

Having been successful in the first Saturday's bets, Graham was able to add his winnings to the investment budget and a couple of quid from his bar wages (the rest being squandered on more coffee and a pack of shortbread biscuits). So, the next Saturday, in addition to revisiting the same betting shops as the week before, he visited the shopping centre in the suburb two tube stops away.

Apart from the essential discovery of three more betting shops, he was pleased to find a large second-hand bookshop. He was looking for a couple of paperback page-turners to be consumed during his daily tube journeys, and a children's book that contained lots of pictures of everyday objects to aid the progress of his language learning. He was sure that mixing visual images and words helped the learning process and the full complement of objects within his room had already been exhausted.

While looking through the stock he noticed a very familiar book – Casino Royale, the first James Bond book. It was such a long time since he had read it, he thought it would qualify as a page-turner but was not sure that he wanted to carry the extra weight of a hardback book. As he opened the book, a vital line caught his eye. It was a first edition – and he remembered hearing that these started to sell for quite large sums of money if they were in good condition and complete with an intact dust jacket, which this one was.

Over the coming weeks, he changed his plans and bought very few paperbacks – buying instead hardback versions of popular authors. Not only useful for passing the journey but also a good investment.

The following week, when his third betting foray took him to yet one more suburb, he found a second-hand furniture shop and spent a couple of shillings on a folding chair. His language lessons would now be more business-like – with both he and Tariq sitting on chairs, and neither needing to sit on the bed.

He also finally got round to jettisoning the half pack of Embassy cigarettes he had found when he first awoke in 1970. 'After all,' he reasoned to himself, 'if I haven't started smoking again after everything that I've been through in these two weeks, I don't think I ever will.'

-

As the term drew to a close, Graham checked his project plan one more time and was pleased to note his progress. On the financial front, he had ploughed his earnings into his betting system and finished the term twenty pounds in credit. He also had an additional twenty pounds 'invested' in one-pound bets at each betting shop on his list for Arsenal to win the league. This would secure him around fifty pounds in May.

He was also pleased with his progress in learning Arabic, and that he had not yet driven Tariq crazy with his continued repetition of keywords and phrases. Tariq and he would never be friends, but he had learned not only quite a lot of the language but also a little about the young man himself.

In one of their early sessions, Tariq stressed that family was very important in all aspects of life, and they had covered many of the words describing family relationships. He learned that Tariq's mother was Iranian, but his father was Iraqi. Hence, he was able to speak both Farsi and Arabic. Apparently, Tariq had always had a passion for language. As a small boy he had, as was the custom, accompanied his father to the mosque every week and had begun to learn the prayers by rote. But unlike most young people, Tariq was not happy with chanting meaningless words. He used his spare time to study the classic Arabic language so that he would understand what was being said. He even spoke about the joy he got from his visits to the mosque as he began to understand what was going on.

Tariq's father was a government employee in Iran, and there was a family sadness that his parents had not been blessed with any brothers and sisters for Tariq. He also seemed to have few, if any friends and was very dismissive of many of his fellow Iranian students. He was quick to express his feelings that felt they were too easily adopting western habits and attitudes and he frequently used the derogatory terms 'coconuts' or 'Bounties' (after the famous chocolate bar) when referring to them – signifying that he felt they were brown on the outside but white inside.

Unsure about how his parents would react, Graham decided not to include any information about this relationship or his progress in learning Arabic on his first visit home at the end of term.

23

He was making good progress in all the different university courses, having overcome early difficulties and he felt confident that his prospects of bettering his first-time 2:2 degree were good.

The only area that was disappointing, certainly in comparison to his first time around, was his lack of progress in making a social life. There was plenty of interaction with other students when he worked behind the bar, and both during and immediately after tutorials, but he still found it very difficult to engage in conversation. He had become more comfortable with the rhythm of speech which he had found so different at first - but was still concerned about expressing any opinions lest they sound more like those of a seventy-year-old than those of a seventeen-year-old. And he was still wary about either using a phrase that was fifty years too early or of not knowing something that any intelligent human being should know from recent experience.

But, lapsing back to his old self, which he tried to do as seldom as possible, he acknowledged that he had spent the last five years of his previous life alone. There was nothing wrong with being OK with your own company.

Any thoughts of chatting up young women – a major preoccupation from his first time around he seemed to remember – was completely out of the question. He was aware of the joke that in 1970 sex had only recently been invented – a product of the recent availability of the birth control pill and its consequent impact on society. This was still a time when unmarried couples living together was almost unknown, and 'good girls just didn't'. He had, he remembered, still been a virgin at this time in his first life and was happy to postpone any activity on changing this status for a while yet.

Strangely enough, at the end of the term when presented with the computer programming project, he remembered it from his first time. There were two choices of programs that the student could prepare. The first choice would produce a calendar for any given year. He even remembered the lecturer's joke that the program had to work for any year later than 1752 when Britain finally and fully adopted the Gregorian calendar, and the student could use his program to verify details of any year up until the one mentioned in the recent hit record – twenty-five-twenty-five.

It was a relatively straightforward task. First, a calculation to determine whether the given year was a leap year, remembering of course that a year ending in double zero was only a leap year if it was divisible by 400. Followed by a more complex calculation to determine the day on which the first of January would fall. After that, it was a matter of printing a neat layout with each month in a large-size script, and a matrix - with days as the column headings and four or five rows of ascending numbers to signify the dates.

Students taking this choice and completing the task (which is what he had done in his first life) would achieve a pass grade for the course. Those aiming to achieve higher honours or seeking to gain extra marks to make up for any shortfall elsewhere should take the second choice.

This choice would entail writing a program that commenced with the input of the league table from the first division of the English Football League, followed by the input of the results of a complete round of fixtures between the twenty-two teams. The program should then output a revised league table.

This task would involve more complex programming: storing an array of numbers, recalculating its contents, then sorting it based on the total number of points accumulated by each team. And then those teams with identical points should be sorted based on goal average (a calculation of the number of goals scored divided by the number of goals conceded).

Although Graham was a keen football fan, he had ducked this more complex task in his first life. This time he welcomed it for several reasons. Not only would it help him towards his aim of getting a better degree, but it would also take up more of his time – especially the many hours that lay before him during the three weeks of the Christmas vacation. It also kindled an idea within him of another project he might tackle later.

But for now, he made sure to pack plenty of data input sheets into his luggage for home. There would be many hours to fill during the Christmas break, and this could be a productive way of filling them.

He was not looking forward to the next three weeks. He knew he should be cherishing the chance to spend time with his parents, who (in his first life) had both died many years ago. But it would be challenging in so many ways. He had spoken to them a few times on the phone in the three months he had been away, and that had been difficult enough. Now he was facing the prospect of almost a month with them and the rest of his family.

'Thankfully, I'll have my project to occupy me,' he thought.

As it turned out, he did his very best to chat with his mum and reassure her that he was eating properly, getting enough sleep, and progressing well in all his studies. It was also good to have some real home-cooked food instead of the institutionalised fodder that formed the mainstay of his normal diet. And he was happy to talk football and drink pints with his father and help him reminisce about his brief experiences in London thirty years previously (during the war). But he continually felt awkward.

Luckily his brother and sister were both young teenagers and going through that completely normal stage of total self-obsession, so they did not bother him much. Just as well, because there was no connection between these two children and the old people that they had so recently been in his memory. Until a few weeks ago both were grandparents, and his sister, who had 'started early' as the family politely put it, and had become a grandmother in her forties, was about to become a great-grandmother.

There was no way he could accept the alternative entertainment of watching television, which is how his family, like so many others, spent most evenings. It was not just the disappointment of watching fuzzy black-and-white images on a twenty-four-inch screen. But the whole experience of watching what was new to everyone else but a repeat to him was a constant reminder that he was out of place. Listening to the radio was perfectly fine – it was so much more like background noise anyway, and the music station played the same music from the fifties, sixties, and early seventies that had remained his favourite and his choice of radio listening throughout his life. And there was no problem with going to the cinema. It was quite nice to see classic films once again on the big screen, instead of the small screen which was the only place you normally got the chance to see them. But television from fifty years ago – no thanks.

He also had little desire to get back in touch with his hometown friends. Even the first time around he remembered how quickly he had become separated from them as a result of his different experiences. He was living away from home in a university environment, while they remained at home with their parents, going to local colleges, or starting their apprenticeships.

He spent many hours during the Christmas break sitting at the dining table, planning, and writing his project. It also gave his mother something to be amazed at and to impress her coffee-morning friends with. Her son was sitting at home writing an actual computer program!

The three weeks passed soon enough, and his project was almost complete by the time he returned to college at the end of the first week of January. After a brief consultation with his tutor and a couple of runs to debug the program, it was ready to present as a completed project. But more importantly, he had also developed in his mind – and sketched out on a few sheets of paper – a further extra-curricular project that he wanted to undertake. One which could play a key part in his future life. He would speak to his tutor about this project when the idea was fully formed.

"You'd better make yourself comfortable, John, because I'm going to tell you a story. A long story. One that you'll find hard to believe – but you'll know it's true because you've been part of it. And then you and I are going to decide how to write the last chapters of it."

Chapter Two - The First Year

Graham resumed his betting project when he returned from the Christmas break. He had unfortunately missed one of the rounds of the FA Cup but was ready for the next. He knew that both Liverpool and Arsenal would win their games (as they were both destined to progress to the final), and he had a larger bankroll available for this round of betting. He had banked his grant cheque for the second term and, by delaying the payment for halls of residence, had a significant sum available.

He had expanded his weekly betting to twenty shops – at five different tube stops - by the end of the previous term. For this enlarged gamble, he visited a further twenty betting shops at the far end of the tube line and placed a pound bet on both teams in each shop.

Having sent a brief note to the college treasurer apologising for his late payment, when he collected the winnings, he paid his hall fees and increased his kitty to nearly a hundred pounds.

But his big chance to make money came when the next round of the FA Cup was drawn. In one of those ties always described as 'the romance of the FA Cup', Colchester United, a team from the lower reaches of the league was drawn to play Leeds United, currently vying for the top spot in the first division. Graham was enough of a football fan to remember it (especially as Colchester was the club nearest to his home). One of the greatest Cup upsets in history. So he was able to get odds of ten to one against Colchester in each of the forty shops on his extended list.

The real coup was when he collected his windfall from each shop. He was able to say, "Wow! What an incredible stroke of good fortune" (or words to that effect) to each betting clerk and "I'll place this unexpected windfall on another long odds bet - Arsenal to win the double this year!"

Even though Arsenal was now one of only eight teams left in the cup and was in a close contest with Leeds United for the league title, the odds against them winning both competitions were still quite high. It was a feat that had only been achieved once in the century, after all.

The completion of these bets and the ongoing bets on Arsenal and Liverpool in every round of the competition, all the way to the final, ensured that his winnings in May would total around £7,000. This might not sound like much - until you realise that its value in the year 2022 would be roughly thirty times higher.

Graham felt confident that when this happened, he would cross off the financial goal on his life project plan. He would have to wait until May, but assuming there would be no change in history between his two lives (which showed no signs of happening) he would have a healthy investment pot. He could now turn his mind to other matters, and he started by developing the idea that had come to him while completing his computer program project over Christmas.

In the middle of the second term, there was a week of very low activity. It marked the changeover from the first-semester timetable to the second, and few lectures were scheduled. It allowed students to complete projects, catch up on anything missed, and prepare for the new courses. Many students used this as a half-term break and visited home, but Graham had other plans.

It did however mark a significant milestone in the UK's history and the event helped Graham's acceptance of his new set of circumstances. In February 1971, Britain ditched its currency system involving twelve pennies to the shilling and twenty shillings to the pound. It was replaced by a decimal system of pounds and pennies - with one hundred pence (or new pence as they were initially called) to the pound.

Although this did not affect Graham any more than any other member of the public – having grown up with the old currency he was happy to move between the two systems. For example, he could work out that an item advertised with a price of 3/8 (which was always referred to as three and eight) meant three shillings and eight pence. He could convert this to a two-digit number, 38, and divide it by 2 to produce 19 – hence its price was 19 (new) pence.

But the change in currency made him feel more at ease. The presence of the old system was one of many factors that made him uncomfortable. But that was now fixed and could be added to the list of factors that were consistent between his two lives. Up until now, there had been only three that were unchanged: people spoke (mostly) the same language, Queen

Elizabeth was the head of state (until the last month of his first life), and the Rolling Stones were still on tour.

As the first step in his next project, he booked an appointment with his tutor the week before the mid-term break. After briefly discussing his progress and reassuring his tutor that everything in both his educational and personal lives was going well, he turned to the reason for his visit. He intended to make the best use of the stroke of luck that his assigned tutor was Doctor Fahd Youseff, head of the computer department.

"As you probably know," he started, "I've completed my programming project for the first semester, and I wanted to discuss with you a personal project I'd like to try." Doctor Youseff nodded and allowed him to progress.

"I have an idea of continuing from the league table project and see if I can write a program to predict football results."

His tutor smiled. "Don't tell me you want to win the football pools!"

Graham smiled in return and shook his head. "No, it's a little bit deeper than that."

The fact that Doctor Youseff knew about football pools, despite having only spent a few years in England and possessing no interest in football or betting, showed how ingrained this activity was in England in the 1970s. The National Lottery would not come into force for another twenty years, and in the meantime, 'the pools,' as they were known, filled the gap and created a national obsession.

Each week people were invited to guess which of the sixty league football games would produce a drawn result. Eight X's had to be entered onto a special coupon, and if you were lucky enough that all eight of your guesses produced a drawn result, you would get a share of the jackpot. If the number of draws was small enough, you might even win the whole jackpot and become an instant millionaire. And at that time a million pounds was a lot of money! All for an entry fee of only a few pence. No wonder millions submitted a coupon every week.

Graham continued with his explanation. "No, there's too much of an element of chance to do that. But I am aiming for financial gain."

Doctor Youseff looked puzzled but was already intrigued. "Go on," he said.

"Every mainstream newspaper has a full page every week showing the games to be played the following Saturday. It shows the recent results of the teams and a prediction for the result of the game. A lot of people pay attention to this before they decide which numbers to choose. What I'd like to do is to gather the same statistics as the newspapers do, and then use this as input to a computer program to predict the result."

"Why would you want to do that if you say the actual results are too random to predict?"

"I would like to approach the newspaper and offer them an exclusive. The first-ever computer-assisted results prediction system. More accurate than any others! I think they might pay something for that."

"And how would you go about it?"

Graham knew he had to be careful with his answer. He had to explain enough to show that he had an idea with a genuine chance of success – but not bore his tutor with too much detail.

"Well, there are six variables for each game. Firstly, the position of each team – the team at the top of the league is likely to beat a team lower down. Secondly, there's the recent form of each team – how well have they done in, say, their last four games? They might have signed a new player or appointed a new manager. This will show up after a few games and their recent form might be a lot better or a lot worse than their overall form. Thirdly, there's the home form of the home team – every team does better in home games than in away games, but the effect is more pronounced with some teams. Maybe because they have a particularly difficult ground for the away team to play on. And lastly, the away form of the away team – some teams have a certain style of play that produces better-than-average results in away games."

He checked that he had not lost the attention of Doctor Youseff before continuing. Quite the opposite, he was visibly interested. "Altogether this produces six variables that constitute the only solid information that's available – and it's how the people who prepare this page establish their prediction. What they need to do is decide how much weight to give to each of the variables. And this is where I believe a computer program will have an advantage. A computer can try hundreds of different combinations of weighting for each variable and show which one gives the best outcome. I'm sure I can produce something that is at least as accurate as their current system."

"But wouldn't you have to prove your method was much better to persuade the newspaper to use it?"

"I don't believe so. If I could show it was no worse, and that they would have the publicity advantage of the only computerised system on the market. I think they'd go for it. Promoting this will enable them to recruit more readers. So, it's got real value for them. And anyway, I'm confident I can show them a better set of predictions as well."

"Sounds feasible, but what do you want from me?" his tutor asked.

"A few things if I may. Your permission to run the program on the university computer and to use some of its storage space to keep the information from one week to the next."

"That should not be a problem – we still have plenty of space available. One of my tasks is to get other departments to use the resource more often – and to share some of the costs, of course. If I ever get so successful that we don't have enough space you might have a problem, but I think I'm a couple of years away from that. Anything else?"

"I'd like permission to ask the data entry ladies to input the data. It won't be much initially – but when I input the results for the season to date, it'll take a few hours."

"I'll need to get permission from the head of the mathematics faculty since they're his employees, but that should not be a problem. They aren't overworked."

"And I'll need help with some aspects of the program – it'll be a pretty big undertaking."

"Of course, I'll help, but I can't give you any time during college hours if it's a private project. But I'd be happy to go through it in the evening if you need help. It's quite interesting by the sound of it. Do you live in college halls?"

"Yes, why?" answered Graham fearing a change of subject.

"It's just that I live close to the halls, and I like to get home early to see my family, so if you'd be willing to come to my house in the evening…"

"Of course, not a problem," Graham answered quickly, knowing that he had already used a significant slice of time and had another issue he wanted to raise.

"Do you think the College will be OK with the publicity if I did succeed with this?" he asked.

"Now that is something I don't know. I'll have to ask."

"They do say that all publicity is good publicity, but I would understand if they thought this was too trivial a use of the college's resources."

"I'll get back to you on that issue. When do you intend to start?"

"I plan to use the break week to do most of the work."

"That seems like a good idea. I'll speak to the faculty head and make sure you're allowed to use the data entry people. Not sure how keen they'll be, though."

"Yes, I expect I'll have to invest in a couple of boxes of chocolates at some time," Graham said with a smile.

Doctor Youseff promised to confirm things as soon as he had spoken to the head of the faculty, and, true to his word, deposited a note in Graham's pigeonhole a day later. Miss Roberts had agreed to do his data input for him, but his work would have to have a lower priority than any of her other tasks.

This was excellent news. Graham had made sure to speak to the two data input staff whenever he had been handing in earlier programs and knew that Jenny Roberts was the junior of the two. He guessed her age as somewhere in her early twenties (although he found that his time shifting had made it difficult to accurately judge the age of young people). He was not surprised that she had agreed ahead of her companion, Elizabeth Kinsella, who was around fifteen years older than her and probably had more responsibilities in her private life.

He wrote a note to his tutor, thanking him for arranging the data input and asking him for a convenient day when he could consult him. He wanted help with running multiple tests and issues concerning data storage and retrieval commands. Although this had been covered in the course, he had not yet had a chance to try it for real.

On the first day of the mid-term break, Graham completed the first part of his program and after his evening meal left the residence hall for a meeting at Doctor Youseff's house. It was a fifteen-minute walk and he arrived at the house at seven pm as agreed.

They went into the back room of the house, which was used as a study. It took about an hour to get a full understanding from his tutor of what he needed to do to get the computer to store and recall his data. When he had a good grasp of the new commands and was making ready to leave, he used the opportunity to ask Doctor Youseff if he would send a letter to the newspaper on his behalf. Graham knew he would need a good way to acquire the data of all the season's results so far, as well as the weekly newspaper predictions. What better way than to ask them to participate in a university project and give him access to their archives? He volunteered to draft the letter and put it on Doctor Youseff's desk – and got the agreement he had hoped for.

As he parted company, he made the briefest acquaintance with Mrs Youseff, who had just put their child to bed and was beginning to prepare the evening meal. He was jealous of whatever was to be served – the smells of eastern spiced food reminded him of tastes he had not enjoyed for many years.

By Thursday lunchtime, Graham had written the additional commands into his program and made his way to the small office shared by Jenny and Elizabeth.

"I believe you've volunteered to do some data input for my project," he said to Jenny – although the office was so small that he was actually talking to both women at the same time.

"I don't know about volunteering, but I said I'd do it," she replied. "And I said I'd even stay an extra half hour if it would help."

"I'm very grateful", Graham said "and I hope these will help fuel you during the work", taking a pack of chocolate digestive biscuits from his bag. He had decided that a box of chocolates might seem too intimate a present, and he had never known anyone who did not like chocolate digestives.

"Thank you. What's this program all about?" she asked

"Oh, didn't Doctor Youseff explain?" he asked and got a shake of the head in response.

"Mind you, I may regret asking because you'll probably show me up if it's something really complicated, and I don't understand," Jenny continued.

"Oh no, I'm sure you'll understand. It's a program that's going to predict the scores of football matches."

"Going to win the pools, are you? Hope you'll remember us when you scoop a million from Littlewoods," Jenny laughed, and Elizabeth joined in with the joke.

"No, I don't expect so – but I'm hoping to sell the idea to a newspaper, so it could be worthwhile."

"Not much of it, is there?" Jenny said, looking at the stack of coding sheets he had put on her desk.

"That's only the test program for the first division. If I can get that working, I'm afraid there'll be a whole lot more."

"Well, I think I'll be able to get that done and submitted before I go home tonight."

Graham thanked her and said he hoped she would enjoy the biscuits. He left the office, pleased to hear that he could return the next day to see the result of the first test.

He noticed for the first time that Jenny was a very attractive young woman. Graham was trying hard to overcome certain difficulties relating to his relations with the female of the species. He had to remove all thoughts from his mind that told him he had a daughter who was older than her. This was one of the few hangovers from his previous life that he hoped to rid himself of as soon as possible. He had to get his brain to think 'I'm just past seventeen, not just touching seventy'. Otherwise, one crucial part of his new life was going to be even more difficult than it need be, and he'd stay a virgin longer than he had the first time!

By the end of the following week, he had a prototype version of his program running and had verified that Doctor Youseff had sent his letter to the Daily Mail asking for help collating the data for the project. A fortnight later he was in their Fleet Street offices for the whole weekend, sitting at a microfilm terminal printing the results and predictions for the football season to date. He talked briefly with some of the staff at the newspaper, most of whom were junior employees, dutifully completing the 'short straw' of the weekend shift. They showed little or no interest in what he was doing but did let him know the names of the key people he would need to approach when his project was ready.

He arranged another evening meeting at Doctor Youseff's house to discuss his progress. Sitting in the study, he was in the middle of receiving a warning that their session would be interrupted when there was a knock at the door, and Mrs Youseff entered, carrying their daughter.

"Pardon me, I must say goodnight to my daughter," Doctor Youseff said and took her briefly onto his lap.

Graham felt something akin to a sharp stab in his chest as he looked at the young girl. He was reminded of the granddaughter that he had last seen some six months ago. Like her, this little girl was a year, maybe fifteen months, old. Quite a beauty, with a dark complexion and dark curly hair, and a wonderful smile as she recognised her father.

"We named her Lana. It's a name that fits both our culture and yours, I believe," the proud father said.

"Yes, there was a famous actress with that name," Graham replied, his memory harking back to his childhood and Sunday afternoon TV showing black and white Lana Turner movies. "She was almost as beautiful as your daughter."

Graham smiled at the child, who looked at him with a look of interest that made him think that maybe she did not see too many strangers in her home.

It was only then that he realised that Doctor Youseff and his wife were speaking Arabic to each other. Suddenly, Graham was very pleased that one of his sessions with Tariq had covered family relationships. Turning to Mrs Youseff he said, "Ladayk aibnat Jamila," (Your daughter is very beautiful). She politely replied with a blush and a very quiet "Thank you," before she briefly said something to her husband, and left to put Lana to bed.

"Where did you learn to speak Arabic?" Doctor Youseff asked.

"It's another of my projects," Graham replied trying to be as nonchalant as possible. "One of the Iranian students is giving me lessons."

"Any particular reason you're doing that?" Doctor Youseff asked, genuinely puzzled.

"I thought it might be a useful skill to have when I leave university, and I do like to keep my mind occupied," Graham replied. He knew his explanation was feeble but did not want to explain his real reasons. He would have to work on his response for the next time his motives were examined.

Doctor Youseff was not entirely convinced with his explanation, but they returned to discussing the programming project. They worked for the next couple of hours on the details before calling it a night.

-

The first unintended consequence of his computer project emerged the following week. Graham received a note from Doctor Youseff asking if he could come to his office for a fifteen-minute conversation. Expecting to be asked for a brief update on the project, he was surprised when his tutor asked if it was OK to talk about a personal matter.

"You may have noticed that my wife doesn't speak much English," was the unusual beginning of the discussion. "I've tried to teach her, but it appears that much like learning to drive, a husband should not try to teach his wife a foreign language."

Graham was not sure where this was leading or how to respond, so he simply nodded and said "Uhuh".

"Fatemeh, my wife, was much taken with how well you dealt with our young daughter," Doctor Youseff continued, not helping Graham gain any further understanding of where he was heading.

"I have younger brothers and sisters," he replied in the hope that this would explain, whilst thinking 'I can hardly tell him that six months ago I had a granddaughter of the same age.'

"Would you consider teaching English to my wife for a couple of hours a week?" Doctor Youseff blurted out. "I would pay you a reasonable hourly amount. I understand you have a job in the college bar, and I would be happy to pay slightly more than that. And if you are unable to say yes, I can reassure you that it will in no way impact any other aspect of our relationship."

Graham sensed that his tutor was a little worried that he might have crossed some line of proprietary behaviour, so he tried to reassure him as quickly as possible.

"I'd be delighted to help your wife. We could do exactly as you ask – but may I possibly suggest an alternative arrangement?"

Doctor Youseff seemed briefly overcome with relief that he had got a positive outcome and so nodded.

"What is your suggestion?"

"As you know, I'm trying to learn Arabic. A fellow student is doing his best to help me, but if I were to spend a couple of hours a week teaching English to your wife, would she give me two hours of Arabic tuition in return? If that's not possible, I'll certainly accept your offer of paying for tuition, but if your wife agrees to this alternative, I'd be even happier".

Doctor Youseff promised to put Graham's suggestion to his wife, and they agreed that the two lessons could start at 8 pm on Wednesday and 10 am on Sunday. These times suited all parties and ensured that Doctor Youseff could take care of Lana, leaving his wife free to concentrate on learning. It would also ensure that Graham was not alone in the house with the two females of the family as this would not be appropriate. He would discover when he arrived whether Mrs Youseff had agreed to the reciprocal tuition arrangement.

Doctor Youseff asked if anything needed to be prepared for the first lesson, and Graham reassured him that he had read about the methods of adult language learning before starting with Tariq and would start with everyday objects around the house.

When he arrived at the house for the first lesson, he discovered that Mrs Youseff agreed to his suggestion and would try to teach him. It worked, and their two-hour sessions became a fixed part of his calendar. Once her shyness had been overcome, he became part of the family, and the Sunday session was extended to include him staying for lunch every week.

The meal was a vast improvement on halls of residence fare. And every week, he spent the hour between the end of the lessons and lunch teaching English nursery rhymes to Lana – much to the amusement of the child and both her parents.

The second unintended consequence of his computer project came a month later.

Having worked through all the prototypes of his program with his tutor and input the results of the season so far, they developed a set of tests to

39

try out different weightings of the input. Finally, he arrived at a set that ensured that his predictions were always as good as the ones in the paper, and usually better. The project was complete, and Graham had the opportunity to sell the idea to the publishers of the newspaper.

He updated Elizabeth and Jenny and thanked them for all the work they had put in. Although it had been Jenny that had done most of the work, he was aware that Elizabeth had also taken some of her colleague's normal workload off her shoulders, allowing her to do the input.

He now had another favour to ask Jenny.

"The newspaper has agreed to meet me next week," he told her. "I'll be preparing a flip chart pad with some diagrams to show them how it works, and there'll be a few of them at the meeting to see it. Can I be cheeky and ask you to take a day off work and come with me?"

"Me?" she asked. "What good would I be? I don't know anything about computers – or football either for that matter!"

Graham was not entirely honest in his reply to her. His life experience told him that an attractive young woman attending a meeting consisting of an all-male middle-aged audience would be of enormous benefit. But he concentrated his reply on the other half of his reason.

"I'll have my hands full showing my ideas. If they ask any questions that I can't answer, it would be good to have someone who can take notes. I'd be very grateful."

Jenny was intrigued, and would not say it, but was also quite keen on a change of surroundings for a day. It would be more interesting than keying in computer data.

"I'll ask my boss if I can have the day off," she agreed.

The following week they met a small group of people at the Daily Mail offices in Fleet Street. Graham carried a rolled-up flip chart pad and Jenny had a new notebook and pen in her handbag. The meeting went well.

Using the experience gained in his earlier life, his presentation focussed on the key benefits they would achieve: publicity, being the first to use 'modern computerised systems' to forecast football results, and the consequential increase in circulation this would bring. He gave a brief explanation of the technical aspects but concentrated on what they would get from it. He showed them his analysis of results versus predictions of the season so far – with his program being marginally ahead of the human method. And when questioned on the relatively minor advantage his system gave, he returned to the key benefit – publicity and increased circulation.

They wanted to monitor his results for the rest of the season, but he told them if they wanted this delay, he would have to offer the system to the other newspapers. He was happy to offer them a short time to think about it before he contacted anyone else - they had, after all, provided the raw data - but he could not wait long. They agreed to get back to him soon.

And Graham was delighted that his colleague (which was how he introduced Jenny) was a perfect, smiling, attractive, note-taker.

On his way back from the meeting, he listened carefully to her opinions of the men they had met – he was delighted that she had plenty to say about who she thought were the real decision-makers. Her observations of the interaction between the different men, some of which he had not noticed, could help as the negotiation progressed.

He thanked her for sacrificing a day of her holiday allowance and, in a brief lapse into his more senior role, said, "I'd like to take you out for a meal to say thank you for everything, but I expect your boyfriend would object."

If she was surprised at his offer, she did not show it. "I don't have a boyfriend right now," she replied.

"So, you could come out for a meal with me then?" he continued.

"Maybe. Where are you thinking of?"

"Well, I don't even know where you live, so I'm not sure."

"Wanstead. Have you heard of it?" she asked with a smile.

"I know it well. I pass through it every day of the week," he smiled back – it was one of the tube stops between the college and the halls of residence. He also thought 'I spend time there every Saturday morning visiting all three of the betting shops in the High Street and a second-hand bookshop,' but thought better of saying anything about that.

"If I'm not mistaken there's a steakhouse called the George in Wanstead, isn't there?" he continued.

"How do you know that?"

"That's something you'll have to get used to if you go out with me. I'm a university undergraduate and we know everything,"

"Really?"

"So, would you like me to buy you a steak at the George?" he persisted.

"Yeh, OK, I s'pose so"

They settled on Friday as a suitable day. Saturday was her night out with her girlfriends, and she had no intention of missing that, especially as the numbers attending these evenings were already dwindling as age, boyfriends, and marriage claimed their victims. She was also insistent that they met at the George, as she did not want him to collect her from home.

Graham enjoyed their evening out immensely. The menu was classic nineteen seventies steakhouse – with prawn cocktail amongst the options for a starter and black forest gateau as one of the deserts.

He let Jenny do most of the talking and learned a great deal about her. She was twenty-two and still living at home. Her father was a train driver on the London Underground and her mother, who had been a stay-at-home mum until her only child finished school, was a supervisor dinner lady in a local primary school.

Jenny had been engaged to a long-term boyfriend but had broken it off a few months ago. She had been to a secretarial college after leaving school and loved her job at the university.

She asked him about his own family, of course, and about his hopes for life after university. He was happy to tell her that he planned to get a job "in the city, working on the stock exchange" and she automatically assumed he would be programming and asked him about this. She showed serious interest in computers and asked his opinion about whether they would continue to be a part of life and whether there would always be a need for people to input data.

He was quick to reassure her that computers would become far more plentiful in the future and there would always be a need for people to put information into them. He knew he was on safe ground to talk about the forthcoming development of Visual Display Units (VDUs) to replace the punched cards and paper tape with which she was familiar.

"Think of a TV screen with a keyboard next to it, with everything you type being shown on the screen in front of you and going straight into the computer."

She was impressed. But he was surprised that she seemed to have no real plan for her life – other than getting married and having children. He tried to persuade her to think about working on her obvious interest in computers and to investigate the possibility of getting some training. But, knowing that this training would be difficult to find, he did not pursue it too far.

He persuaded her to increase her knowledge of wine. Initially, she had said that "she'd tried it a couple of times but hadn't liked it". So, he ordered a bottle of Mateus Rose, and after a brief discussion with the waiter about the correct pronunciation of 'Mateus', was pleased to note that Jenny liked it, and her drinking a couple of glasses added to the ease of their conversation.

They were still in full flow of conversation when they finished the meal and when he offered to walk her home, she accepted. After walking for a few minutes, he asked her how much further the journey would be - explaining that it was important for him to know.

"About a mile from here," she said, "Why is it so important?"

"Well, I think we have a few crucial decisions to make before we get there"

"Such as?"

"Is this going to be a one-off event, or are we going to risk going out together again?"

"If we went out again, I couldn't let you pay for everything again, you've only got a student grant and I have a pay packet. We'd have to go Dutch."

Graham smiled to himself. He hadn't heard the phrase 'going Dutch' for some considerable time. 'Do people still say it in the twenty-first century?' he wondered. 'I don't suppose it matters,' he thought, 'I'm stuck in the twentieth century, anyway'.

"Yes, I agree. If we went out it couldn't be somewhere as expensive as the George. It'd have to be somewhere much cheaper like that Chinese restaurant we passed," he suggested.

"I've never been to a Chinese restaurant. I wouldn't know what to order, or what to do with those chopstick things," she replied.

He was tempted to show surprise that she had never been to a Chinese restaurant but remembered that by the age of eighteen first time around, neither had he. And using chopsticks was very much part of the Chinese restaurant experience in the 1970s – the world had grown up beyond this by 2022.

"It's not a problem," he reassured her, "My parents have taken me a couple of times. You can order a set meal, and the waiter will show you how to use the chopsticks." And then, after a brief silence, "Does that mean you'll have a Chinese meal with me next Friday?"

She agreed, trying to act a little coyly – but they both knew they were having fun, despite being an unlikely couple.

"Do we have any other important decisions to reach, because the next turning is my street," she asked.

"Yes, one sensible one – which is whether I still have to call you Miss Roberts in front of your work colleagues."

"Oh yes – I'm not sure I'd want them to know about us going out just yet."

"That's decided then – and I'm not at all offended that you don't want them to know about us."

She looked a little worried when he said this, but then understood he was just pulling her leg.

"Any more decisions to make? This is my parents' house."

"Only one more – we need to decide how to end the evening. I was thinking of something like this," he said quickly and kissed her. He was pleased to feel her respond – as much as she probably dared to, knowing that her parents could be watching from behind the curtains. She turned, put her key into her front door, and disappeared before he could say, or do, anything more.

On his way back to the station and throughout his tube journey, he smiled more than he had at any time since the start of his second life.

The newspaper people were good to their word and called him a week later. They asked him to return for further discussions, which he took as a wonderful buying signal. Ten days later he was back in the offices of the Daily Mail and was told that they wanted to go ahead but had some lingering doubts. He suggested that they agreed to pay for it so long as the results for the rest of the season continued to prove its accuracy, and they accepted this compromise. Subject to the price being acceptable, of course. They asked him how much he was asking for the use of the program.

Graham had reckoned that a good price would be the cost of an average person's wage - £1,000 per year – but in anticipation of them haggling and beating him down, he opened with an offer of £2,000 a year. They accepted it, and Graham immediately knew he had set the price too low, but it was too late to do anything about it now.

He agreed to take Jenny for another steak dinner to celebrate. They had been steadily dating for almost a month by now, meeting not only every Friday evening but also spending Sunday afternoon together, visiting venues in the vast playground that London offered them. And Jenny had let her friends into the secret, so he was able to call her by her first name at work too.

The following Friday they watched a film at the local cinema before a late evening drink in the pub close to her home and he noticed that she seemed distracted. Their main topic of conversation had been the exciting news that her parents had booked a holiday abroad for the forthcoming summer. They had never been abroad before, and Jenny was full of the details about them getting passports, planning to get foreign currency – Pesetas for Spain – and a dozen other sub-headings to this great adventure. Graham had to bite his tongue concerning his own frequent visits to Spain and managed to mount a show of some excitement on their behalf.

As the evening progressed, he could tell that something was on her mind but was not able to find out what it was. When they reached her front door, she evaded their usual goodnight kiss, and instead opened the front door.

"Mum and dad are away tonight – they won't be back till tomorrow lunchtime. Would you like to come in?"

Of course, he would, and he told her so.

Once they were both in the front room, she asked, "Is this better than standing on the doorstep?"

"Not sure", he replied, "so far I'm down one goodnight kiss."

She came to him and gave him a long, passionate kiss.

As they separated, he asked with a smile, "Do I ravish you here on the sofa, or do I get invited to the holy of holies upstairs?"

"Can you wait five minutes before you follow me?" she responded.

"Yes - but be sure to leave the light on and the door open, I don't want to have to break it down."

Graham waited patiently for five minutes then followed her upstairs. She was already in bed, so he quickly undressed and as surreptitiously as possible, placed a pack of condoms on the bedside table, before joining her beneath the covers.

'Getting your girlfriend pregnant when you are a penniless student is daft enough. Doing it when you're also a time-traveller must surely qualify as the most idiotic thing imaginable', he thought.

The experience of having a seventy-year-old mind in an eighteen-year-old body had never been more enjoyable. He took time to make sure she was ready for every move he made – running his hands over her body, stroking, massaging, exploring, and arousing. He murmured words of admiration and encouragement, and when she was finally ready, slipped inside her and made love - slowly and gently at first, before accelerating as she encouraged him on. She came in a noisy burst of delight and surprise, and he followed seconds later.

They cuddled and soon slept. They woke in the early hours of the morning and made love again, more relaxed with each other, and again when they woke at the more normal start of the day.

He had to leave by mid-morning – in case her parents arrived earlier than their promised lunchtime ETA. They kissed one last time before confirming their meeting time and venue for Sunday afternoon.

He thought long and hard on his journey home to make sure of his feelings. He had not taken undue advantage of the situation – he'd done nothing against her will, and she did seem to have enjoyed herself. And he was reasonably sure that he had not been her 'first'. No, he had nothing to reproach himself for. But there were going to be problems ahead, he was sure of that.

They met at three the next day - a warm Sunday afternoon. Graham had taken advantage of a great deal on a cruise along the Thames. When he added up the early-booking discount, the pre-season discount, and the student discount, it was too good a price to miss! It was something they'd both looked forward to and the day was sunny enough to be on the open deck enjoying this unique view of the capital city.

Eventually, during a lapse in their conversation and a break in the commentary on the boat's speaker system, Jenny said "I really did enjoy Friday evening."

"Yes, it was a good film, wasn't it," he said and got a justifiably firm slap in response.

"You know what I mean," she said, and then, after a brief pause, "I wish we could do it more often".

"Well, we could, if you came to my place," Graham replied.

"What, spend Friday evening in your room?"

"Or Sunday afternoon. You are allowed to have sex in daylight, you know."

Another well-earned playful slap followed, but a moment later, she said, "Well, we could try, I suppose."

A week later they met at the less-than-glamorous location of the tube station close to the halls of residence. There was a frisson of excitement – they were meeting for the explicit purpose of having sex, and the special nature of the encounter was increased as Jenny was one of the very few women entering the men-only residence. They made their way to his room, where clothes were removed and the two of them squeezed into his single bed.

Later he made coffee, and both his mugs were used together for the first time other than during an Arabic lesson. After coffee, there was time for more kissing and cuddling, and what it led to – before they got dressed and he walked her home. And a new pattern for their Sunday afternoons together was set.

Their relationship continued - surviving the enforced break over the Easter vacation when Graham returned home for three weeks - and lasted well into the summer term. But he noticed an increasing feeling that Jenny was not totally happy with the way things were.

One Sunday, as she made ready to leave his room, she declined his offer of accompanying her home – it was still daylight and she told him he did not need to see her home safely. She suggested he use the time to study for the end-of-year exams that were a few weeks away.

Kissing her goodbye, he noted that she had turned down the chance to spend an additional forty-five minutes in his company - which confirmed his fears that she was unhappy with the arrangement, and possibly with the whole relationship.

The following Sunday, on their way from the tube station to his room he pretended that he had run out of coffee and asked if she would like to stop at the café, which she agreed to. It was his excuse to pointedly let her know that she did not have to come directly to his room every week. It was not that he didn't enjoy it (which he did rather a lot) but that she should not feel obligated. This seemed to reassure her but did not dispel his lingering doubts. He could tell that she was unhappy with the lack of direction in their relationship and knew all too well that there was nothing he could do.

He thought long and hard. Their Friday nights and Sunday afternoons were still fun – but she was looking for a relationship that was going somewhere, and theirs wasn't. The following week he took a drastic step.

They paused again at the café, and he told her that they would have to stop seeing each other. He blamed the imminent exams and the subsequent summer break which would separate them for months. He also reminded her that he would be in college for two more years – with no prospect of earning any money.

She had been thinking similar thoughts, but her reaction surprised him. She agreed that they had to break up – but would like to make love once last time. He could hardly believe his ears and checked that she was serious.

And so, after making love in his room one more time, she got out of bed, dressed, kissed him, said goodbye, and walked out the door. The only way he could explain her actions to himself was that this gave her the permanent memory that she had walked out on him – which she had obviously done in a physical sense, if not in a literal sense.

He was surprised at how much the breakup affected him - but was sure it had been the right thing to do. He had been mostly truthful about the reasons – not only was there no chance of their relationship going anywhere in the next couple of years, but he was also unsure if he would be ready for a full relationship even after that. Could he ever find a partner who would tolerate his unique situation?

The only way he had not been truthful was when he used the excuse of their being parted through the summer vacation. He had no intention of going home for the twelve weeks between the end of this term and the start of the new academic year. But that was not the real issue. He had done everything right in the way he had told her, hadn't he? Didn't someone once say something about 'Tell me on a Sunday?'

Thinking this to himself, he found the perfect distraction. Not being a big music fan, he hadn't thought about it before – but he was sure he could remember the words to several songs that had not yet been released. And 'Tell Me on a Sunday' was the perfect example. Unable to sleep that night, he sat at his desk and wrote down his memory of the lyrics of the song. An hour later he was sure he had them all. He even thought to himself, adjusting the line that Eric Morecambe would use to such great effect, a few years later, 'I'm sure I've got all the right words, but not necessarily in the right order.' He smiled to himself at this, and his devilish plan.

He changed only one phrase in the song, replacing 'Don't call me at three a.m. from a friend's apartment' with 'Don't leave a note in my pigeonhole in the maths department'.

The following day he saw Mike, the editor of the college student newspaper, and asked if he was looking for content for the next publication. "I'm always looking for content for the next publication" was the wearied answer.

"Well, you'll be pleased to know I've written a little piece of trivia about the breaking up of relationships," Graham told him.

"That'll be a big hit. Very popular sport at the end of the summer term – breaking up. I'm sure it'll go down a storm," Mike replied, giving his best impersonation of a world-weary newspaper editor.

Graham passed him the piece of paper containing 'his' work – in the form of a poem - with an introduction stating how appropriate this might be as so many relationships seemed to end at the end of a college year. He waved away the offer of payment for the pint he'd just pulled for Mike.

"If you're going to publish my first piece of work, then that pint's on me. Consider it my thanks for the wonderful start you've given to my literary career".

The following week he bought half a dozen copies of the student newspaper containing his poem. One copy found its way anonymously to Jenny, a couple were sent home to his mum for bragging rights, and the others were filed away. 'I wonder if I'll ever get to have fun with that in a few years when the song is released,' he said to himself. 'Should be interesting telling the author that he's copied it from a student newspaper and owes me all the royalties. Might even make myself a few quid.'

"So, what you're telling me is that there are two or three or maybe more bodies buried, or maybe cremated, with – what was that phrase you used? – oh yes, low-level electrical activity in their brains, is that right?"

"Yes. That's what has kept me awake at night these last five years."

Chapter Three - Almost a First

He had over £7,000 in his account by the time the football season ended. He made four trips to the betting shops to collect his winnings, concerned about carrying so much money – and intended now to execute his plans for investing it.

First, he arranged with a colleague to join his house-share over the summer. His landlord was happy to get a small amount of rent during the summer when he expected to get none, and so that the house would not be left empty for twelve weeks, allowed Graham to use one of the rooms for a small fee.

Despite his large bank balance, he knew he would need every penny he could lay his hands on for his plan. So, he got a job at the largest of the three betting shops in the local shopping area where the manager recognised him, having had a few conversations when taking his bets over the previous months. He was an ideal candidate for a summer temp – he understood betting, was intelligent enough to perform the calculations needed, and was not only cheap to employ, but happy to work for cash-in-hand.

He set about making his investment. He had now spent nine months in this time and could see that the obvious place to put his money was into bricks and mortar. The difference between nineteen seventies house prices and those fifty years later made this a 'no-brainer' to quote one of his most hated phrases.

He needed to find accommodation for the following year – halls of residence were open only to first- and third-year students – and he had been warned to plan as soon as possible because there was a shortage of suitable accommodation in the area. Which was the only clue he needed as to exactly how to make his investment. He was going to be a live-in landlord!

The staff at the local estate agent took some persuading that he was a real buyer, him being so young – but a well-rehearsed story that his parents wanted to buy the house as an investment convinced the agent to take him seriously.

There were plenty of properties matching his requirement – three upstairs bedrooms, and two downstairs rooms – and he was able to drive a hard bargain as a cash buyer. The agent soon found him a suitable property and the wheels were put in motion.

His work week at the betting shop was Tuesday to Saturday. He suffered immense frustration that he could not do any shopping on a Sunday, since the legislation to allow seven-day opening would not be passed for many years yet. So, he crammed everything into Monday – usually including a visit to the estate agent or solicitor and the local second-hand furniture shop to see how they were getting on with his list of requirements.

He also was able to chat with a local builder who was a frequent customer at his place of employment. He got a quote for a new kitchen and bathroom, putting locks on the bedroom doors, and giving the whole place a lick of paint. 'If I have to share a bathroom and a kitchen with strangers for the next couple of years, then at least I'll make sure they start out clean and tidy' he thought.

True enough, the purchase, legal fees, building works, appliances, furniture, and fittings took more than his total savings – and he had to rely on the good nature of the builder to wait until a week after the term started for him to complete his payment. (In his unusual position as both flatmate and landlord, he was able to insist on his tenants paying the term's rent in advance. They were all paying it out of a grant cheque that they received at the start of the term, so why not?)

It was ready on time (just) and his tenants were pleased to find everything so new. He continued with his story of the house being owned by his parents – it gave him useful protection against anyone taking advantage of his position as both landlord and fellow tenant. More than once he had to say "I've asked my parents, but they've said no."

The downstairs bedroom was rented to Tony and Andrew – who were not 'a couple', just two of his fellow undergrads who had shared a room in the halls of residence and were happy to extend the experience into the second year to save money. Graham had told them his plans, and they'd been happy to be relieved of the task of flat-hunting.

The back bedroom upstairs was rented to John and Amanda, who definitely were a couple. They initially baulked at the relatively high rental he was asking for and were not overly impressed by the new kitchen or bathroom. But when he agreed to replace the two single beds in their room with a double bed free of charge, they were sold.

As well as inventing rich parents who had lent him the money to buy the place, Graham also invented an older brother who gave him a set of guidelines for a successful student flat-share. (Whereas the rules were actually based on his own memories of the good, the bad, and the ugly parts of his experiences of flat sharing than his first life). Simple rules like each person having dedicated space in the fridge (Large fridges were not yet on the market in the UK, so Graham had installed two fridges in the kitchen to make this easier). They also agreed that each one of the five of them would be responsible for preparing the evening meal and cleaning up after it on a specific weekday. His brother's guidelines were accepted by his fellow residents and proved to be extremely useful.

The term started with the single room unlet for a week until the force of nature that was Maggie arrived. None of them had met her as she was starting the second year of an arts degree and they were all science students. Her extrovert personality was only matched by her striking appearance. A shock of natural red hair grew long, free, and extremely unkempt. It was either flowing behind her or mostly hidden by a large black felt hat. And she was always to be seen in a floor-length skirt, of which she seemed to possess one of every colour known to man.

She explained to Graham that she had intended to share a flat with some friends from her department but there had been some issues - which meant she had to change her plans at the start of the year. She was not able to share in the meal preparation rota because she did not eat meat. (He noticed that she did not use the word vegetarian and wondered if it had not yet been invented or just not yet widely circulated). She also let him know that she would spend the occasional night away at her friends' flat which was a short drive away.

The 'short drive' phrase revealed that she had a car – which was extremely unusual for a student at that time. And it was no ordinary car, of course. It was the only soft-top Morris Minor that Graham ever saw. It was dark blue, and on the rare occasion that the British weather allowed the top to be lowered, had a passing resemblance to a Victorian baby's pram.

Graham was skint. He had sunk every penny – including his grant for the next term – into the house. There had been one or two unforeseen issues with the building work which had stretched the budget to breaking point, and he had to beg a hundred-pound overdraft from his bank manager. But he was able to pay it off within a month with the advance rent from his tenants. From that point onwards he started to build his finances, and never looked back.

Life in the house passed without incident for the first term – Graham kept busy with his job behind the college bar, his session with Tariq, and the visits to Doctor and Mrs Youseff. He had kept up one visit a week during the vacation and resumed twice weekly visits at the end of November, having stopped them entirely during the month of Ramadan.

His Saturday was no longer filled with visits to betting shops, but there was food to buy, washing to do, and the paperwork and issues relating to house ownership which all combined to keep him occupied.

Graham noticed that Maggie was experiencing a few problems at the start of the second term in early January. She was spending far less time with her friends at the other flat and rarely stayed there the night. She was much quieter and was often alone in her room for the whole evening. He was concerned – he was concerned that she might be experiencing mental health problems as systems to cope with them were much less in evidence in the 1970s than they were fifty years later.

He spent a few evenings chatting with her. It turned out that quite a few things about her were different from the norm. She had taken a year off between school and university – which was nowhere near as common as it would be twenty years later. For most of that time, she had worked for her parents, who ran a small garden centre. They had helped her pass her driving test very young so that she could help with deliveries. Then for the last three months of her 'gap year' (although the term had not yet been coined), she had travelled to Italy, France, and the Netherlands, visiting art galleries and museums in preparation for her fine arts degree. On her return, she had still enough money saved to buy herself a car.

He also discovered that the reason for her less frequent visits to her friends' flat was that she had split up with her boyfriend. In fact, the reason she had abandoned staying there at the start of the year was that her original plan to share with her boyfriend had been quashed at his request as he did not yet feel ready to commit to living together.

'She should have seen this as a warning sign,' Graham thought. 'It's just not natural for a teenage guy to turn down the opportunity of sharing a bed with his girlfriend every night.' But he said nothing.

Every Sunday evening, he had the same task to perform. He would sit at the desk in his bedroom with a copy of that day's newspaper, opened at the football results page. Every result had to be entered onto a computer coding sheet, followed by the list of the following week's fixtures. About one hundred and twenty lines of code, together with instructions for it to be run with his stored program for results predictions. On Monday he would deliver the sheet to the data input team, who would enter it into the college mainframe. He would collect the output on Tuesday, check it for accuracy, and put it into an envelope to be collected by the newspaper courier that evening.

All part of his self-imposed list of tasks that helped him to keep busy and steadily build his bank balance.

On this particular Sunday evening in late January, he received a fresh reminder of the reasons for these two self-imposed objectives of building a bank balance and keeping busy. Listening to the radio in his room, he heard the breaking news of an incident in Londonderry. A protest march – part of the ongoing 'troubles' in Northern Ireland - had turned violent and casualties had resulted. Some of the protesters had been shot dead in an incident that came to be known as 'Bloody Sunday'. A stain on the reputation of the British Army, soldiers of which had fired the rounds that resulted in the deaths of fourteen unarmed civilians, and injuries to many others. As he listened to the distressing news, Graham was reminded that legal action was still taking place one month before his jump back in time. The event cast a shadow that would linger for over fifty years.

News like this – tragedies, especially those that could feasibly have been avoided – always caused problems for Graham. He knew that there was nothing he could do to prevent these events. He had felt similar thoughts the previous year when hearing of a disaster at Glasgow Ranger's football ground when sixty-six people had died.

These incidents triggered memories of others that he knew would happen and he was powerless to prevent. Multiple shootings in Dunblane, Hungerford, and Manchester – the third one being particularly poignant as one of the victims had been a work colleague of his.

He would think of the episodes with single but tragic victims like Jamie Bulger, Milly Dowler, and Maddie McCann. Some events were in his locality and so stayed in his memory – the schoolchildren killed in Soham, the multiple murders in Ipswich, and the tragedy of the Bamber family. All avoidable. And could he do anything to prevent any of them?

Or could he do anything to hinder the progress of the evil monsters that he knew were around? When did Peter Sutcliffe start his campaign of murders and attempted murders? Had Doctor Harold Shipman already begun his string of killings? Graham seemed to remember accusations that he had been killing for years before he was found out. But he knew that he could do nothing – even when Shipman had finally been arrested, many of his patients refused to believe him to be evil, even in the face of overwhelming evidence. What chance of doing anything now? And when did Fred and Rosie West get together and start their awful path of evil? These thoughts would bounce around his head and leave him saddened and frustrated.

He reminded himself that he had planned his life the best way he knew to take advantage of his knowledge and do as much good as he could. If he could accumulate enough wealth, he would be in the best position to use it to do good and to tackle evil when he was able. Wealth brought power and with it the opportunity to influence matters. Without it, he would be powerless to do anything. Remembering that aim, after several minutes of unhappy thoughts, he was able to return to his coding.

Having seen Maggie's details on a registration form when she moved in, Graham remembered that her birthday was February 14th – Valentine's Day – and wanted to forestall any problems she might have on that day. The coincidence of a birthday, Valentine's Day, and the recent loss of a boyfriend would be bad enough. Add to that the possible lack of friends to go out with on the night (since they were most likely to be going out with their boyfriends) and you would have a classic cocktail for depression.

So, he bought her a present and, when she confirmed that she was not planning to go out that evening, he presented her with a gift-wrapped package. It was something he hoped would amuse and distract, and possibly start a conversation. A cactus in a plant pot.

"I thought you could do with some company," he said. "He doesn't have a name. You'll have to choose it."

She enjoyed the joke. He had also bought a bottle of bubbly with the intention of everyone in the house sharing a toast to her birthday, but. nobody else was at home that evening and they ended up sharing it between the two of them.

At the end of the evening, Graham intended to give her a small birthday kiss on the cheek and leaned towards her. She intended to give him a small kiss to say thank you for her present, and their lips met. Two small kisses became one rather large and lengthy kiss and healthy teenage lust took over.

Moments later they were in his room, tearing clothes off each other as he heard her say the four words that any young man would want to hear at the time: "I'm on the pill."

His relationship with Maggie helped to make his second year the best of his three years at university. He and Maggie became very close and spent almost all their free time together. They agreed to have some separation – she would still visit her friends once a week, and he would continue to have his weekly session with Tariq and both his weekly visits to the Youseffs. But soon enough they agreed they would have to visit each other's parents. They went first to hers – both accepting that the moral code of the time meant they would be placed in separate rooms for both nights of their stay. And to avoid causing any unnecessary concern, they agreed that they would not let the parents know that they lived at the same address (Graham learned the address of Maggie's friends just in case).

And when they visited his parents, similar rules applied. But he also had to come up with a cover story relating to the funding of the house purchase. He invented an uncle who was the black sheep of the family who had been the real lender of the money for the house purchase – and made sure that Maggie would never mention it. As far as his parents were concerned, he was just an ordinary tenant, not a landlord.

The academic year sped past. Before they knew it, it was exam time again and they helped each other study and revise, where they could, and sympathised with each other when exams seemed harder than expected.

They agreed to stay together for the summer – it was a no-brainer as Maggie had found a job in a major museum in London. As she put it, "It pays the square root of bugger all, but the experience is invaluable and it's something that will look good on my CV."

Graham was able to pick up the same summer job in the betting shop, and they spent every spare moment together, revelling in the privacy that resulted from the other housemates all going to their respective families during the break.

At the end of the summer, Maggie told him she needed to go home to her parents for a week without him, which he readily agreed to. He needed some time alone to arrange matters to do with the house and his new course choices for the final year. But it came as a complete shock when Maggie returned and told him she wanted to end their relationship and move out.

She explained that she had not actually visited her parents but had been on some form of retreat for the previous week. She had deliberately booked this to help her to sort out her life and to plan for the vital transitional year that was imminent. This year would mark the change from her being a student to being a fully-fledged adult, and decisions had to be made about what she would take with her into the adult world - and what would be left behind.

"Graham I've loved our relationship and the time I've spent with you. You are probably the most interesting and unusual guy I'm ever likely to get close to. But be honest – you don't see us as a permanent part of your life, do you?"

He could not disagree. Despite getting very close to her for the last six months, he had at no time ever thought of telling her his one big secret. And he guessed that somehow this was something she could detect.

He had noticed the rather obvious change in her appearance that accompanied this change in her life. Her hair had been cut shorter and properly styled – he had even complimented her on it. But sadly, it appeared that he was on the list of things that would not be joining her in her adult life.

She moved out and left him scrambling to find a new tenant and placing urgent calls to the college accommodation office.

And so, his last year at university was considerably less enjoyable. He put his nose to the proverbial grindstone and concentrated his efforts on getting the best degree he could. He tried to minimise his distractions. There was always something that needed doing with the house – paperwork, bills, minor repairs, and so on. There was also the work he had to do to run his computer program every week and ensure that the output was ready for the courier to collect. He remained convinced that his skills in Arabic would be valuable – the situation in the middle east remained unstable and the nationalisation of the Iraq Petroleum Company was just one of many events that would later be seen as straws in the wind that were leading to an oil crisis. He was as determined as ever to continue with his study of Arabic and started learning to read the language as well as speak it – it was certainly a challenging diversion.

When the FA Cup Final came around, he resisted the temptation to place a bet. He was not one of those people who remember all the results of all the big games, but everyone remembered Sunderland's long-odds victory over Leeds that year. But the fear of being recognised and refused at a betting office outweighed the temptation of easy money.

He also had a quiet smile to himself at all the fuss being made in the media about the introduction of Value Added Tax to replace Purchase Tax. "Don't worry guys, you'll soon get used to it," he said aloud to the radio when he was sure nobody could hear him.

The last term of the academic year meant not only final exams but the even scarier prospect of trying to find a job. There was the 'Milk Round' where various large companies and organisations toured the universities promoting themselves as potential employers. Graham engaged in discussions with two of the major banks, both of which showed considerable interest in him as a potential employee. Graham also sought out some of the smaller companies in the financial world that were looking to employ graduates and was very much taken by one in particular.

The company was Paternoster & Co. It had originated as a stockbroker, and this was still its main business – but it was actively trying to add activities that would come to be known as 'wealth management' to its business – and it was this area that attracted Graham. He researched them and found they had also been heavily involved in the early financing of North Sea oil exploration. He felt this company, its activities, and its development strategy might be an ideal fit with his plan.

The attraction was mutual, and, following a couple of rounds of interviews, he found himself in the fortunate position of receiving job offers both from this smaller company and one of the major UK banks. He puzzled briefly over the advantages of the smaller company seeming to offer him more of what he wanted in a career, and the larger company offering a better benefits package, (particularly a fixed low-rate mortgage which he knew would be immensely valuable in the near future). After some thought, he took the obvious step and asked the smaller company if they could match the larger company's offer. They revised their offer accordingly and he accepted.

He had to negotiate the end of his agreement with the newspaper for his pools prediction program. Unfortunately, he would now neither have easy access to the university computer nor (he assumed) would he have the time to run it either. His need to end the contract put the paper in a strong negotiating position, and in the end, he had to accept a pay-off of just one year's income in return for signing over the ownership of the software he had created.

During this busy and stressful period, Graham had to confront one other decision – a decision he knew in his heart of hearts that he had already made, but wanted to mentally cross off his list, just to be sure.

In his first life, he met his wife while working at the company he had joined directly from university. They had met a year after he joined when she started her induction programme and spent the first month in his department. He needed to confirm to himself that he had decided not to contact her in his second life. Even though they had shared over thirty years until her untimely death, he just knew that trying it over again would not work. How could a relationship succeed when he knew everything about her, while she knew nothing about him? Could anyone live with someone who knew just about everything that was going to happen? Finally, there was the fact that he was now a completely different person from the one she had fallen in love with. No, his decision was the right one. He would not communicate with her in any way.

"Do you know what keeps me awake at night? A family. A son, a daughter, a daughter-in-law, a son-in-law, and four grandchildren. They were there when I went to sleep, but when I woke up, they were all gone. Completely wiped out. No longer in existence. That's what has kept me awake for the last fifty years!"

Chapter Four - The First Rungs on the Ladder

His final year of 'all work and no play' (well, almost) paid off and he achieved his goal - an upper second or 2:1 degree.

He had hoped that his hard work might have got him a first but realised that the distractions of his computer project, learning Arabic, and managing a property (as well as having a very time-consuming affair in his second year) had probably derailed that. But he still had the delight of witnessing the pride in his parents' eyes when they attended the degree presentation ceremony in late 1973 in the presence of the Vice Chancellor of the University, the Queen Mother.

By then he had been working for a couple of months in the city of London.

Paternosters was a well-respected city firm that could trace its existence back to its founding in 1823. It was one of the last independent investment banks in London, and the last to remain a private partnership. The latest (and, it later turned out, sadly the last) of the family to manage the business was Bernard Paternoster – whose vision was leading it from its sleepy state where it was best known for its illustrious clients to a place on the leading edge of the financial world.

Despite the current parlous state of the financial market in the UK, the company was still investing in youth and talent, and developing programmes and capabilities that would later lead to it being heavily involved in financing the development of the UK's North Sea Oil reserves.

Unfortunately, the offer of a low-rate mortgage that had helped him accept the job offer was conditional on him completing a three-month probation period. So, he had negotiated a deal with a developer of some new flats in an area of east London that was beginning the process of 'gentrification' and was able to rent a place with an option to buy. He had needed to move out of the student environment – and consoled himself that although he was now having to pay rent for the first time in his life, he was able to get two additional rental incomes by letting his room at the student house. He had to move closer to the job as he expected it would be demanding of his time and energy and the shorter commute would be sensible.

And he was right. He moved into a world where working long hours was the norm. And there was so much to learn. A plethora of terms, abbreviations, processes, and practices. It was challenging and demanding – just what he wanted.

Moreover, his pursuit of the Arabic language brought him an opportunity.

One October afternoon, about two months after joining the company, he was called to a meeting in the office of the senior partner. He had no idea what the reason for the meeting was, and entered a vast office, in which even the presence of a huge oak desk, well-stacked bookshelves, and a drinks cabinet thinly disguised as a globe still left copious space. He was surprised to find that the only other person present was the great man himself.

He sat on one of the large leather-covered visitors' chairs and accepted the offer of a cup of coffee, which was duly delivered by an ancient secretary a few seconds later.

"I'm told you have some skills in Arabic," was how the discussion was opened by the senior partner – a middle-aged man whose dress sense was so far behind the times that he looked like an escapee from a Charles Dickens novel.

"Yes, I learned a little while I was at university," Graham replied.

"Could you conduct a conversation in the language?" he was asked.

"Yes, a simple conversation. And I can read a little of the language. But I can't write it."

"I don't believe that will be necessary. Why did you decide to develop this skill, may I ask?"

"I thought that it might be possible that some of the Arab countries would be looking to invest in the London Stock Exchange, and if I could communicate better with them, it might be a useful skill for my employer," Graham continued.

"Well, young man, it seems that you were quite prescient. We have a meeting next week with some people from that part of the world who are looking to invest, just as you described. I must assume that we are not the only company they will be investigating as suitable partners, so your skills might be of use. Perhaps you could join us at the meeting."

Graham was mildly amused by the phrasing 'perhaps you could join us.' As if he could ever refuse.

"Certainly, sir, I'd be delighted to", he replied. (He had been warned that the senior partner expected to be called 'sir', and he had no problem in continuing the ancient practice.)

"I will get my secretary to send you the details". He was dismissed.

The meeting was a week later. There were three delegates from the potential customer, who introduced themselves with a lengthy and grand-sounding title for their enterprise. 'They've not yet developed the term Sovereign Wealth Fund, but that's what it is alright,' Graham thought.

The senior partner introduced himself to the visitors and explained that although he would, of course, be paying close attention to their requirements, their main point of contact would be Robert Ellington, one of the firm's leading fund managers, whom he introduced. Robert read out his impressive track record of fund management and then indicated Graham to introduce himself.

All he could speak of was his recent honours degree from London University, and then added, "Yumkinuni 'aydan altahaduth bibaed allughat alearabia." (I also speak a little Arabic)

The leader of the customer delegation, Abdulrahman Al-Aboud, turned to his two colleagues and spoke in Arabic, *"We must be careful. This young man can understand everything we say to each other,"* which produced some mirthless laughter.

Turning back to Graham, he continued, *"How did you learn the language? Do you have a family connection?"*

"No, I had some friends at university who taught me a little and I followed this by doing some study," Graham replied.

"Your study seems to have been successful – and hopefully will be of some use if we do business together."

And so, their dialogue ended, and the meeting reverted to the English language and Graham made no further contribution to the meeting.

As the meeting concluded, the leader spoke in Arabic again for the first time since his brief exchange at the start. Addressing his colleagues he said, "Kan hadha liqa' jayid ma sha' allah", which produced nods and affirmations of agreement from them. Turning to Graham, he continued, "'Atatalae 'iilaa liqayik 'ukhraa 'iin sha' allah," and left the room with a hint of a smile on his face.

With just the three of them now in the room, Robert asked him what had been said at the start of the meeting and Graham told him.

"And what was that at the end of the meeting?" he asked.

"He said to his colleagues that the meeting had been a very good one, by the grace of God, of course," Graham replied, "and he told me that he looks forward to meeting me again - if Allah wills it," he answered.

"Them and their bloody Allah," Robert exploded, combining his frustration at his lack of understanding with a hefty dose of prejudice.

"Well, you had better hope that 'their bloody Allah' as you put it, *does* will it," Graham replied. He knew he was being too forceful but was not happy at the stress he was being placed under and the lack of sympathy he felt he was receiving. "Because if he doesn't will it, you can be sure that nothing will happen." And then, trying to lighten the atmosphere. "And anyway, you should remember that whenever you say Hallelujah, in church or out of it, then you are saying praise be to Allah yourself."

The senior partner broke into the dialogue to dissolve any tension and ensure they were all pulling together. He congratulated Graham on helping to break the ice at the beginning and said he felt sure that he had made a valuable contribution to the success of the meeting.

A week later, there was a second 'invitation' to visit the office of the senior partner and Graham found Robert Ellington already there when he arrived. He was once again directed to one of the leather chairs and plied with a cup of coffee by the secretary.

"I've had a rather unusual communication from Mr Abdulrahman Al-Aboud," he said, directing himself to Graham. "His son is visiting London next weekend with some of his friends, and he has asked me if you could show them some of the sights."

He paused, and Graham thought he was probably expecting him to jump in and say something like "Of course, sir, I'd be delighted to do that." But he hoped to convert this opportunity into a negotiation rather than an open-ended commitment, so he said nothing. He had learned from his sales experience in his earlier life that there was nothing like the pressure of silence. 'The first one to speak loses' was a phrase he remembered hearing from a veteran salesman.

"We were rather hoping that you might be able to do this," Mister Bernard continued.

"Do you believe that it will actually help move the deal forward?" Graham asked, after the briefest of pauses, knowing the answer, but needing it to be confirmed by both the other men.

"I do believe it will," was Mr Bernard's reply, backed up by confirming nods from Mr Ellington.

"Of course, I would like to assist," he replied, "but I do need a couple of things clarified beforehand."

"And what would they be?" This time the reply came from Robert.

"Would I be expected to fund any of their activities? Buy meals, pay for drinks, that sort of thing."

"I believe we would make it clear to Mr Aboud that as a junior member of our team, you would not be expected to pay for any activities for the group. And, of course, any expenses you incur would be reimbursed by the firm," he continued, turning to his senior for a confirming nod, and at the same time answering one of Graham's intended questions.

"I also believe it might be useful for me to speak to Mr Aboud's son beforehand to find out what activities he might enjoy," he continued and was assured that this would be arranged.

"It might also be sensible for you to arrange membership for me at a casino - if my brief knowledge of young men from that part of the world is reliable. I believe membership is needed to gain admission, and gambling is one of their favourite pastimes." Graham continued and gained immediate agreement from his superiors.

"Is there anything else?" Robert asked.

"One more thing. If this is to contribute to the success of the deal, I believe it's reasonable for me to receive some reward based on the success of the deal."

Graham knew this request would be unexpected. His previous twenty-one-year-old self would never have had the nerve to make such a request – 'but that was then, and this is now,' he thought.

The two partners looked at each other and the senior took on the task of answering.

"I'm sure you are aware that it is not usual for us to give any points to a junior member of staff. You should know that success with this company does involve more than just the normal nine to five."

"Yes, I do understand – and I believe you'll find if you ask my department head that I've always contributed more than the nine-to-five, sir," Graham replied, "And isn't the company built on the principle of receiving reward for adding value?" He was, he knew, somewhat cheekily quoting words from a recent speech given by the senior partner and written up in the company newsletter.

"If I'm to give up some of my weekend, that should merit additional reward. And if this is a success, I expect that this weekend may well not be a one-off request. I believe that the middle east is known for the large size of some of the families."

Again, Graham left the silence in the room to work in his favour.

This time it was Robert who spoke first – he could see this impasse harming what was, after all, his deal.

"Mister Bernard and I will have a discussion and get back to you," he promised.

"Excellent," Graham said. "I'll look forward to hearing your answer."

A few days later his third visit to the senior partner's office took place. This time it was a one-to-one meeting and there was no coffee served.

"Mr Ellington and I have discussed the unique situation posed by our potential client and have agreed to offer you an additional reward in return for your extra-curricular activities - if the deal goes through. You will receive a quarter point on the deal, and this will carry with it two conditions. Firstly, you are to tell no other member of staff that you have received this award. This is an absolute exception to our policy, and I want to impress the importance of confidentiality."

Graham nodded his head, maintaining a suitably grave expression and hiding his delight.

"And secondly," Mister Bernard continued, "you need to understand that this reward will be added to your personal trading account. While it's technically yours to dispose of how you will, it's considered to be bad form for you to withdraw it. We expect you to invest it through the firm and to merely take out of your account any profits, leaving the capital secure."

Graham knew that profits on deals within Paternosters were expressed in 'points', referring to percentages of the value of deals. And the deal they were working on was expected to produce an investment of ten million pounds. The firm's commission on this would be two percent per annum – two hundred thousand pounds of fees. The partner on the deal would receive one or more 'points' – a point being one percent of the value of the deal in this case worth two thousand pounds.

In other words, he had just been offered a bonus of five hundred pounds a year, a quarter of his current salary.

With the expectation of more deals to follow - and possibly more involvement as he progressed his career - Graham was more than happy with this offer and was quick to say so. He expressed both his gratitude to Mister Bernard and his complete agreement with the conditions imposed. They shook hands and he left the partner's office. The following day he took a step he had been waiting to take but had felt unjustified in taking until now. He applied for one of the new-fangled things that had recently become available in the UK and a week later received his first credit card.

Using it was such fun. Watching the retailer place the card carefully in the little machine, inserting the multi-part transaction slip and cranking the handle to imprint the raised letters of the card onto the form. The cardholder was then asked to sign the document which carried handwritten details of the transaction, his signature being carefully checked against that on the back of the card. The card was then returned to the owner, while the retailer deftly separated the set of forms, throwing the single-use carbons into the bin, returning the top copy to the cardholder, and placing the other two copies (one for the retailer and one for the credit card company) into his till. Such a far cry from the touch-sensitive wireless terminals of the twenty-first century, it was like

71

participating in a cross between a retail purchase and an ancient Japanese tea-drinking ceremony.

-

Ali Aboud, the son of Abdulrahman, proved to be rather cagey when Graham telephoned him the next day. All he would express in terms of his wishes and those of his colleagues for their forthcoming trip to London was that they wanted to see the major sights and experience how English people lived their lives. He and his colleagues would attend morning prayer early on Saturday and would be ready to meet Graham around noon.

They met in the reception area of the Dorchester Hotel on Park Lane, where the young men were staying. Graham relayed back to them that their wishes were to see all the sights and he suggested that they took a sightseeing trip on a London bus – it should give them a quick overview of all the major sights and help them decide the agenda for the second day.

At first, they revelled in sitting on the open top deck of the bus – a double-decker bus was such an iconic part of the London experience, and they were pleased to experience it. But despite the thick jackets they were all wearing, they soon found a bright British October day to be a little too chilly, and after getting off to take the obligatory photos in front of Big Ben, the rest of their journey took place in the comparative warmth of the lower deck.

As the afternoon wore on, they began to realise that Graham was a guide and not a chaperone. They opened up a little more and told him some of the things they most wanted to see.

The recorded commentary as they passed the Tower of London seemed to grab their attention. Graham was not sure whether it was just the historical detail, or that this was where English rulers once arranged for their opponents to be beheaded, that grabbed their interest. It was rapidly decided that a visit should form part of the itinerary for the following day.

At the end of the tour, in response to how they wanted to spend the evening, they replied that they wanted a 'typical English meal'. Resisting the urge to inflict fish and chips on them, Graham suggested a restaurant he knew in Chelsea that specialised in 'English Cuisine', and they reserved a table – giving themselves a couple of hours break to freshen up.

Over dinner, their relationship warmed further, and they admitted that they would like to visit an English pub – an institution of which they had heard so much. Graham asked them about the contradiction between this and his understanding of their religion's ban on alcohol. They implied that there could be an exemption if it was part of the overall tourist experience – and made sure that this was only on the condition that this part of the itinerary was not reported back to Graham's business contacts, which of course he was quick to assure them would be the case. He suggested that they have lunch the following day in a riverside pub – a traditional Sunday Lunch with a traditional pint of English beer.

This allowed him to ask about one of the other activities he understood was forbidden – namely gambling. In response, they asked if he could also include this on the plans and exclude it from any report he gave. He stole the saying from another famous venue and told them that whatever happened in London stayed in London – which brought a healthy laugh from all.

And so, they visited the casino as the last stop on their schedule for the day. It was rapidly apparent that for some of them, this was not their first visit to such an establishment, and they settled down for a session at the roulette wheel.

Having abstained from drinking alcohol for the whole day, Graham asked them if they would be OK with him leaving them for a while so that he could have a drink at the bar, and they had no problem agreeing.

He joined the only other guest sitting at the bar and they fell into conversation. His bar friend told him that he too was here on a work-related social event, but that his luck had not been so good, so he was nursing a drink while his colleagues continued losing their money.

His new-found friend was of average height with a stocky but muscular build that indicated time spent in a gym or some similar fitness training. His prominent eyebrows spoke of scar tissue from either boxing or rugby, and his slightly posh voice covering a regional accent Graham could not quite discern, all indicated a public-school upbringing.

He accepted the offer of a drink and introduced himself as John Bishop. Graham smiled, thinking that his new colleague bore no resemblance to the lanky Liverpudlian comedian and chat show host that he associated with the name.

"Something funny?" John asked him.

"Don't suppose they see too many bishops in here," Graham replied, and John laughed his agreement.

They chatted for a few minutes about nothing in particular and parted when the drinks were finished, Graham reuniting with his charges and watching them enjoy another hour at the table before finally boarding taxis for the journey home.

By the end of the following day, after lunch and an afternoon at the Tower, he felt satisfied that he had completed his business mission – the young men gushing with praise at how he had looked after them and had filled their trip with everything they had hoped for. It might even have laid the foundations for friendship with some of them.

He hoped the positive feedback would be relayed to their parents, as the next meeting with Mister Aboud senior and his colleagues was planned a week later when Robert Ellington was due to present Paternoster's proposals. Graham's request for a copy of the proposal before the meeting was grudgingly complied with, and a copy landed on his desk just before five pm on the day before the meeting. He asked one of the secretaries for a favour – if he was to make any comments on the proposal, he would need her to type his suggestions first thing the following morning. He was pleased and relieved when she agreed to come in early.

Strict company security procedures meant that he was not able to take the report home with him. So, he had to stay at his desk late into the evening, reading the report and writing three suggestions for additional paragraphs. He cursed the absence of laptops and the internet (for the first, but not the last time in this rerun of his life), which necessitated his reliance on the secretary arriving early the next day. Thankfully she was true to her word, and his memo including the suggestions was on the desks of both Mr Bernard and Robert Ellington when they arrived for work at nine.

A phone call asking him to meet with them immediately followed.

"I like your first suggestion," Mr Bernard said. "We should make a point of stating that we will show sensitivity to their culture and not invest in any company which makes any significant part of its earnings from the sale of alcoholic beverages, nor any that is involved in betting. That's good, you should include that Robert".

Robert Ellington tried hard to show magnanimity and to conceal the fact that he had delivered the report so late to Graham.

"But what's this second suggestion? We should acknowledge their greater understanding of their regional area and therefore we will not invest in any company that has significant interests in or is controlled or managed by any country in the middle east. Why would we do that?"

"It's a way of saying that we will not invest in any Israeli company without actually stating it, sir. It will please our potential customers, but should it ever become public knowledge, this choice of wording should not cause us any problems." Graham replied.

The two senior men accepted the suggestion as it did not seem to impose any restrictions on what they would probably do anyway.

They were less sure about his third recommendation. He noticed that the report ended by stating that their offer for the investment of this tranche of money was solely in the form of stocks and shares – their core expertise. They would spread the risk by investing in markets all around the world but would not invest in any other form of asset. Graham suggested that they extend this to state that they would consider a broader spread of investment – into areas such as property – if further investment advice was sought.

When asked to justify this, he was on shaky ground – being only able to state that he thought that these clients would be very positive about investing in tangible assets. Moreover, if Paternosters did not offer them this class of investment, they might go elsewhere for advice and partnerships. He was not sure whether the opposition to this suggestion was genuinely rooted in their stated lack of skills and experience in this area, or out of a fear of parts of the physical infrastructure of London passing into foreign ownership.

This suggestion was not accepted. 'You're going to have to get used to it,' he thought to himself. 'I know I'm right – they'll be buying up chunks of this city before you know it, but I only know this because I've already seen it. Sometimes I can't show you that I know what's going to happen - without telling you that I know what's going to happen," but he did not voice his opinion.

And the deal was done! The next time Graham visited the senior partner's office was for a celebratory glass of bubbly with Mr Bernard and Robert a week later. Their toast was, of course, to this being the first of many. As they finished their brief celebratory drink and left the office, Robert Ellington spoke briefly to him.

"I'm sorry I was a little late in delivering that report to you – it won't happen again."

"No problem – all's well that ends well as I believe someone once said. Next time I'll make my suggestions just to you so that you can incorporate them before he" Graham nodded his head towards the door of Mister Bernard's office, "gets to see it. OK?"

"Yes, thanks – and you can call me Bob – everyone else does."

This last comment was music to Graham's ears. In a world where methods of addressing a colleague were often the most significant indicator of status, he had just received a promotion. It had no monetary value, but Graham appreciated its true worth.

His remark that his services as a tour guide would not be a one-off experience also proved to be correct. A month later he was contacted (via the senior partner) by another of the negotiating party who also had a son planning a visit to London.

This time his conversation with his potential visitor was less guarded. "Ali told us what a great time you organised for him and his friends. Can you do the same for us?" was a simple way of summarising the conversation, and that is what Graham did.

The only surprise over the two days of the tour was that he once again bumped into John Bishop at the bar in the casino. It appeared that John's boss thought that team-building days should occur more often. John, though, was less than delighted but had to go along for the sake of team spirit. He asked what Graham was up to and gave his sympathy to a fellow sufferer of weekends lost to office politics.

Graham's real surprise came when John rang him at the office a few days later. "I've been chatting to my boss about our conversations, and he'd like to meet you. He thinks that there are some ways we might be able to help each other, and he's prepared to buy both of us a good lunch if you could take the time out," was the proposal put to him over the phone. Graham seldom took a full lunch hour and had no problem checking with his immediate superior.

"A friend of mine who works in the civil service has asked to chat with me and says it might be good for business, you don't mind if I have a long lunch for once?" It was not a problem, Graham always put in more than the required hours.

The lunch took place at Simpson's in the Strand. John introduced his boss over pre-lunch drinks, only ever referring to him as boss, so Graham never got to find out his name. They introduced Graham to the unique tradition of Simpson's basement bar: cold draft Bass, drawn straight from the barrel and served in silver tankards. He found it thoroughly enjoyable and risked using the word 'morish' which neither of his companions had heard before and assumed to be city slang.

John's boss explained that he headed up a special department in the Foreign Office that dealt with furthering British business interests in the Middle East. He had been most interested in John's description of Graham's work and was sure they could achieve more by working together than separately.

The pitch was put to Graham carefully, slowly, and highly effectively. They could feed business intelligence to him and he to them. The information they could give him might be sporadic, but of high value when it was available, whereas he would provide them with a more consistent feed of more general information. Nothing confidential, of course, nor would they want him to reveal anything potentially harmful to his employers or his customers. Just the kind of general tittle-tattle and gossip that his clients might recount to him about their home countries. Potentially it might be very valuable to the Foreign Office in building a picture of what was going on out there. After all, it was so difficult to get any reliable information on who was up and who was down, and the importance of family was just so huge.

They offered a current example of what they could do for him. A large government construction contract was due to be announced in the next few days, and they knew which of the two firms that had bid for it would be successful. John passed Graham a sealed envelope and told him he could take it as a sign of their good faith. What they wanted in return would be a report from him whenever he could give them a page of information that he was hearing from his contacts. They appreciated this would be taking his valuable time, and, stressing once again that he need never breach any confidence, they would be prepared to deposit a hundred pounds into his bank account (which would of course be tax-free) whenever he sent them such a report. They thought it could be every month or so - that sort of frequency.

Graham asked if he could have some time to think it over, and of course, they said he could – John would ring him in a week – and he could certainly take the envelope with him anyway.

After the longest lunch break of his life, Graham returned to his office, opened the envelope, and read the name of a well-known building company. He decided to talk things over with his boss, and, in the privacy of his office, gave him a very slimmed-down version of the conversation, omitting the exact nature of his proposed cooperation, but making sure to give the information about the construction project.

The way that his boss snatched up this information – he was more aware of the competitive bidding than Graham had been – and his obvious intention of using the information for gain - helped Graham to make his decision. The attitude of his boss could be expressed as 'I can understand why you're doing that – thanks for letting me know.' There was no hint of 'This might not be the right thing you are doing,' or 'Are you sure you plan to go ahead?'

Graham reconsidered the proposal. His plan was all about building his fortune so that he could use it to help others, wasn't it? And this exchange of information would help him grow his capital base more quickly – both from the regular payments and from converting the information he received in return.

He had not yet decided how to invest the five hundred pounds in his capital account from his points on the middle east deal. So, he decided to invest it in shares in the winning construction company. Their twenty-five percent leap in value when the contract was announced a few days later was the final convincing factor. He would start reporting to John and so called him the following day to let him know, using a public phone box to make the call, a fact that seemed to amuse John.

On the phone call, he made one additional request – asking that the hundred-pound fee be index linked to the rate of inflation He knew that inflation was likely to be running at twenty percent for the next few years and would rapidly erode the value of the payment. But he gave the reason that it would be better if the amount varied every month – just in case anyone ever looked into his accounts. John agreed.

He produced his first report a week later – exercising great caution in both its content and delivery. He acquired a second-hand typewriter and decided to keep a carbon copy of the report. He also wanted to minimise the chance of his fingerprints or DNA being gifted to them, even though he did feel a little silly typing the report and addressing the envelope wearing Marigold gloves.

The report contained the gossip from his recent weekend as an acting tour guide, plus the information that negotiations for a second contract between his employers and their middle eastern customers were scheduled to begin soon, speculating that this might involve investments by the delegates of their personal funds in addition to the official government funds that had been contracted for previously.

He posted it to the address that he'd been given and was pleased to see the funds hit his account a few days later. This also confirmed to himself the need for caution. He had at no time given his bank details to John – he was expecting to receive a cheque by post, but somehow, they had obtained his full account details. He was now sure that whatever department of government he was cooperating with, it was not the Foreign Office.

To top off his run of good fortune, during the next meeting with the Arab clients, they asked if Paternosters had any suggestions for a partner to help them with a major infrastructure project. Graham was able to inform them that a certain large company in the UK had recently narrowly lost a bid for a major infrastructure project. They might find that the business had geared up for this project and would bid very competitively for a project to replace the one they had not been successful on.

At a future meeting, they learned that their customers were very pleased with the suggestion and that the company had indeed been able to secure a contract with them which would be announced soon.

Selling the shares in the first construction company, realising his profit, and investing in the one that soon announced a major contract in the middle east gave Graham's funds a further bump upwards.

-

Graham's career progressed very satisfactorily for the next few years. More deals were done with customers from the middle east. Governments, large commercial organisations, and occasionally private individuals with surplus sums to invest, all came to Paternosters to find a safe and profitable home for their money.

On a personal level, his funds grew steadily. Salary and profit shares from his employers, rent from his student home, and payments received for information given to John's employers (whomever they were) enabled him to build a healthy bank balance as well as enjoy some of the many entertainments that London had to offer.

Working in a high-pressure environment produced the occasional strain and, despite his easy-going nature and his determination to keep a low profile, he became involved in one notable conflict. His colleague Michael was, in the opinion of Graham and several of his colleagues, an obnoxious misogynist. When Margaret Thatcher stood for the leadership of the Conservative Party, Michael was vociferous not only in his objection to her but also in his confidence that his beloved Party would never elect her as leader.

Graham had vowed to himself never to use his knowledge of future events to harm another individual. Winning money from bookmakers was an exception – they were organisations, not individuals. Besides, they were always well-off – as the old saying went, 'you never see a bookie on a bike.' But he decided to make an exception to his vow in the case of Michael. He pushed him to make a very public bet that she would not be elected as leader and made sure it was for a sum of money large enough to really hurt him. He was delighted to win – and immediately and publicly donated his winnings to a charity that had been formed for the victims of the recent Moorgate tube crash.

He was also asked to make occasional trips to the Middle East whenever it was in the interests of Paternosters to court both existing and new clients in that part of the world. At first, he was accompanied by a colleague, but as time went on, he almost always travelled alone.

He found the novelty soon wore off. He had occasionally visited this part of the world in his first life – but that had been to 'westernised' destinations, dealing only with the local branch of major multinational companies. Now he was dealing with the locals.

He found the countries to be monochromatic. Everything was just grey. And nobody brought up in England could ever be comfortable in a place where it was colder inside a building and warmer outside. He had never been a fan of corporate or hotel art – but when all the buildings you spent all your time in were devoid of any decoration whatsoever – except pictures of the head of state – you missed the framed prints that were everywhere in Europe.

The saving grace was the relationships he was building with his clients. He respected their culture and took whatever opportunities he could to learn more about the region. Their hospitality was exceptional. Forsaking alcohol for the duration of each trip was a small price to pay for the experience.

Naturally, he heard tales from fellow travellers – usually in the security of an airline lounge and often to be taken with a very large pinch of salt – of how their hosts had subjected them to a visit to a public flogging or a public execution. He never had any experience like this – and often wondered if there was a link between them being treated this way and their boasts of attending embassy and private parties where the booze flowed like water. 'Perhaps the disrespect flows both ways,' he thought, 'or perhaps they treat me better because I'm helping them make more money.'

Only on one occasion did one of his contacts open up to him about his feelings towards this type of Westerner. He learned a new Arabic word when his host referred to these people as 'miskeen'. Not knowing the word, other than a translation as 'beggar' which he thought was inaccurate Graham asked for an explanation, and his host switched to English. "They are people who have lost their values. And as a result, they have no value," was his thoughtful response.

While home, he did not live a monastic lifestyle. Although he worked long hours, there was still time for relationships, but none of them lasted long.

The year 1977 contained a few milestones for Graham. The phrase 'Space Shuttle' entered the language and the film 'Star Wars' was released. He thoroughly enjoyed seeing this once again on the big screen, obtaining tickets to an early screening for himself and his girlfriend, Beverly.

While these minor matters might not seem important, they allowed him to add key phrases back into his vocabulary. He could now say 'may the force be with you,' or 'I'm running around like R2D2' or 'these are not the droids you are looking for,' (with a different word substituted for 'droids' in the phrase – which was always delivered in an impersonation

81

of Alec Guinness's voice). Removing these verbal trip hazards was very helpful to a time traveller, and each year more were eradicated.

His latest girlfriend, Beverly, was the first woman he had dated who was younger than him, which to him felt like a significant step in his 'normalisation'. A full year younger and, like him, something of an outsider. She had joined Paternosters' graduate entry program, having taken a year off after completing her degree. An outspoken Yorkshire woman - her forthright personality, the bright clothing she always wore, and her northern accent all marked her out as different.

They were watching the TV news together one evening and saw the police appealing for information about the man now being referred to (by the press and public but not the police themselves) as the Yorkshire Ripper. Beverly became unusually serious as she explained to Graham from her own experience how frightening it was to be a woman in Leeds – and the terror that would persist while this man remained at liberty.

It was all the prompting that he needed. He decided that this was an ideal opportunity to find out if he really could change the course of events for the better. He would try to intervene and see if he could help to get this man caught more quickly.

Of course, he remembered Peter Sutcliffe was the name of the Ripper. But he also remembered watching a TV program shown years after his death in prison, which had uncovered information about his earlier life. There were several crimes that he had been linked with before his killing spree, but he had never admitted them, and they were not pursued by an overstretched police force after his capture.

Graham also remembered the information that the investigating team had shown aspects of heavy bias. In particular, they paid almost no attention to information coming from outside Yorkshire and heavily prioritised locally sourced input.

So, he took a day off and travelled by train to Leeds. He wanted to deliver his information in a way that would appear to be locally sourced and to see how the case was being reported in Yorkshire itself.

He bought a copy of the Yorkshire Post in Leeds Railway Station and headed outside to the first vacant public telephone box on New Station Street. He dialled the Yorkshire Police Hotline number on the front page of the paper and read the statement he had prepared:

"The man you are looking for is Peter Sutcliffe. He is a local man, a lorry driver living in Batley with his wife. They are childless and she does not know about his activities. He wears boots to work. He does not only attack prostitutes. He has attacked other women and men in the past – hitting them several times on the head with a hammer, just as he did with these latest victims. If you look at your records, you will find some unsolved cases which contain details about him and a photo-fit from multiple victims. If you do not arrest him, he will attack other prostitutes and non-prostitutes."

He replaced the receiver before there was any chance of questions. Not being sure how quickly or easily a phone call could be traced, he moved to another callbox, dialled the number of The Yorkshire Post, and asked to speak to Pat Threlfall, the journalist whose name was on the main story on the current edition.

While he waited to be connected, he wondered briefly if Pat was male or female, before saying aloud to himself "Don't be silly, Graham, this is still the nineteen seventies – of course, it's a man." And so it turned out to be.

He read out the same statement that he had given to the police and refused to answer any questions. He did add one other thing to his statement. "Pat, I'll give you my name. It's Derek Brinkley. Of course, that's not my real name, but it's the name I'll use if I contact you again," and rang off. He returned to the station and took the next train back to London.

Graham had sat next to Derek Brinkley throughout primary school – it was a name he would not forget, and he was confident it could not be traced to him, just in case.

He did not expect his intervention to show any immediate results, but as 1977 moved into 1978 he was disappointed at the lack of progress. But he had a very busy work life, a flourishing relationship with Beverly, and further financial complications to distract him.

He had received a compulsory purchase order for his student house. The road widening that had flashed into his memory on that first day of his second life was now due to occur, and his house was part of a row that was to be demolished to make it happen.

Graham decided that he would use this windfall to fund a purchase of a new apartment. He wanted a place with more space – hoping that there might one day be a partner for him to share it with – and a view of the river was something he had always desired.

To make sure he had enough money for the necessary furnishings, he decided to make one last trip around the betting shops. 1978 was a year engraved in his memory as the only time his home team, Ipswich Town, had won the FA Cup. As they entered the competition in January 1978 languishing in the lower reaches of the first division, he was able to get good odds against them winning the trophy for the first time in their history.

Digging the details from his college papers, he visited all forty betting shops, placing a ten-pound bet at each - and looked forward to collecting eight thousand pounds to furnish his new home. He even dared to dream that if he could involve Beverly in the choice of some of the furniture and décor, she might be persuaded to move in with him.

Two months had passed since his visit to Leeds, and with no results apparent, he decided to make a second attempt. He had no more information to impart – but thought that a second reinforcement might assist – especially if it was given in writing rather than just by 'phone. He even decided to invest in a new typewriter – his paranoia about the possibility of the typewriter being matched with his notes to John Bishop fuelling this decision.

He helped reduce the expenditure when he saw the secretary in the outer office showing off her new Wang word processor. As her redundant 'golf ball' typewriter was heading for the scrap heap, he contacted the office caretaker, and passed him a couple of the new, small pound notes. A box containing the perfectly usable device was on his desk that evening.

He typed a letter containing exactly the same words he had used in his earlier calls, making sure that no fingerprint or DNA traces could be transferred to the paper or envelope. He would send an anonymous version to the police - and a separate copy from Derek Brinkley would go to Pat Threlfall at the Yorkshire Post. And, to make sure that they received due attention, he repeated his trip to Leeds to put the envelopes into a local post-box and ensure they would be locally franked.

Then, in mid-1978 while he and Beverly were choosing a sofa for the lounge of the new apartment, Peter Sutcliffe was arrested and charged with the murder of nine women. Graham felt reasonably sure that in his first life, there had been thirteen victims, and he could feel happy that he had saved at least four lives by his intervention. He and Beverly duly celebrated that evening.

But his plans did not work out completely as he had hoped. That July celebration marked the high point of his relationship with Beverly, and two months later their relationship ended, leaving him to complete his move into his new home alone.

He was never completely sure why the breakup happened – she was very vague about her unhappiness with his obsession with money, his lack of real commitment to their relationship, and even the 'funny way' he reacted whenever she mentioned the Ripper. He had heard the phrase 'lack of commitment' before - and knew this would always be a problem. He could only guess that his guilt at not being able to tell her about his successful contribution to the arrest of Peter Sutcliffe must have shown, and probably accounted for the 'funny way' he had reacted.

He began to think he would never find a partner in his second life. But he decided to make one last connection using the work he had done to aid the capture of Sutcliffe. He rented a private PO Box at a nearby Post Office and sent a letter to Pat Threlfall.

I'm delighted to hear that Peter Sutcliffe has been arrested and that the streets are once again safe. Congratulations on your part in bringing this about.

I would like to offer you more assistance in the future. I cannot always promise to be as useful as I was this time, but I do believe that I sometimes see things that others cannot, and I would like to put this ability to good use whenever possible.

Please feel free to communicate with me at this address and allow me a few days to respond.

Regards
Derek Brinkley

He received a letter in his PO Box a few days later:

Dear Derek

Thank you for your letter and for the information you provided. I too am delighted with the success.

I plan to shortly take up a new position with a national Sunday newspaper and will contact you if I believe you might be able to help me.

Regards
Pat Threlfall

Graham was not at all surprised to hear of Pat's progress – his success would have brought him national attention, and the breakthrough to a national paper was every local reporter's dream. A few weeks later, he read about Pat's new appointment. It was the start of a long and mutually useful relationship between the two of them.

-

Graham was doing his Saturday morning housework when he heard it. It was several seconds before he realised the significance, but there it was, being played on the mid-morning show on Radio Two – "Tell Me on a Sunday". He immediately stopped what he was doing and went to his boxroom and started rummaging through his college papers. It took him nearly half an hour to find the copies of the college newspaper with his poem. He put one into an envelope and prepared to start the fun of getting his share of the action.

The following morning, he asked his boss if he could have access to the company's law firm to assist him with a private matter. He was prepared to meet the costs but hoped to receive preferential treatment based on the volume of business placed by his employers. He received the go-ahead, having given a brief background explanation of why he needed the assistance, and enduring the reaction.

"Never saw you as the poetic type," his boss remarked with a broad smile on his face.

The process was long and tedious, as he had expected. First, he had to explain the circumstances of his original composition to the lawyers. Then he had to wait for them to present an adequate case to lawyers representing Universal Music Publishing Group (who had published the song) and to receive a response. Then he had to prove that he had actually published the words eight years previously, and a court action had to be threatened. All the time everyone knew that publicity would be unwelcome for both the publishing company and the composer and that a settlement was inevitable. Finally, a demand had to be made for a huge amount in compensation, before eventually, a settlement for an ongoing royalty payment was reached.

The music company preferred to offer an ongoing payment as it would ensure his secrecy – the royalty being null and void if the secrecy was broken. Breaking the secrecy, and thus bringing attention to himself, was the very last thing that Graham wanted, so he readily agreed to this form of compensation. He had found the whole thing to be an interesting diversion as he had expected, and the royalties formed a welcome addition to his income stream.

He also had an ongoing distraction in the correspondence between Pat Threlfall and Derek Brinkley. He was not able to help with every request Pat made – and he made a request about once a month – but he was able to provide useful input and 'steer' Pat's stories in the right direction. He gave him the tip-off to follow the police investigation into Cynthia Payne, letting him know that a rich treasure trove of column inches would be found there. And when a taxi driver reached the final of Mastermind, Graham suggested that Pat should line up an exclusive interview – just in case the man won (which of course, he did.)

He also let him know that the young Diana Spencer was soon going to be making serious steps towards becoming the next queen (just as he was able to let him know many years later that she was taking serious steps to NOT become the next queen.)

These were serious deposits into the favour bank, and he was able to cash in on them on one occasion.

Graham was enjoying a very close relationship with Jay. She was known to the public by a different name but to friends and family, she was always

Jay. They had met at a party thrown by a mutual friend and had quickly begun a close relationship that proved that opposites do sometimes really attract. She was a presenter on children's TV, but her good looks, lively personality, and obvious intelligence enabled her to broaden her role with appearances on panel games and chat shows. She was assuredly destined for bigger and better things.

Although attitudes had changed considerably during the 1970s, she felt that the public was still not ready for a children's TV star to be living with someone she was not married to. So even though she spent a large part of her spare time at Graham's new flat, she had not fully moved in with him, and still maintained her own place.

It was no surprise that when her agent, Penny Vallens, wished to contact Jay one Friday evening she called Graham's number. He handed the phone over and went into the kitchen to clear up the remnants of the takeaway meal they'd just enjoyed and to refill their wine glasses. The calls between Jay and Penny were usually long and lively, so when he returned to the lounge, he was surprised to hear her quietly giving monosyllabic replies, "Yes, … sure, … will do, …. no, … OK…." before soon hanging up and trying to hold back tears as she turned towards him.

"What's the matter?" he had to ask.

Looking into the distance she mumbled, "It's all over. Everything. It's the end, I know it."

He pressed her for more., and she wiped away her tears and looked at him.

"It was a long time ago… I was very young…. There was a party. Some people brought some drugs and some stupid things happened." She paused and Graham let the silence hang there for a moment.

"Someone took some photos," she continued, "and now they're going to be in the papers. I'll be finished." Then, seeming to take a decision "I've got to go home."

She got up and put on her coat and shoes.

"Don't you think you'd be better here?"

"No, I need to be alone for a while."

"OK – if you think that's the right thing to do, but let me get you a taxi, and then I'll call you in a couple of hours - and you'd better answer or I'll be round there banging on the door, OK?"

She gave him the weakest of smiles and nodded. "OK" and a few minutes later left.

Graham put on his coat and headed out. He needed to urgently talk to Pat Threlfall, and he did not want him to be able to trace the call. Reaching a nearby phone box he dialled Pat's number and was not surprised to find he was in the office at this late hour on a Friday.

"Pat, it's Derek here. I need your help on something", he began.

Pat was surprised. His communication with Derek had all been by mail until now, so he knew this was something unusual.

"Pat, I've had a call from a good friend of mine, Penny Vallens. Apparently, one of the papers is going to run a story that will be very upsetting for one of her clients. Do you know anything about it?"

Pat was very guarded in his response but confirmed that it was indeed his paper that was planning the story.

"I need you to do me a favour, Pat, and leave Penny's client's name out of the story."

"But, Derek, Penny's client IS the story."

"I understand – with her it's page one, without her you're on page ninety-four, possibly below the fold," Graham continued, hoping to keep the conversation friendly.

"That would be a real problem, Derek. Quite a few people already know about this."

"I understand, Pat. But there's a huge difference between a few people knowing, and the details being plastered across the nation's breakfast table on Sunday morning. That would ruin a young woman's career and I've promised Penny I'll do everything I can to stop it. You know that if you do this little sacrifice for me, I'll make sure that you still get all those tips you find so useful. You wouldn't want them going to anyone else instead, would you?"

Graham's threat was obvious, no matter how nicely he put it, and when Pat replied "I'll have to see what I can do, Derek. I can't make any promises," he was confident that he had achieved his aim. He thanked Pat and promised he'd be back in touch soon.

An hour after he returned home, Pat received a call from Jay. She was a lot more upbeat than when she'd left earlier.

"Penny just called me – she says they've changed their minds and they're not going to run the story," she told him.

"Well, I think you'd better get back here. There's a bottle of wine with a little left in it. Or maybe I should put some bubbly in the fridge."

They embraced as soon as she came through the door, and shortly afterwards, took the bottle to bed with them. It was an hour or so later that she said, "you knew, didn't you?"

Graham tried to maintain ignorance of what she was on about, but she persisted. 'Damned women's intuition' he thought.

"You knew they were going to withdraw the story. It's the only explanation for how you reacted before I left, and when I returned. How did you know?"

He knew that she would not stop her questions until he said something and so he replied "Look Jay, I've told you what I do for a living. I make a lot of money for some very rich people, and they are very grateful to me for that. I just called one of them and asked if he could do me a favour in return. And it seems like he was able to."

Having thought about it for a few minutes, she decided that this was enough of an explanation and told him she was very grateful – and proceeded to prove it.

Strangely that night was the beginning of the end of his relationship with Jay. She became more guarded in the things she said to him. She asked him more questions – and when he was unable to answer as completely as she wanted, she grew more unhappy.

'Another occasion when the seeds of defeat are sown in the moment of victory,' he thought to himself when a couple of months later she ended their relationship.

-

The end of the 1970s meant that it was time for the next stage in Graham's plan. He had more than established himself in Paternosters. There was a steady flow of business coming from the middle east, and he was involved in some way with each of the deals.

His guided tours of London were now only an occasional diversion. He'd broadened them out for some of the returning customers, including visits to football matches – back then tickets for top-flight football were both affordable and available – to museums or art galleries, and even the odd visit to a Sunday afternoon 40-over game of cricket in the John Player League.

But most often the return visit of his customers gave rise to small dinner parties, where business and pleasure were mixed. His reservoir of gossip was topped up and, after filtering, passed on to his government contacts.

His business relationships survived the difficulties in relations between the UK and Saudi Arabia in 1980 when a TV documentary with a less-than-flattering portrayal of the Saudi royal family was broadcast in the UK. And when the fuss caused by this programme had all blown over, he received the rare honour of being invited to the banquet held at the Saudi Embassy when King Khaled visited the UK.

His income from Paternosters, the rental income from his flat, the royalties from his composition, and the monthly government pay cheque, put him in a position where he could afford a comfortable lifestyle and start to build a sizeable nest egg. He now planned to spend the next few years building a considerable sum of money that he could put to good effect after taking early retirement.

As a first step towards this goal, he asked to discuss his future with his boss and Mr Bernard. He expressed his desire for a new challenge, having spent six years in his current role. He suggested that the firm should consider creating the role of an in-house expert for the rapidly growing computer market. IBM had recently released their first Personal Computer – which was to become known as the IBM PC (although it would not be available in the UK for another year) and this gave credibility to this market sector. Graham spoke with enthusiasm of his belief that there would be substantial growth in this area in the coming years. He felt it was such an important sector that the company should have a specialist in the area, as they did in each major business sector.

He could sense that his arguments were not entirely convincing to his audience – them being a few years older than him and possessed of both ignorance of and hostility to such an innovation as a personal computer. However, his track record spoke for him – and when he managed to convey a hint of his wish for a change, their fear of him moving to a rival swayed their judgement.

He proposed that he would have less involvement in the middle east business and become the in-house man for IT (an acronym for Information Technology that he had to teach to the partners). He wrote a job description that would allow him to visit the key industry conferences – all of which would occur in the USA – and to write investment recommendations for the firm.

The response from the partners (who had to hold a meeting to discuss a change of this nature) took a little longer than he had hoped, but he was patient. And when the response was conveyed to him, it was better than he had anticipated.

His recommendation for the creation of a new division coincided well with the company's overall strategy to build an in-house database that would gather crucial information on the companies in which they might be requested to invest on behalf of their clients. There was also obvious potential for these companies to list their shares on the London Stock Exchange – and this was a terrific potential for Paternosters. However, Mr Bernard informed him in an informal meeting in his office there was one problem with appointing him to head the business unit.

"You'll be going over the heads of some of our employees in our US subsidiary when you do this, you know. And they are not accustomed to being told what to do by anyone except a partner in the company."

Mister Bernard held up his hand to prevent Graham from countering this objection and continued, "However, we have come up with a way of overcoming this barrier. We would like to offer you the position of partner in the company."

It was an unusual step for Paternosters to appoint someone so young to a partnership, and it was an indication of the value placed by the company on him (and the revenue he was bringing in). He was delighted to accept and in his new role indulged his pleasure in visiting the USA. He especially enjoyed visiting Paternoster's US offices as a partner. He'd spent a large part of his first life being told what to do by American bosses and this role reversal was very enjoyable. He travelled in business class and attached a few days of holiday to each trip, refreshing his knowledge of the country from his first life.

He put together his first set of recommendations after his first visit to the Comdex conference in Las Vegas at the end of the year. The first entrants in the new company IT database were Microsoft and Intel. Graham drew up a summary of the current strengths and weaknesses of each and recommended them as good investments. Both were exclusive suppliers of key components of the new architecture – based on the IBM PC - which was rapidly becoming an industry standard. He also wrote a report on Apple and recommended investment in their shares, since they still held a significant part of the market and had maintained control of their proprietary design. His final recommendation was Motorola, the supplier of the chips which Apple needed for their computer.

In truth, he was post-justifying by picking names that he recognised as still being in business in the next century. Hence, he recommended against investments in some of the companies that were hot at the time – such as Digital Research, producer of the then leading operating system, CPM, and Micropro with the world-leading Wordstar product. Graham knew both would soon disappear. Instead, as he grew the company database, he included unknowns such as Adobe and Novell, which he knew would continue for many years.

And as he made his repeat visits to the computer conventions in the USA, he added more companies to his recommendations - companies that he knew would still be there for many years to come. He was careful to also mix in some which would flourish briefly and then pass – such as Lotus and Compaq.

Investors whose funds were managed by Paternosters would put a small part of their investment into these fledgling companies – and despite the excellent returns that began to be shown, the cautious approach of fund managers would keep individuals' exposure to a minimum.

Graham's own investments were not shackled by this caution – and he began to switch all his investments to IT companies. Not surprisingly, the value of his portfolio began to multiply significantly.

Back in the UK, he continued a lower level of involvement with the ever-growing list of middle east customers, meeting the key personnel (and occasionally their extended families) on both business and social levels.

He deviated once from his pledge to do no more betting. In 1981 he spent a week's holiday in Leeds, watching the famous Botham Test Match. He could not resist the legendary occasion in the middle of the five-day game when bookmakers offered odds of 100-1 against an England victory. He placed a £10 bet intending to cover his expenses for the week, which he did when the match was won by England following Ian Botham's incredible performance. But Graham resisted the temptation to place a higher bet, fearing that this might bring him unwanted publicity.

He watched various milestones pass, each of them freeing up part of his vocabulary and knowledge. He witnessed the miners' strike, Torvill and Dean, the introduction of the twenty pence and pound coins, Band Aid and Live Aid, Chernobyl, the Falklands War, and AIDS – all for the second time. Each of these contributed to a changing world and helped him feel less like a stranger in his own land.

His new responsibilities at the office allowed him to have a PC on his desk – and he made sure to be one of the early adopters of mobile telephony as he moved gradually toward a world that he could feel more familiar with.

He continued to feed scraps of information to Pat Threlfall, whose career at the Sunday paper grew from strength to strength. Mostly it involved Graham responding to messages sent to his PO Box – steering the various investigations when he could remember them from his first life but giving no feedback on the many occasions when he could not remember them.

He was finally able, via his Derek Brinkley alias, to give Pat Threlfall a scoop and return the favour he had received concerning his friend Jay. In August 1985 the newspapers reported a horrific event involving multiple murders at an Essex farmhouse. The first reports conveyed the police's initial belief that it was a murder-suicide committed by Sheila Cafell, but Graham knew differently. He was able to give Pat the tip-off that the culprit would be identified as Jeremy Bamber (Sheila's adopted brother) and so enable Pat's paper to report the story in an entirely different tone.

And Graham made one attempt to use his knowledge to influence events when he was shocked into remembering a tragedy that could easily have been avoided. The event occurred when he took his girlfriend to Bruges for a short holiday. It was partly to make up for his lengthy absences over the previous year when so much of his time (and of everyone around him) had been taken up with the reorganization of the UK Stock market that became known as the Big Bang.

The holiday however necessitated first achieving another personal milestone that he had postponed for too long - passing a driving test. Living and working in London and being able to afford a taxi when public transport was not appropriate, he had never felt the need to own a car. So, when his girlfriend suggested that they hire a car and take a trip to Belgium he was too embarrassed to admit that he couldn't legally drive. He had to rapidly contact a local driving school and arrange some lessons.

The initial conversation and first lesson were somewhat of a surprise to the instructor. As soon as they met, Graham stated that he did not need to learn to drive - but needed to learn how to pass a test. The instructor may well have heard the claim before but was taken aback when Graham drove during the initial lesson. After all, he had probably never had a pupil who had fifty years of driving experience. Thankfully the instructor was flexible enough to change his approach and, after a few lessons to get rid of bad habits, Graham passed his test in time for the trip to Belgium.

Graham had been to Bruges for both personal and business travel in his first life, which raised two issues when he agreed to go there with his girlfriend.

He always knew that he could not revisit any holiday location that had been special to him and his wife, and there were a few places around the world that were in this category. It would feel wrong to go to any of these destinations in a different life with a different woman, but Bruges was, thankfully, not on this list. It would have been difficult for Graham to explain why he could not go there again without opening a can of worms he intended to keep firmly closed.

He also had to dis-remember all that he knew about the place. Having told his girlfriend, "I've never been there, it sounds like a great idea" meant that he had to feign ignorance from then on. But feigning ignorance had become second nature to him, and the short holiday was enjoyably spent on the canals, in the shops, bars, and restaurants, and in the hotel room.

But there was a huge shock waiting for him on the return journey. Driving onto the ferry, Graham noticed the ship's name: "The Herald of Free Enterprise." and was immediately reminded of the disaster that this ferry had been involved in when leaving the port of Zeebrugge. He racked his memory for the date of the accident but could only recall that the disaster had occurred on a weekday in the second half of the 1980s.

In the unlikely but possible event that this could be the very day of the disaster - once onboard, he pretended to feel a little unwell and insisted on standing on the outside deck as the ship set out on its journey. In answer to his strong request, his girlfriend stayed with him, and he only 'recovered' when the ship was well clear of the harbour.

Having been so forcefully reminded of the disaster, he wondered if he could do anything to prevent it. But without knowing the actual date, his options seemed to be very limited. The best action he could think of was to write letters to the Managing Director and Chief Safety Officer of Townsend Thoresen, the owners of the vessel.

His letter claimed that he had seen severe lapses in safety procedures on one of their ferries. Knowing that the disaster was caused by the ship leaving the dock before the bow doors had been secured, he thought it acceptable to report that he had seen this happen, even though he had not. He was sure that most people would find a claim of this nature – a ship setting out with a sea-level door wide open – would be impossible. But sadly, he knew that it would happen - with tragic consequences.

He received replies assuring him that such an event was not possible, and a couple of years later listened in horror to the news reports as the disaster unfolded. He thought about publicising the correspondence with the company but reasoned that it would achieve nothing other than unwanted publicity for himself. He wished he had done more to save the unfortunate passengers but knew that the intransigence of the company's management was the main contributory factor.

"I've also got a little story to tell you, Graham. It's not something I would have thought of telling you – but there's part of your story that makes me think you'll be very interested in this. It'll answer some of your questions, and probably raise a whole lot more."

Chapter Five - The First Disappointment

From the earliest days of his second life, Graham knew that he would have to try to prevent the Hillsborough disaster. As a football fan, he had been deeply saddened by the death of ninety-seven people at an FA Cup semi-final. The disaster had been caused by a surge of spectators into a standing area of the ground when a gate was opened by police match controllers immediately before the start of the game. The rush of people had caused a crush at the front of the enclosure resulting in multiple fatalities, many of them children and young people. And the tragedy was compounded by the establishment cover-up that followed. The inquest into the deaths had produced a very unsatisfactory outcome and the bereaved families had to fight a campaign lasting some twenty years until its verdict was corrected.

He could not remember the exact year of the tragedy – he knew it was in the late nineteen eighties – but he had drafted his plans and was waiting for the draw that would put Liverpool and Nottingham Forest in the same semi-final. This would then give him about a month's notice to execute his plans.

On Monday, March 20th, 1989, the draw that paired these two clubs was made, and Graham knew the time had come. He had been reasonably sure when the weekend's results had left both of these two clubs in the final four, but waited until Monday to be certain.

Now he could once again curse the absence of the internet as he sought to find an opportunity to visit the ground before the game itself. He had to telephone Sheffield Wednesday, the team that played their regular fixtures at this ground to find the details of their next home game.

The good news was that it was against Wimbledon, a team with a small following, so there would be no difficulty in getting a ticket. The bad news was that it was a mid-week game so he would have to take a day off work, and, more importantly, conduct his reconnaissance in the dark.

He had pondered possible actions to disrupt the event, and had, after considering various alternatives, come up with a plan that had a 'belt and braces' feel to it. He felt that there were two ways he could affect the course of events. He could try to change the flow of people into the stadium before the match - because the timing of this flow, and the police response to it, was the root of the whole tragedy. And he could make sure that the police handling of the day's events was headed by a different person, which would hopefully alter the way they responded.

That evening he took his project plan out of his filing cabinet and reviewed it one more time. He then made two calls.

The first was to leave a message for John Bishop requesting a meeting as soon as possible. The second was to Pat Threlfall, using his Derek Brinkley alias.

"Pat, I need a favour. There's a senior policeman in Yorkshire by the name of David Duckenfield. I need a recent photograph of him, and I need to know his home address."

Pat was naturally inquisitive as to the reasons for this unusual request, but the only response he got was, "this is personal and there won't be much of a story, but I'll tell you what I can as soon as I can, OK?"

Graham thought silently to himself, 'Please God, there won't be much of a story.'

He finished with a request. "Pat, nobody else needs to know about this, do they? I know you want me to keep sending you those useful titbits. So, not a word to a living soul. Is that a deal?"

"Sure thing," came the reply.

The meeting with John took place a few days later at their usual meeting place.

"John, I've got a favour to ask, and an unusual one at that," he began.

"I need to have a face-to-face meeting with a crime boss in Manchester. It's a personal issue for a friend of mine, and this is the only way I can do anything to help him out. I know you have these types of connections and hope you can trust me enough to arrange a meeting and not ask any questions."

"You'll have to travel up there, you know, these guys don't come south for anything," John replied. He was curious to know the reasons for this unusual request but figured he would eventually find out the reason - one way or another.

100

"I'll go wherever's necessary. All I need is enough notice to make the journey. It's that important. And I need it to happen as quickly as possible."

John agreed to do his best, and a few days returned Graham's call.

"You need to be in the bar at Manchester Piccadilly Station at eight pm tomorrow. Find a table by yourself and you'll be contacted."

"How will I recognise him?"

"You won't. He'll recognise you."

-

David Duckenfield was a name known to all football fans. He was the match commander on the day of the disaster and admitted his errors at the inquiry. Errors that led directly to the disaster, but which went unpunished in the courts. Graham planned to remove him from the equation in the hope that a different commander might take different decisions on the day.

Graham was sitting alone, as directed, the following evening in the grim railway station bar with a pint of beer and a folded newspaper on the table in front of him, and a small briefcase between his feet. He had placed all his trust in John and just hoped that the person he met would be real, and not an imposter.

When a tall thin middle-aged man sat down at his table and said, "You wanted to talk to me," he was oddly reassured. Surely a man who carried so much menace in delivering such a simple sentence could not be a fake.

Graham pointed to the folded newspaper. "There's an envelope in that paper with the name and address of a man. He's a senior policeman in Yorkshire, and he needs to be the victim of a serious mugging within the next week. Enough to put him in hospital for a week – no more, no less. I'm told you're the man who can arrange this, and I'm willing to pay what it takes."

He had rehearsed the speech several times in the hope of delivering it without showing the nervousness he felt. And this nervousness was not improved by his companion's response. He leaned towards Graham and grabbed his wrist hard enough to cause pain.

"And why shouldn't I just tell you to stick your money up your middle-class arse and fuck off back south where you belong?" he asked.

Graham had anticipated some pushback and had prepared his response.

"Look I know I'm out of my depth. I'm a southerner and I don't belong here. But this man must be punished and I'm rich enough to pay for it. You know I've got enough influence to make this meeting with you happen. Whoever asked you to meet me is someone you don't want to disappoint. So, when I'm asked by the people who set up this meeting if everything was OK, I want to say yes. And you would rather I gave positive customer feedback to these contacts – because they are the sort of people even you don't want to piss off."

There was a brief period of silence while his answer was digested, and his wrist was released.

"It'll cost you five grand."

Even Graham realised that this was an extortionate amount, probably more than double what would be paid to the person who did the job, but it was within the range he had expected. He opened his briefcase in which there were five envelopes with the numbers one to five on them. He extracted the one with '5' written on it and quickly placed it on the table. It was picked up by his contact, who spoke no more before leaving.

As he sat on the train on his way back to London, he was confident that the first part of his plan was successfully in place. David Duckenfield would not be the match commander at the forthcoming semi-final and therefore would not make the catastrophic mistakes in crowd control that even he admitted had contributed to the death of ninety-seven people.

He had wondered whether his course of action was fair and reasonable. The man had not yet made the mistakes, and therefore could not deserve the injuries he was to receive. But on the other hand, he would have one week in hospital and a few more weeks recovering from injuries. The alternative would be to spend the rest of his life under suspicion and racked with guilt. Surely that was fair, wasn't it? Anyway, it was now too late to change the plan. The 'belt' of Graham's 'belt and braces' strategy was now in play. Next, he had to get the much more complicated braces into place.

On Wednesday, April 5th, he caught an afternoon train to Sheffield, dressed in jeans, a T-shirt, and a light jacket. He carried a large vinyl bag, which he placed in the overhead rack as he took his seat in the first-class section of the train. A quarter of an hour before arrival at Sheffield he took his bag with him to the toilets and locked himself in. He removed a pair of jeans that was large enough to wear over those he was already wearing, and a knee-length coat that he wore on top of his jacket. A small wedge went into one of his shoes. The vinyl bag folded down to almost nothing and was placed into a plain carrier bag which contained a flattened cardboard box, a roll of Sellotape, a pair of scissors, a pair of gloves, and some birthday gift wrapping.

Graham, now a fat man with a limp, wearing a long coat and carrying a plain carrier bag, emerged from the toilet and got off the train as it rolled into Sheffield station. He limped his way to Hillsborough stadium.

At the ground, his first call was at the supporters' shop, where he purchased a few items of team merchandise which went into the carrier bag with its existing contents. If it was searched by security personnel when he entered the ground, his story would be that he had bought some souvenirs as a birthday present for his nephew, and he planned to box and wrap them after the game.

But the fat guy with the limp was not searched. He bought a ticket and made his way into the Leppings Lane end of the ground. If anyone watched him for the next half an hour, which thankfully they didn't, they might have been concerned about his digestion. He went from one Gents' toilet to the next until he had visited every one of them in that part of the ground, then took his seat and watched the game.

Graham had idly speculated that if he were ever to tell the story of this day – which he sincerely doubted would ever happen – he could insert a funny line, "And the worst part of the whole day was having to sit through a whole Sheffield Wednesday game." It was certainly a dull game, but the story was very unlikely to ever be told.

Fifteen minutes before the end of the game, he joined some of the pessimistic Wednesday fans and made his way out of the stand. His immediate destination was the toilet which he had selected as best suited for his plan. He entered the cubicle and closed the door, donned the gloves, reconstituted the box with the aid of strips of Sellotape, and filled it with the football merchandise, scissors, and remains of the tape, before sealing it. He then wedged the box behind the toilet cistern in a position where he was confident that it would be unseen by a regular visitor to the cubicle - but quickly spotted if a search was conducted.

Leaving the toilet when the game finished, the carrier bag now only contained the vinyl bag and the gloves, and the fat guy with the limp joined the other fans making their way to the railway station. Once on the train back to London, he immediately entered a toilet and removed his outer jacket and trousers, took the wedge out of his shoes, placing all the items into the reconstituted vinyl bag. A thin guy without a limp, carrying a vinyl bag, took his seat in the first-class compartment for the return journey to London.

Reaching Euston station, he walked south towards central London and rewarded the first homeless person he saw with a new pair of jeans, a coat, and a pair of gloves. The two empty bags went into the next rubbish bin he passed, and he caught a taxi home.

Later he placed the rest of the clothes he had worn that day into a black sack and took a midnight walk to deposit it in a builder's skip a couple of streets away from his flat.

Part one of his plan to disrupt the flow of human traffic at the semi-final had passed as smoothly as he could have wished and he now had ten days to wait for the vital second stage of his plan, with only a few details needing to be checked in the meantime.

-

The cup semi-final at which the tragedy was due to happen took place on Saturday, April 15th with a 3 pm kick-off. Early that morning, Graham left his flat, wearing a reversible jacket that he had chosen specially. It was dark on one side but much lighter when turned inside out and could be worn with either side outwards. It would play a key part in his plan.

He used his credit card to buy an all-day London Underground ticket at his local tube station and travelled to Marble Arch, where he visited a nearby café for a hearty breakfast, making sure to keep the receipt. Leaving the café, he walked east along Oxford Street, stopping to buy a pen at one shop and a tie at another. Small items that could easily fit in his pockets, the receipts for their purchase would be timestamped and prove his presence at these shops, and his progress eastwards along Oxford Street through the morning. Reaching Bond Street tube station he entered and bought a second all-day ticket – using cash this time – and used this ticket to travel to Ealing Broadway at the end of the line.

Ealing Broadway was about the furthest west one could travel on the tube network, and he planned part of his activities there in the hope that it would misdirect any future investigation away from his home turf in the east of the city.

But he also chose it because he remembered from his days of visiting betting shops that there was a particular pair of phone boxes close to the station in a dingy alley off the Broadway and close to a slightly less dingy pub. If there was a prize for the phone boxes in London that were the least likely to be visible to a CCTV camera, these two would be serious contenders. More importantly, because there were two of them, it gave him the best chance of finding one empty at the right time to make his call.

He reached the North Star pub at twelve-twenty-five, as planned. He had a specific time in mind for his call if he was to achieve his aim of significantly changing the flow of human traffic that day at Hillsborough. The stadium's gates would normally open at 1 p.m., two hours before the scheduled kick-off. He aimed to delay this kick-off by about forty-five minutes.

Once inside one of the phone boxes, he calmed himself, took a handkerchief from his pocket, placed it over the mouthpiece, and called the main number of Yorkshire Police.

He spoke the few vital words slowly and clearly. "There's a bomb at Hillsborough football ground. It's in the Lepping end of the ground and it will go off before kick-off. You will have to postpone the game."

His preparation for this call had included learning a script and repeatedly listening to tapes of an Irish comedian to improve his imitation of an Irish accent. He was hoping that the current level of bomb threats and actual bombings in England was high enough that even his amateurish attempt would invoke a police search of the ground.

He had chosen the time carefully. The message would be forwarded to police at the ground, a search conducted, and the suspect package found and declared to be a hoax. Hopefully, the gates would then be opened. Estimating that this whole process would take about an hour, the call had to be made at twelve-thirty to delay the opening of the gates by at least half an hour and thus change the flow of people into the ground.

He was as sure as he could be that once the very poor imitation bomb had been found, the police would decide this was a hoax and allow the game to continue. They would not want to postpone the game and have thousands of disappointed fans roaming the streets all afternoon. But there would be a delay.

This delay, and the absence of the planned commander for the event that he had caused, was all he thought he could do to disrupt the whole event and change the outcome.

As insurance against his call to the police being dismissed, he placed a second call to the Yorkshire Post newspaper and read the same script, using the same change of voice. Before leaving the phone box at twelve-thirty-five, he reversed his jacket and put on a cap, scarf, and sunglasses from his bag, which he discarded on his way back to the station.

He crossed the road junction, walked the few yards uphill to the station, and arrived just in time to board the 12:45 train to Oxford Circus, the busiest station on the London underground network. He had visited Ealing Broadway earlier in the week to verify that the phone boxes were still where he remembered and to establish a way to enter and board the train with minimal chance of appearing on CCTV. He trusted that this, coupled with his change of appearance between arrival half an hour earlier and his departure would make him more difficult to trace if he was caught on camera.

His near-perfect timing allowed him to board the last carriage of the train just before departure. Then, between Ealing Broadway and Oxford Circus, he changed carriages four times, moving up from the last carriage to the fourth – making it less likely that any casual observer would remember him sitting in the same carriage for a long period, and ensuring that he was in the closest carriage to the exit on arrival. He was also fortunate that the change of drivers at White City was perfectly timed, and the train completed the twelve-stop journey in twenty-four minutes.

At Oxford Circus station he moved quickly to the escalators, walking steadily up the left lane and climbing forty-four steps to minimise his time. He then went directly to exit number one where a climb of thirty more stairs took him directly to the entrance of TopShop.

Inside the shop, he removed two polo shirts from the rack closest to the entrance and presented himself at the nearest Pay Point. He made sure to keep a copy of the receipt, with its time stamp clearly shown.

He had carefully planned this part of the schedule. If he was ever to be investigated, it would show that the time between the second phone call and the purchase of the sweaters was thirty-four minutes. This time would be very difficult to achieve by anyone casually recreating the journey and was as close to achieving an alibi as he could hope. He had even bought two polo shirts on the previous visit, making sure they were the correct size. The ones he had purchased in haste might not be.

He disposed of his second all-day ticket, made a few more purchases in stores east of Oxford Circus, and then used his original ticket to travel back home from Tottenham Court Road Station at the eastern end of Oxford Street. The next day, two non-fitting polo shirts and a reversible jacket were on a rail in a charity shop – and a scarf, hat, and pair of sunglasses were dumped into a waste skip.

He hoped that if his activities on the day were ever to be investigated, it would show him breakfasting in Marble Arch at the western end of Oxford Street, and then moving east along the street making occasional purchases, including one at a store located on Oxford Circus, before reaching Tottenham Court Road Station and using the same ticket to go home.

He was feeling exhilarated as he prepared to make his nocturnal excursion to the waste skip, as the semi-final had been completed without incident and the disaster had been successfully averted. But he was brought crashing to earth as the TV programme was interrupted by a breaking news story.

A major accident had occurred in West Yorkshire, involving a coach carrying supporters back to Liverpool from the FA Cup Semi-Final. The coach had collided with other vehicles, including a petrol tanker. Details were sketchy, but many serious injuries and deaths were expected.

Graham knew that this accident had not happened in his first life. Of course, there was a perfectly logical explanation. Because of the disaster and the resulting abandonment of the game, this particular coach would not have been on this stretch of road at this time. But he could not help thinking that maybe this was a variant of the 'Butterfly Effect' he had heard of.

Was fate making an adjustment? Were the people killed in this road accident some form of compensation for the lives he had saved by the avoidance of the original disaster? He would never know, but he suspected this was the case. He recalled something he'd read in his first life – possibly some university or institute research. The article speculated that time travel was possible and that the 'Butterfly Effect' did not exist because it would be corrected by some form of quantum theory.

These were the thoughts going through his mind as he went to dispose of his clothes. He had not known of any similar reaction to his only other intervention – securing the early capture of Peter Sutcliffe. But that had only saved half a dozen lives – and if there had been some multiple death in Leeds at that time, he would not necessarily have heard about it. And anyway, the lives he had saved were mostly street prostitutes. Not that their lives were any less important or valuable – but if they were to be considered in terms of their potential impact on the future, they would have a relatively low life expectancy and a small chance of producing offspring, so maybe a correction had not been necessary.

But what he had done today had saved ninety-seven lives, many of them young people. So, the potential impact was much larger.

After drinking a couple of very large measures of his favourite single malt, Graham fell into an uneasy sleep. He followed the news coverage on TV throughout Sunday. Eventually, the death toll reached fifty-five, and after much solitary thought, he was able to console himself with two facts. The number of people killed was significantly lower than in the first disaster. And, painful as this would be to all the affected families, closure (a word he hated but could not think of a substitute for) would be achieved much more quickly. There would be an investigation, reasons for the accident decided, recommendations made, and actions taken within months. It was even possible that the person or persons to blame would be identified. There would not be a wait of over twenty years for a satisfactory inquest verdict as had happened the first time around.

And there was one further outcome of the day's events. The work that was created for the Yorkshire Police because of the major accident meant that several other issues received little or no police action. The list of these incidents that were neglected included the matter of a bomb hoax call received immediately before the match. No further action was to be taken on this matter.

-

As the calendar page turned, the decade changed from the 1980s to the 1990s, and the possibility of him being linked with the events relating to

Hillsborough diminished day by day, Graham knew that the next stage of his plan must soon come into place.

He had always envisaged that his time at Paternosters would eventually come to an end. He was soon to hit forty and, if his memory was correct and his plans could be effectively achieved, that was when the next phase of his life should start.

He knew that what he was waiting for would happen early in the 1990s, but, as ever, was unsure of the exact date. What he had forgotten, and hence was unusually shocked by, was a bomb attack on the Stock Exchange in the summer of 1990. The building and surroundings were evacuated after the IRA telephone warning was received forty minutes before the explosion, so nobody was even injured. But the detonation of a bomb that had been estimated to contain between five and ten pounds of high explosive, was an unpleasant shock to him and his colleagues, nonetheless.

But the events that would lead to a change of life for him, and to so much more for many other people, began to unfold on October 4th, 1990, when the Chancellor of the Exchequer, John Major, persuaded the Prime Minister, Margaret Thatcher, that the UK should join the ERM – the European Exchange Rate Mechanism. Financial commentators were split on the wisdom of the decision. Some predicted success and some foretold of disaster. Graham knew that the latter was to prove true.

He began to move both his own money and that of his clients into positions where they would not be adversely affected by the catastrophe that would shortly occur. In discussions with his colleagues, he recommended that they do the same, and his influence was such that his advice was followed by most.

In the past he had prevented his clients from risking their investments, making sure they were never exposed to any one technology company's shares. Now, he made sure that any investments he made on their behalf concerning the outcome of the UK's membership of the ERM were properly hedged. There had to be no chance of problems if the situation did not play out as he expected and remembered it.

However, in the same way that he had risked his portfolio on his knowledge of how certain high-tech companies would succeed, so he was able to execute a strategy for his shares when it came to planning for the

ERM meltdown. He planned to invest all his money in a one-way bet against the UK government.

Matters came to a head on September 16th, 1992. Graham had made all the necessary transactions on his accounts as the government fought in vain to hold its position in the face of overwhelming odds. In one day, it raised the official interest rate from ten to twelve percent and then fifteen percent, before finally admitting defeat and, at 7 pm, withdrawing from the ERM.

It became generally known that George Soros, the famous international financier, made billions of pounds that day. Graham was not in his league, but, by the end of the day, he had made a very large amount of money – as you should expect to do if you sit in a casino making bets all day knowing what number is going to come up at each spin of the wheel.

He stayed in the office late into the evening as the markets continued to react to this huge U-turn by the chancellor of the UK Exchequer. He unwound the positions he had taken for himself and his clients, before going home alone and drinking a couple of large measures of an eighteen-year-old malt whisky he had been keeping for just this occasion. It was partly a celebration of his winnings, partly a farewell toast, and partly a jolt of Dutch courage for the actions he needed to take the next day.

Make no mistake, before these events took place, he had already been a very wealthy man – but that day he moved to a level of wealth that was exceptional even for the traders and financiers he worked with. The total of his accounts at his employers, and the ones at a few other financial institutions that he kept secret, made him a multi-millionaire.

The atmosphere in the office the following morning was, to say the least, a little strange. For his colleagues, it was unlike anything they had ever known, but Graham had one experience in his first life that had prepared him for this feeling.

In 1997, during his first life, while living in a Kent village, he had gone into his garden to survey the damage on the morning after the great storm. He had set about repairing the fences and dealing with the broken limbs of trees and other garden items that had been damaged the night before. There was a unique feeling of companionship with his neighbours who had similar tasks to complete - they talked with one another across broken fences and joined in shared effort and teamwork to tackle the larger breakages.

That's how he felt the day after the financial storm that had just passed. The financial world had been hit by a metaphoric tornado, and his co-workers were experiencing shock and embracing a combined will to repair the damage. But he noticed his colleagues were reacting strangely to him. Even though his finances should have been secret, word had leaked out of the personal gains he had made, and he was suffering the consequences.

'It's just as well that they don't know the true extent, including the accounts I've got with outside organisations', he thought, 'because then they might be really angry!'

In a world where making money was a religion, there was some admiration for what he had (reputedly) achieved for himself the previous day. Making money was to be praised and envied. But there was also a certain disdain. He had, in the minds of many of his colleagues, profited by 'betting against the home team'. There was some discomfort with this act of disloyalty, and many were not speaking to him in the friendly fashion that they normally would.

He was not totally surprised; he had never felt that the company he worked for was a great home of team spirit. He had even referred to his group as 'not so much a team but more of a shoal of piranha that just happens to be in the same river at the same time.' So, this coolness he was experiencing did not faze him.

He knew it was not going to last for long, anyway. He arranged an appointment with the senior partner, who agreed to see him at the end of the day. Graham never got to find out whether the meeting was so readily agreed to because Mister Bernard was worried about the team spirit or the embarrassment that might be caused to other staff members by the large amount of money he had made. Graham solved both problems for him by announcing his wish to resign.

The senior partner's reaction was one of considerable surprise. If there was some relief there, because two problems had just been removed from his list, it did not surface. After overcoming his surprise, he asked Graham to reconsider, and when this was unsuccessful, suggested that he should take some time off to recover from the strains of the past few days before making a move that he might regret.

The considerable reticence that Mr Bernard had shown to accept and implement Graham's decision was completely driven by concern for the company. There was fear for the impact that the loss of Graham might have on their business – particularly business emanating from the middle east. Graham was quizzed about his plans and the questions betrayed the main concern – had he received a better offer from a rival?

Bearing in mind the events of the previous few days, and the reaction of other members of staff, it was agreed that Graham needed and deserved a break before making any final decision. They decided to meet again in two weeks so that a plan of action could be put in place to suit all parties.

That evening, the office was empty as Graham bade a silent farewell. He had three items on his immediate action plan.

He wanted a break, that was sure. The worry that his plans might backfire had been a strain and, unusually for him, sleep had been an elusive experience for several nights. Then he wanted to move house. He planned a complete change of lifestyle, and nothing would better signify this than to move from his current city-centre flat to a more rural location. But most of all he wanted to address an issue that had been lurking in the back of his mind for a long time. He needed to find out if there was anyone else who had experienced the same time shift as he had.

He also had longer-term plans to find a good use for all the money he had made, and would continue to make, from his knowledge of future events. But that part of his plan needed to wait a little while. The urge to see if there was anyone he could talk to – which he believed was only possible with someone who shared his experience – had been growing in him for years, and now he felt he had the time to put a plan into action.

He wondered if he should wait a while before starting the search, but the plan had been in his head for such a long time, he knew exactly what he was going to do, and it took only a few minutes to write the advertisement:

Harry Potter, The Spice Girls, The Kardashians, and Boris. Do you know who they are? And do you know about the iPad, Tracy Emin's bed, the Angel of the North, and Covid? If you do, I would love to meet you. Please Reply to …

He opened a second PO Box at his local Post Office to avoid the risk of Pat Threlfall making the connection with their communication address. He put this address at the end of the advertisement, together with a code that signified the newspaper in which it was placed. He then spent the day booking the advert into every national daily paper and the key regional papers of the UK for every day for the next month.

The second task was accomplished on Saturday. He visited the local travel agency and simply stated "I want to go on a holiday for two weeks. I want to get away from it all and I want to go as soon as possible."

A helpful member of staff quickly established that price was not an issue and made a few suggestions. The one that offered the quickest departure was a cruise around the Mediterranean visiting key historic and archaeological sites. One of the exclusive suites on the ship was available - and the idea of being aboard ship and difficult to contact appealed to Graham. He also remembered the cruises he had been on with his wife in his first life and thought that the level of activities associated with this cruise – lectures on board as well as the site visits – would be an ideal way to make sure he was kept artificially busy. He did not want to dwell on his recent activities and the nagging worry that his advert posed him. He knew that either he would receive a reply, or he would not. He was not sure which was the most concerning.

He set sail on the cruise two days later.

The holiday certainly took his mind off things – he had not realised what impact he would have on some of the passengers. The presence of a single, straight, wealthy man (whom it turned out was not averse to the company of slightly older women) caused quite a stir among the many middle-aged single female passengers. Graham quickly discovered that he had to engage in a shipboard romance with one of the eligible ladies to avoid being almost literally chased by all the rest. It certainly took his mind off his other worries!

His return on Sunday evening heralded two important events for the following day – a discussion on his future with Mr Bernard and a visit to the Post Office to collect any replies to his advert. Both events could have been a source of worry, but the exhaustion from his exertions of the previous two weeks meant that sleep was not a problem.

He did not even check his answerphone until waking up the following morning. The message told him that he was invited to a meeting at ten am in the office. Although it was possible to visit the Post Office first, he decided that it was best postponed until after the business meeting. 'Focus on one major issue at a time,' he told himself.

The meeting was with Mr Bernard. Just like the old days, he thought, just the two of us in the big leather armchairs enjoying excellent coffee and biscuits. He allowed the senior partner to make the running initially. It was obvious that the firm was driven by fear of his skills and his contacts being used by one of their rivals. So, they were prepared to be very flexible in making an arrangement that would prevent this.

He was quite happy to sign a 'golden handcuffs' agreement with them and to commit to attending the office a minimum of twenty days in the next year and to "undertake reasonable additional tasks designated by the senior partner, having been given a suitable period of notice". The daily rate they were prepared to pay was a figure so high that many would describe it as quite obscene – but he knew that he justified it, and it would enable him to devote yet more money to the good causes he planned to espouse.

Having signed the appropriate paperwork and entered a couple of dates in his diary for the first two days that he would be needed at work, he took a taxi to the Post Office.

A large bundle of letters was presented to him, and he was pleased that the walk to his flat was short enough that he was not tempted to open them before he reached home.

Piling them on the dining table, he took a knife from the kitchen drawer and began opening them. There were several pieces of junk mail, advertising almost anything imaginable, and they were quickly filed in the bin. Then he tackled the more personal ones – with envelopes bearing both handwritten and typed addresses. Some were obscure; some were obscene; some offered him various types of therapy for what they assumed were his problems. He placed them in a pile, planning to re-read them just in case there was anything that might show up on a second careful re-read. But he was not hopeful.

Finally, there was one that made sense. He read and re-read it several times.

"But I return to the subject of your Petty Officer, or rather your mother-in-law's Petty Officer. The image he transmitted was sent across a wavelength we do not understand. One which we cannot detect, but I believe it may be akin to the wavelength we are transmitting in our experiment. But – and this is the crucial part of my theory - the message that he transmitted crossed over time. What was seen – by your mother-in-law - was not the image of him in his current state – it was the image of him some ten years earlier"

Chapter Six - The First (and Only) Real Relationship

The letter was hand-written, and his first impression was that this was a woman's hand. It was neat and precise, and was headed with an address that read simply "Worthing, Sussex." Dated one week ago, the code on the envelope showed that it was responding to an advert in The Times.

Dear Sir/Madam

In answer to the questions posed in your recent advertisement I can state that Harry Potter is the boy magician; The Spice Girls is an all-girl pop group whose members are Baby, Ginger, Posh, Scary, and Sporty. All I know about the Kardashians is that they are a group of young women who are famous for being famous. I believe the iPad is an electronic device made by Apple. Tracy Emin's Bed was an exhibit at the Tate Gallery and The Angel of the North is a sculpture by Antony Gormley. The only Borises I can think of are Boris Yeltsin, President of Russia, and Boris Johnson, Mayor of London (although I'm unsure as to why you deem either of them important).

I am unaware of the meaning of Covid.

Before agreeing to meet, I would like to know a little more about you, including proof that you also know the answers to the questions, and the reasons you wish to meet.

You may reply to me at the following address (quoting a PO Box Number in Worthing).

I look forward to hearing from you.

Yours faithfully

Carol

Graham rushed to get a reply to her, deciding to follow her lead, and handwrite his response. This was one of the most important letters he would ever write and deserved great care, but his heart ruled his head as he responded in haste. He dashed off his reply and headed immediately for the local Post Office to send the letter by the fastest method. He would have used one of the express couriers he was familiar with from the financial world, but the destination of a PO Box made this impossible.

Dear Carol

Thank you for your letter - I'm happy to answer your questions.

Harry Potter's best friends are Hermione Grainger and Ron Weasley. Half a dozen books and films made his creator, J.K. Rowling, a very wealthy woman. After the break-up of the Spice Girls, Posh Spice, whose first name is Victoria, married the England footballer, David Beckham, produced several children with unusual first names and began a second career as a fashion designer. Tracy Emin's bed will be (or was) nominated for a Turner prize but was not successful and the Angel of the North is (or will be) situated in Gateshead.

I'll happily explain Boris and Covid when we meet.

My name is Graham and the reason I know the information above is that I am living my life for the second time, as I suspect you are. I have used my knowledge of future events to acquire considerable wealth but unfortunately have never been able to form a relationship with another person because of my unusual situation.

I placed the advertisement in the hope of discovering if any other people shared my situation, and to date, you are the only responder.

I would be delighted to meet you at any location and time, and in any manner that suits you. I understand your caution but hope you will be able to agree to meet as soon as possible.

I look forward to hearing from you.

He signed the letter "With Best Regards"

While waiting for a reply he re-read Carol's letter and wondered what he might gather by reading between the lines. The language was very correct, and there was a hint of a sense of humour with her comment about the Kardashians. Carol's inability to identify Boris or Covid at first puzzled him, but after some thought, he presumed it meant that she had ended her first life before 2016. Her use of language showed intelligence and her caution implied that she had an understandable concern about revealing her situation. He was thoroughly intrigued and almost excited at the thought of meeting her.

He could hardly wait for a reply to his follow-up letter and checked his postbox every day. Meanwhile, he commenced the other one of his immediate plans for his early retirement.

Living in a flat in London completely suited his lifestyle while he was employed in the city, but now he planned a slightly less urban lifestyle. He wanted to remain close to London for both business and social reasons, but also planned to have some time on his hands and wanted some ready ways of using it. The ideal location would be immediately west of London. He had always enjoyed the view of the Thames from his flat, and for this reason, and to provide himself with an extra hobby, he wanted a property with access to the river. A small boat moored at the bottom of his garden would be a suitable and pleasant distraction.

Two other motives produced one other requirement. The property had to have a swimming pool, and if it was not currently usable all year round, he would spend the money necessary to make sure it could be. One reason was that he had grown used to having convenient access to a pool – his apartment boasted a health club in the same complex and he had swum almost every day as a perfect form of relaxation and exercise. He also reasoned that a pool at his new house would be an attractive feature for his young nephews and nieces with whom he had sadly had so little contact over their lifetime. He intended to issue invitations to his brother and sister and their families as soon as he could find somewhere to tempt them. So, he started visiting estate agents while waiting for the all-important reply to his letter.

A reply arrived a week later. Once again, the letter was headed with only "Worthing, Sussex" and the date. It was short and to the point.

Dear Graham

Thank you for your reply and for answering my questions.

If you can come to Macari's Coffee Bar on Worthing seafront at 10 am on Saturday, wearing something red and displaying a copy of The Times, I will make myself known to you.

Regards

Carol

Receiving the letter on a Thursday meant there was not enough time to guarantee that a reply might reach her, so he had to just go.

Despite the many meetings he had had in his life, each with its level of risk – the presentation to the Daily Mail when he was in university, his first interview at Paternosters, his meeting with the senior partner when he asked for a profit share, and so many more – the pending encounter with Carol made him feel more nervous than anything before. Scared that some last-minute traffic problem might delay him, he travelled to Worthing on Friday evening and took a room in the Chatsworth Hotel, a beautiful Georgian building close to the seafront.

Once he had checked in, he took a walk along the seafront and found Macari's some two hundred yards from the hotel. He felt a strange superstition that prevented him from entering the café before seeing Carol the following day. So, he returned to his hotel for a meal, and despite the wonderful comfort of one of the best rooms, his anticipation for his morning meeting ensured that he experienced the worst night's sleep of his life.

He arrived at Macari's ten minutes early the following morning. In 1992 there was not the plethora of choices of coffee that would become commonplace a few years later, and he was pleased to be able to order just a plain black coffee. Resisting the temptation of the wonderful choice of ice creams that were the house speciality, he took a seat at a table that had a clear view of the entrance, straightened his bright red tie, and laid his copy of The Times on the table in front of him.

When a woman entered alone some ten minutes later, he was confident that this was Carol. She chatted for a few minutes with the person behind the counter. 'Obviously a regular customer,' Graham thought and almost held his breath until she had purchased a milky coffee, suitably frothed, and carried it to his table.

"Are you Graham?" she asked quietly. She was about five feet six; her pleasant face showed no signs of makeup and was dominated by a pair of dark-rimmed glasses that were a little larger than they should have been. Her raven black hair was dead straight, parted down the centre, and was worn shoulder length. She was dressed in a knee-length woollen skirt and a jacket of the same mixture of blue and brown colours over a cream blouse. She struck him as a woman who could be very attractive if she tried – but one who probably never tried.

"Yes, I'm Graham. You must be Carol," he replied, trying to produce a welcoming smile, and fearing that his face betrayed his nerves more than his welcome.

There was the briefest of pauses as neither of them seemed to know what to do next, so he extended his hand, and she shook it.

His "Please sit down," produced what he thought was an equally nervous smile from her. She placed her coffee on the table and sat opposite him.

"Thank you for agreeing to come here to meet me," she said. "Did you have to leave very early this morning?"

"No, I came down last night just to be sure that I didn't have any last-minute problems, I'm staying at the Chatsworth," he replied, hoping to show how important the meeting was to him.

"Oh yes, you said you have considerable personal wealth, didn't you," she replied, and he felt there was just a hint of criticism – or was it disdain – in her reply. There was an awkward moment of silence.

"Would it make sense if I told my story first?" he asked and noticed she relaxed a little when agreeing – he guessed she had worried about going first.

Making sure that they could not be overheard, he began his story with his jump from 2022 to 1970. She listened carefully and silently at first, but as he progressed, she began to ask questions. Firstly, asking him to go back to what he had been doing on the last day of his first life, and then quizzed him about how he had reacted to the jump. It was obvious that she was seeking a comparison with her own experience.

He told the story as fully as he felt he needed to. He covered his early betting on football, his career choice, his easy path to wealth, and his retirement plans. He did not mention his attempts at changing events and did not go into any detail about any of his relationships. He wanted to get to the end of the story as soon as reasonably possible so that he could hear hers. Even so, with her questions and his explanations, it took over forty-five minutes to complete the telling, by which time they had both finished a second cup of coffee.

At this point, Carol asked to be excused while she visited the bathroom. He kept his eyes pinned on the door, fearing that she might yet escape but was reassured when she returned.

She did not seem comfortable starting her story, so he asked if it would be easier for her if they took a walk along the seafront and she readily complied. The fresh air, on a day that was cool but not unpleasant with a gentle onshore wind, seemed to help her open up.

"My jump started on October seventh too – but in twenty-twelve, exactly ten years earlier than yours," she began. "I'd been to visit my solicitor because my divorce had just come through and there were some final issues to deal with, and, as she put it 'I had to start planning my second life'. Wow – if she had only known," Carol gave an edgy laugh and paused for a few seconds. Graham sensed that there were some difficulties for her in retelling the story, so he stayed quiet.

"My marriage had been a total disaster, and it had been very difficult for me to get out of it. But my solicitor had been an enormous help and had become a close friend. There was quite a lot to get through, and we worked until lunchtime when she took me out for a meal and a few drinks to celebrate. Then I went home and slept – I did feel extremely tired, but I put it down to the stress – and maybe one too many glasses of wine with lunch."

Graham could hear and sense that she was lengthening this part of the story, probably because the next part would be difficult. He allowed her to continue at her own pace.

"I landed in July nineteen eighty-two. Not my eighteenth birthday, unfortunately. My wedding day. As I said, my marriage had not been successful. In fact, it had been a bit of a nightmare. The man I married had been so different once we were married. He made me quit my job and I had almost no contact with any friends or relatives. So, here I was, back there again at the start - what's the saying, dazed and confused - and about to walk down the aisle with a man that I had grown to fear and loathe. I can tell you I didn't react well. I simply refused point blank to go through with it.

Of course, my mother told me it was just wedding day nerves and that I'd get over it. She said I had to think of all the people that were waiting and the journeys they had taken to get there. How selfish I was to even think of cancelling it. She stopped short of saying how much money she and my father had spent – but I knew that was in her mind too. But of course, I wouldn't budge, and I wouldn't explain why I was suddenly so sure it was such a bad idea. You know how crazy it would sound."

Graham was quick to agree with her. "Yes, you're right. I've never felt able to tell anyone in the twenty years since it happened, have you?"

She shook her head and stayed quiet while they walked a few more yards.

They had walked quite a way and Graham wondered if it was right to allow her to continue the story, knowing that every step they took would have to be taken again on the reverse journey. But he felt that this was difficult and it was best if she got through it, so he said nothing. His only contribution to the flow of the story was to keep murmuring "Mmmm, yes, or aha," at the appropriate moments.

"The pressure didn't stop with the cancellation of the wedding. My relationship with my parents, especially my mother, deteriorated rapidly after they had to call off the wedding and make my apologies to everyone. I'd refused to come out of my room until they'd all gone.

I didn't cope well with anything for a while. To cut a long story short, I was in a mental health facility soon after and stayed there for some time. Eventually, they felt I'd recovered sufficiently. I had time to adjust to the fact that I really was living my life all over again and more importantly that the one good thing that came out of the marriage – my son Adam – not only didn't exist, but he also wouldn't ever exist. That was hard, I can tell you. But they let me out, and I had to decide what to do with my new lease of life.

I'd been a teacher before the non-wedding. Of course, I lost that job when I had my 'difficulties' so I looked for a new job. With what was on my record, it wasn't easy, but eventually, I was offered a job at a small private girls' school here in Worthing. The pay was dreadful, but they were prepared to take a risk with me - they probably had little choice with the money they were offering - and so I took the job, rented a little house down here, and here I've been ever since.

I still have difficulties. Certain dates will always be a problem for me I guess – my wedding day, my son's birthday, October the eighth, you know."

At the mention of October the eighth, she turned and offered a weak smile to Graham. It was the first time she had fully acknowledged his existence since they began walking. She paused briefly and he realised she had lost track of where they were and how far they had walked.

"Shall we walk back?" he asked to fill the void that had suddenly developed. She nodded.

She stayed silent and Graham picked up the conversation, "You had a much more difficult time than I did. I was very lucky to land where and when I did. I was presented with a blank page. First week at uni, there was nobody there that I knew. It must have been very difficult for you." He looked at her and she nodded, appreciating his acknowledgement of her difficulties.

"I had difficulty relating to my parents when I went to see them at the end of term," he continued, "and I'd had months to prepare. I can't imagine how I'd have coped with what you had to face."

"What did you leave behind in your first life?" she asked after another period of silence.

"I had a family. Two children, and four grandchildren. My wife had already died a few years previously, but the grandchildren were a huge miss. I've tried to put them out of my mind – it gets easier as the years pass, but there's always something to surprise you when you least expect it."

She nodded sympathetically.

"So, you're still a teacher at this school?" he asked to try to continue the story.

"Yes, you could say I lead the ultimate quiet life," she continued, emitting another short laugh that was totally lacking in humour.

"Nobody else in your life?"

"Not really. I have some friends at work, one, in particular, has been very good to me. My job keeps me busy; I volunteer at the school, you know school fetes and the like, and I also give some time to a couple of good causes. And I enjoy reading my copy of The Times cover to cover every day – which is where I saw your advert. Which brings us back to the present."

They walked for a short while in silence. Neither seemed to be sure what the next step was.

"There are a few things I'd like to ask you about your jump if you don't mind," Graham ventured.

"Yes, thank you for letting me tell the story uninterrupted, it wasn't easy. It took more out of me than I thought it would. I'd like to answer your questions but to be honest I'm feeling a little tired."

Graham could see that she was wilting and withdrawing into herself and decided not to push.

"We could stop for lunch if you like," he suggested but she shook her head and told him she wanted to go back home and rest for a while.

"Could we meet again this evening? We could have dinner at the hotel."

"Yes, of course, you have all that money. Can I call you later?"

He decided not to respond to her second jibe about his money but knew that the subject would have to be tackled shortly. He gave her a card from the hotel and wrote his name on the reverse side.

"Call me when you're ready to talk some more – and maybe we can at least enjoy a meal together."

"That would be nice," she replied, and Graham was pleased to note that the remark seemed sincere, and she came as close to a real smile as she had since they first met.

They reached the coffee bar on their return journey and parted company.

Graham returned to the hotel, ordered a sandwich from room service, and turned over the morning's events in his mind; killing time, waiting, and hoping for Carol's call. Her story was so full of potential danger points that he would have to negotiate the conversation very carefully. He wanted to find out more about her jump (as they had seemed to agree to call the event that they had both experienced). The exact ten-year gap between their two events was uncanny. There also seemed to be certain similarities between the way each of them had spent the last day of their first life – he particularly wanted to explore this aspect.

He re-examined his motives. Why had he set up the meeting? He had not really analysed his thought process, but he knew that it was driven by two factors. The first was the search for some explanation for what had happened. But maybe more important was the desire to have one person with whom he could totally share his story, and maybe even more. Having spoken with Carol he could now see that these impulses were what had driven him – and would continue to drive him, to find some resolution.

At six o'clock she called him, and they agreed to meet in the dining room at seven-thirty. Graham felt more nervous than he had been for any first date. It was so important that he and Carol hit it off, and although they had so much in common, there were also huge differences. He would have to overcome her natural resentment for the ease with which he had been able to adjust – and the financial gains he had made from it. Both factors might stand in the way of a relationship – of any kind – between them.

He showered, changed his shirt, and went tie-less into the dining room.

When Carol arrived, he noticed that she had made a little more effort with her appearance and seemed a little more relaxed. He risked planting a kiss on her cheek, and she accepted it.

Their conversation stayed trivial for several minutes, discussing the restaurant and its menu, the hotel, its history, and general stuff about Worthing. This enabled her to do most of the talking and to relax, which is what he felt was needed.

He then gave her an amusing run through some of the replies to his advertisement and moved on to explain that Boris Johnson had become Prime Minister (which caused her to utter the word gobsmacked – presumably overheard from one of her pupils – for possibly the first time in her life).

He also gave a brief overview of the Covid pandemic, which also produced a shocked reaction from her – and an intriguing remark "Perhaps I didn't miss out on too much by leaving the party early."

This allowed him to ask her more about the final day of her first life and to talk more about his last day. They were both intrigued by the similarities in the way they had spent the day and the uncanny time difference of exactly ten years between the dates. As they discussed it, another similarity emerged. The location of her solicitor and his financial adviser appeared to be very similar. Neither could remember the exact address, but both were sure that it was somewhere in east central London, and they agreed to research the exact addresses.

After hearing more details of Carol's last day, Graham expounded a theory that there was another coincidence – if that was the right word.

Her meeting had concerned the end of her marriage, and her jump had taken her to its beginning. His meeting had loosely concerned the end of his adult life (three score years and ten) and his jump had taken him back to the start of adulthood. As he made this link, he added to his explanation. He told her how his financial adviser had asked him about his plans for his seventieth birthday – knowing that it was the following day. The conversation then moved on to a discussion of their best and worst birthdays. He mentioned his eighteenth birthday, spent in the company of strangers without so much as a single drink bought for him.

Carol linked this with her memory of having spoken at length to her solicitor about how happy her wedding day had been, in contrast to how unhappy had been the marriage that followed.

They certainly felt there were links there - it was a little shaky, but they agreed it was something to work on. They would each look into the address of the place they had visited on their respective last days to see if a more complete picture could develop.

"I'm on half term next week so I can look into it on Monday," Carol remarked. They exchanged telephone numbers and agreed to speak as soon as they had more information.

They talked some more about the difficulties of readjustment, both realising that there were many more topics for them to share. As the meal and the conversation came to an end, Graham decided to let Carol know how nervous he had been about the whole idea of contacting her, and how pleased he was with the outcome so far. Carol was delighted to hear this – she thought she was the only one who had been wary and said so.

She declined his offer of a drink after the meal, explaining that she had found the day very tiring and the two glasses of wine she'd had with the meal was already a lot of alcohol by her standards. He offered to order a taxi to take her home, but she asserted it was unnecessary as she had less than a mile to travel. He absolutely insisted on walking her home, and she conceded after a brief period of token resistance.

They walked half a mile along the seafront in the opposite direction to their morning walk, turned right, and walked back three streets to her small, white-painted terraced house. Their conversation touched on several issues and finished with an agreement to decide where and when to meet after they had researched their respective last days.

This time Carol leaned first and kissed Graham on the cheek. He felt it was a perfect end to a meeting he had been both keenly anticipating and thoroughly dreading.

As he walked back to the hotel, he realised that Carol was not the only one who had found the day emotionally draining. He went straight to his room and was asleep minutes later.

Back at his flat on Sunday afternoon, he set about researching his last day and the visit to the IFA. He remembered the name of the person he had met but knew that would not be of any use – they were not due to meet for thirty years from today's date, and the man would still be at school. Unfortunately, he could not remember the name of the firm he worked for – maybe it began with a C, but he could not be sure. So, he found several lists of financial adviser firms on his computer but could not recognise any.

He tried to remember the meeting. They had been to a pub – on a crossroads, he remembered, with entrances on both streets, one of which was quite busy. That was not much use, it could apply to hundreds of pubs in that area of London. They had met in a large, new multi-storey building, of which one floor (or maybe part of one floor) was rented by the company he visited. But where was it? He had travelled on the underground to a station with which he was familiar from visits to one of his customers. At last, it came to him - Old Street.

He leaned back and tried to recall something else, but that was it – all he could remember was a large new multi-story building within walking distance of Old Street. Carol had said she would do her research on Monday, so he resisted the urge to call her and decided to wait until Monday evening when he dialled her number.

She had made similar progress to him. She remembered that the address she had given to the taxi driver when she visited the solicitors was City Road. But although she knew the name of the solicitors she had visited, there was no listing for them anywhere in the vicinity.

They were pleased with their progress, and Graham suggested that they should visit the area as soon as possible. With Carol being on half term it was agreed that she should travel up to London on Wednesday morning – he would meet her train at 10 am and they would go together.

They took a taxi to the junction of Old Street and City Road and walked up City Road. But it was not at all helpful. They walked several hundred yards but the large multi-story building that they both thought they remembered was not there. Not only was it not there, but the buildings that it was to replace, had not yet been demolished,

"Now what shall we do?" said a crestfallen Carol.

"Well, we've been up and down the City Road, so I guess the next step is to go in and out of the Eagle," Graham replied, quoting the nursery rhyme.

Carol laughed, more than his joke deserved. But it was the first light-hearted remark that had passed between them, and the protective layers that they had both built were slowly coming down.

"How about I take you out for a nice lunch?" Graham asked and was pleased to receive rapid consent. He hailed a taxi and gave the address of his favourite Italian bistro – which he had patronised often enough on business to be confident of getting a good table.

The lunch went well, and their conversation warmed further. He asked if she had any more time available on her half-term break, but she had to regretfully let him know that she had agreed to one day in school, and one day of volunteering, and she also had a whole day of marking to do.

This was her second mention of volunteering, so he had to ask what she did. It could have produced a negative turn in the conversation as she explained that she volunteered at a local women's refuge – repaying the help she had received with her difficulties in her first life. But he turned it into a positive by referring to his plans to put to good use some of the money he had accumulated. He asked her if he could funnel some of it to her cause. She agreed to consider it.

Not wanting to lose the momentum of their dialogue, Carol agreed to meet again on Saturday.

"Same time same place as last week?" Graham asked and she agreed. They shared a cab to Victoria Station and, as he said goodbye to her at the entrance to Platform 2, they shared their first kiss. It was platonic – but progress was being made in a relationship that was developing despite challenging circumstances.

He was in the same seat as before when she entered the coffee bar on Saturday morning, but without the red tie and the copy of the Times. This time their conversation ranged more widely. They went over the ground covered, quite literally, in London and agreed that there seemed no purpose in pursuing that thread any further. It seemed likely that they had both been in the same building on the last day of their first life, but until the building was built, there seemed to be little hope of progress.

They also agreed that they could not think of any other way of pursuing the mystery of how it had happened. They started to open up to each other about the various difficulties they had experienced. The discussion was prevented from becoming too downbeat by the occasional funny story they could each tell, about inadvertently referring to a future event, or using a word that had not yet entered the vocabulary, and the strange reaction it had produced.

Carol asked if he had ever tried to use his knowledge to change events, and so he told her the story of his reporting of the Yorkshire Ripper and an edited version of his intervention at Hillsborough. (He omitted the bit about removing David Duckenfield from the equation as he thought this might be too much for her to swallow.)

He supposed it revealed something of the sheltered life she had lived in her first life, as she had not even noticed the complete change in the Hillsborough story – but said nothing. He received the expected answer when he asked if she had done anything similar. He received a sad and slightly sorry 'No' in response.

As they moved from the coffee table to their walk along the seafront, he began to tell her his latest news.

"You remember I told you I was looking for a new house?" he started.

"Oh yes," she replied, showing more interest than she had been doing for the previous few minutes.

"Well, I think I've found it. It's just what I want and where I want it. It's owned by an American couple – he's the head of a computer software company and they need to move back to America quickly. So not only are they willing to offer a very good price to a cash buyer like me, but they also want to leave a lot of their furniture behind. And they've only been living there a couple of years, so it's all in pretty good condition. A bit modern for me – but it's useful because I'm going to need a lot more furniture than I have in my flat."

"Is it a big place then?" she asked.

"No, it's just four bedrooms – and being Americans, they've put in an extra one and a half bathrooms,"

"What's half a bathroom?"

"I'm not completely sure – I think it's probably what we would call a shower room or a cloakroom. You can see for yourself if you want. Would you like to come and have a look at the place?"

He had landed on the perfect invitation for her. Looking at a house was, she thought, an easy way of continuing the careful steps of getting to know Graham. She would have felt uncomfortable with a proper date. The meals they had shared had been pleasant enough – all of them had had a kind of business agenda attached to them – but a traditional date would pose other issues. She had been concerned about how they would proceed, and the idea of looking around someone else's house seemed ideal.

That evening they had dinner together again and talked about their frustrations with all the things they would like to change but couldn't. The disasters both small and large that they could do nothing about, the villains they could not expose, either because they did not know the exact date on which something would happen – here Graham broke off and talked about his experience with the ferry disaster – or because there seemed no way of pulling the right lever to stop an event from occurring.

Carol asked if he would be willing to try to prevent other disasters - despite his disappointments over Hillsborough and the ferry disaster - and he agreed he would. He felt sure she had a reason for asking the question, but she denied it when he asked.

Once again, Graham walked her home. They agreed that he would call her during the following week to let her know the arrangements for visiting his proposed new home, and they shared a warm kiss on her doorstep. She made no move to invite him in, and he did not attempt to push forward. 'If this was any other date, I would have tried to get invited in,' he thought. But this was no ordinary date. If he and Carol were to continue to meet, their relationship would have to be very special.

He was thinking, 'We're two white mice in a laboratory. The only two of our kind as far as we know. If we're to stay together we'll have to be very, very sure it's right.' But he did not share any of these thoughts with her, yet.

When Graham called her on Wednesday to confirm the arrangements for her visit, she was surprised at his requests.

"You'll need to bring a change of clothing and your swimsuit," he said. She had to ask why.

"You're going to have to travel to Slough by train, then I'll have to drive you to the house, and if you want to have a decent amount of time to look at the place, there's no way you can get back to Worthing the same day."

"And I suppose you've booked a fancy hotel with a swimming pool then?" she asked, remembering that he had spoken of his love of swimming as a form of exercise and that money was never an issue for him.

"Don't worry – there are two separate rooms," he replied.

It was only after the call had finished that she realised they had agreed on which train she would catch, and on which train she would depart on Sunday afternoon, but not the details of the hotel. But it didn't matter – she had nobody to tell, anyway. And while she was aware of the 'gathering proximity' of their relationship, it was still under control. In fact, one of the things she liked about Graham was that he seemed very happy to move at her pace – even though it was a very slow pace for some.

Graham collected her from Slough station on Saturday and they made small talk for the twenty minutes it took him to drive to the house. Turning off a narrow lane, a short driveway led to the house, which stood on a little less than two acres of land, accompanied by two outbuildings, only one of which was visible from the front of the property.

"The building on the left is the granny annexe," he explained. The main house has got four bedrooms and the aforementioned two and a half bathrooms. Downstairs has been made into an open-plan area: lounge, dining room, study, and kitchen all in one. And it's furnished American style – which means there's lots of space and not a lot of furniture in there."

"You've missed your calling. Sounds like you could have made a great estate agent," Carol interrupted. Graham was more than happy with her mocking him in this way – he had not heard her make too many humorous remarks in all the time they had spent in conversation, and this surely showed she was becoming more relaxed in his company.

He took the keys from his pocket and opened the front door.

"Where are the owners? How come you've got the keys?" she asked.

"You remember I told you they were keen to sell quickly?" he asked - surely a rhetorical question as he gave her no time to answer before ploughing on.

"Well, we reached a deal where I'd rent the property for the time it takes to complete all the legal stuff. So, in a way, it's mine already." Graham could not suppress a smile as he imparted what he thought was excellent news whilst causing some amazement at the same time.

He conducted a tour of the property and explained that he had not had time to move his furniture here, only a couple of suitcases of clothes and a box of possessions. Two of the bedrooms did not have a stick of furniture between them, but the other two were both fully equipped, one with a double bed and one with a king size.

Downstairs the rear of the house comprised a full glass wall, which could be opened partially or fully, and gave a terrific view of the back garden leading down to the river. A pathway led from the back of the house to a featureless outbuilding, and he beckoned her to follow him.

Opening the door of the building revealed a good-sized swimming pool. He put his hand in the water, "Good, the heating's been on long enough, it's perfect. I'll get this building altered as soon as I take possession – I want it to be able to open out and be used as an open-air pool in the summer."

Apart from general sounds of approval, Carol had said very little as they had toured the house and now the garden and pool.

"Do you like it?" he asked.

"You're very lucky to be able to afford a place like this," was her guarded reply. Graham was reminded once again he would have to continue to tread carefully on the issue of his financial status - unless and until the relationship between himself and Carol moved on.

"But isn't it rather a lot for you to manage?" she asked, sweeping an arm to convey the house, gardens, and outbuildings.

"It comes with a special added feature," he replied with a smile, "the Prescotts."

"And what, exactly, are the Prescotts?" she said, returning his smile.

Graham explained the conversation he had had with the previous owners who told him that they had 'inherited' Mr and Mrs Prescott with the house. Mr Prescott looked after everything outside – tending the gardens, doing minor repair jobs on the buildings, and letting the owners know when any major job needed outside help to be hired. And Mrs Prescott was, apparently, the world's most flexible housekeeper – cleaning and tidying when and where it was needed, helping in the kitchen with dinner parties, and either helping or directing Mr Prescott as she deemed necessary.

"I've met them, and they're delighted to carry on looking after the house and me - its new owner." He felt that she was less than happy with this aspect and so changed the subject rapidly. "But I'm not being a very good host," he continued, "I managed to find the local supermarket this morning – you must be ready for lunch unless you've already availed yourself of British Rail's wonderful catering?"

"Lunch would be a great idea," she replied.

There was a fresh baguette on the worksurface in the kitchen, and Graham took a range of cheese, dips, sauces, and nibbles from the fridge. "Can you root around and find plates and things?" he asked. "I've no idea where anything is kept."

They took their food to the dining area. There was enough of a view for them to watch the various pleasure boats, both private and commercial, that passed along this stretch of the Thames. With a little persuasion, Carol shared a bottle of chilled Chablis with him, and they chatted easily in what was their first ordinary conversation. They talked about the various things that happened during the week, and the stories that were in the news. But since this mainly comprised bombs, strikes, and financial disasters, they soon switched to talking about her school and her pupils – a subject she always found easy to speak about.

It was a pleasure not to spend the whole time talking about time travel, and he hoped it marked a further step towards them having a more normal relationship, even though he was not yet sure what that relationship might be.

Maybe it was the effect of the wine or his persuasive personality, but he managed to get Carol to agree to go for a swim with him. It also helped him over a hurdle he imagined might be difficult. "You can change in the guest bedroom. It's yours for the night and you'll find a long towelling robe hanging behind the door. It's quite all right, I stole it from a posh hotel," he quipped.

Leaving the dishes in the sink, he changed quickly in his room and made sure he was at the pool before Carol arrived.

After a relaxing swim, which Carol found surprisingly enjoyable and "wonderfully decadent" they returned to the house. He dried and dressed quickly and went downstairs to fathom out the dishwasher. He set it to go with the light load of their lunchtime dishes plus those he had previously put in from his breakfast.

Music was playing on the stereo when Carol appeared and he was sitting on the sofa, looking through a local magazine. He passed it to her and asked her to choose a restaurant for their dinner that evening.

"Any you fancy," he offered, "on one condition. You don't look at the prices on the menu when we get there. The one thing I've learned from visiting here a few times is they are all extortionately priced."

She selected one and passed him the details.

"I trust you found your room acceptable?" he asked.

"It's perfectly adequate, thank you," she answered.

That evening, they walked up and down the quaint high street of Burnham village before taking their table at the Italian restaurant Carol had chosen from its advert in the local magazine. It was pleasingly (and surprisingly, for that part of the world) unpretentious, serving excellent food and providing a welcoming atmosphere.

They returned to the house and Carol refused his offer of an alcoholic nightcap, expressing the opinion that she had already drunk more that day than in a normal week – possibly a normal month. After a brief period of puzzlement, she managed to find a way to get a drinkable cup of coffee from the complex American coffeemaker in the kitchen.

Graham felt that normally, now would be the time to 'make a move' but reminded himself once more that this was no normal relationship. He was therefore not surprised when Carol announced that she was tired and would be retiring to the guest room. Graham finished his glass of Remy, turned out the lights, and went up to the main bedroom.

One of the few possessions he had brought from his flat was a digital radio as he liked to listen to late-night radio before going to sleep, and he turned it on and got into bed.

After a few minutes, there was a soft knock on his door, and Carol entered after he'd said "Come in."

She was wearing a floor-length dark blue nightdress and matching robe. Lace trimmed and silky, but not silk, it suited her pale skin tone and dark hair extremely well. 'As sexy as Marks and Spencer will ever get' Graham thought.

"I would like to be close to you," she said, a sad look on her face. "But I think I've forgotten how. There has been nobody for so long…"

He beckoned her to sit next to him on the bed, and she complied, resting her head on his shoulder as he put his arm around her. Then she began to cry, softly and continuously as he held her.

Graham understood. She was crying for the losses suffered, the loneliness and isolation, the continual sense of not belonging, the fear of the unknown, and all the other symptoms they shared. While there may be others who had experienced what they had been through, neither of them knew of anyone. As far as they were concerned these feelings were shared by them alone in the whole world. She was not the only one in the room shedding tears.

And in this manner, Carol fell asleep in his arms. He laid her head on a pillow, eased the bedcovering over her, and fell asleep next to her.

He remained as still as he possibly could when he woke and waited until she awoke soon after.

"I'm sorry, I didn't expect our first night together to be quite like that," she said, turning towards him.

"No," he replied, "I'd expected it to be more like this," and gently kissed her. She responded warmly. Slowly, gently, and carefully they began to make love, and it was unlike any sex he had ever experienced. What it may have lacked in passion and aggression it more than made up for with feelings of deep and close connection. He knew that this was something that would be very special and suddenly felt confident that their relationship would be close and lasting.

Throughout the day, interrupted only by brunch and by more lovemaking, they planned out the first steps of a shared future – carefully as befitted their unique situation.

Carol agreed to stay every weekend at Graham's house until her school broke up for the Christmas holiday. And they agreed that if everything was still going well, she would spend the whole four weeks of the Christmas holiday with him. She politely declined his suggestion that he should visit her in Worthing during the week – she was insistent on keeping the two parts of her life separate for the present. And on that theme, she said that she would want to return to Worthing once a week during the holiday – her friend Tilly had been very good to her, and she did not want to abandon her or the refuge where they both volunteered just yet.

Graham agreed to her requests, realising that she was still emotionally fragile in so many ways. He had been given the precious gift of someone with whom he could share his unique situation, and he wanted to handle things with kid gloves. But he insisted that she let him buy her a month's rail ticket so that she was not out of pocket – and let her know he wanted to meet Tilly soon. But she was not so quick to agree to that.

The weekends leading up to the year-end flashed by, and then it was time for them to spend some serious time together. They walked the local countryside. They ate meals at pubs, in restaurants, and at his home. They took day trips to the sights of London. They relaxed on his boat and tried - and failed - to come up with a name for the maritime equivalent of The Mile High Club. And in between he drove her to and from the railway station, enjoying the goodbye and welcome back kisses on each trip.

On Christmas Day he gave her just one present as they had agreed.

"It's actually two presents, but I think you'll understand," he said as he gave her the gift-wrapped parcel. It was a silk version of the night dress and gown she had worn on their first night together. It was beautiful, expensive and, he soon discovered, she looked wonderful in it.

"Your present is actually two presents as well", she said as she handed him a wrapped box. On opening it, he saw immediately that she had bought him the current Giles Annual. This had a special significance as he had told her that he was a big fan of Giles cartoons, something he had inherited from his father. His mother had bought his father the annual every year of their married life, and he knew that by giving him this present, Carol was sending him a strong message of hope for a shared future.

But as he lifted it out of the box in which she had packed it, he saw a second present below. From the wartime cover design, he recognised it as the 1946 collection – the first one published, and a truly rare and expensive item.

"I've got a confession to make," she said. "I bought you an old book at the second-hand bookshop near me. I go almost every week and the owner gives me a discount on the book I buy when I return the previous week's. I told him about your fascination with Giles, so when he found this edition in a collection of books he bought, he called me and gave it to me for a very special price – and I traded the other book back in, so I haven't spent as much money as you might have thought."

The combination of the two presents was very special to Graham.

"You know, we kind of got together because of the worst birthday I ever had, and now it looks like we're starting by sharing the best Christmas I've ever had," he told her and enjoyed the look of happiness she bestowed on him.

Not surprisingly, as the holiday came to an end, they discussed their future. In response to his request, Carol told him that she would be handing in her notice at the start of the new term, would leave at the mid-term break, and move in with him "if you'll have me" she said. It got the obvious reply about his willingness to have her whenever she wanted.

But she still wanted to go back to Worthing – not every week, but from time to time. Graham said that he wanted to buy her house in Worthing from her current landlord and transfer the title to her.

"In case this ever goes wrong, you'll have the security of knowing you've always got somewhere to go to – a roof over your head."

Carol was uncomfortable with him spending money on her, but he reminded her for the first of many times that the wealth he had accumulated was almost totally because of his time-travelling accident – and as such, it kind of belonged to her as well. In the end, she agreed.

She made it plain that she wanted to continue to work, and he suggested that she could either find a job in a local school or enrol with an agency. There should be plenty of supply teaching opportunities – the area was not short of private educational establishments. Alternatively, she could help him to assemble his plans for a charitable foundation which would be focused on giving his money to deserving causes. She had been a little worried about letting down the women's refuge where she volunteered each week, and Graham helped to win her over with the suggestion that this organisation could be one of the first causes they helped, possibly with funds earmarked for the recruitment of a paid helper to replace her.

In the end, she joined his company on a salary equal to what she had been paid by the school (her idea, which Graham was happy to agree with), and the first grant she oversaw was to the Women's Refuge in Worthing.

There was one final condition Carol laid down – and told him it was utterly non-negotiable. She would never marry him. It was not what he expected to hear, and it was stated in a manner that did not brook any discussion. But it was a condition he could live with.

They spent the next few months furnishing the house to their liking, discovering that they shared deeply conservative tastes. Very few possessions moved from her house in Worthing, which she continued to visit almost every month, staying overnight. Graham thought this a little unusual but was more than happy for her to continue as it kept her happy and grounded. On the nights she was away he would usually work – reading and preparing papers for his office visits and ensuring that his investments continued to produce exceptional returns to fund charitable work.

Graham's idea was to help small charities manage their money to achieve better returns. He planned to donate his time and expertise to them, as well as donating money. He also worked hand in hand with the Paternosters Charitable Trust which had been formed to provide matched funding or support to charities in which members of the firm were actively involved or which had a close connection with the firm. Using the trust's connections, he was able to ensure that when setting up investments for the charities, the financial organisations concerned waived all their fees. This, together with Graham's expertise enabled them to get the best possible return on their investments, whether small or large.

He and Carol focussed on small charities that came to their attention via the media, the recommendations of colleagues, or whatever. They would offer a donation and contact the principals of the charity, who were usually the parents of a child or the relatives of an adult whose misfortune had triggered the start of the charity. Some recognised that they needed help in managing funds and asked them to become involved in this way, which they were happy to do. Others merely took their money and gave their thanks – and that was OK too.

And they holidayed too. Graham was keen to revisit many of the places he had visited on business, particularly in the USA, and get to know them a little. Carol had a list of places she had longed to visit – and reminded him that she had had two lifetimes of longing. And then they both discovered that they fancied some more off-the-wall pastimes like taking a canal boat across England.

And they shared time with his siblings, nieces, and nephews, who welcomed the chance for a free holiday in a place with a swimming pool, a large garden, and a boat on which to take trips down the Thames. If a trip to London was not magical enough for a child, then a trip to London on your own boat certainly was!

-

Graham was not sure when he first noticed that Carol had an unusual interest in Diana, the Princess of Wales. As their relationship grew slowly and steadily, it became more obvious. There was nothing wrong with it, just one of those things that you noticed when you spent a lot of time with someone. He wondered idly if she saw some strange connection between herself and Diana – the outsider in every group, the quiet one, the one who permanently seemed to be on a different wavelength from those around her. The feeling probably went back into her first life too, he thought, when she was perhaps trapped in some form of golden cage herself, not unlike the Princess of Wales would claim to be.

He realised, as he was sure Carol did, that there would be a tragic end to this, and after the impending divorce of Diana and Charles was announced in 1996, he knew that the days were numbered, although he was not able to remember exactly how long it would be until her tragic end.

He was to learn soon enough, as one evening, after cooking him one of his favourite meals of spaghetti with scallops, accompanied by a beautiful Sauvignon Blanc served at the perfect chilled temperature, Carol said she wanted to talk to him about something serious. Having reminded him about his previous success at changing events such as Hillsborough and the arrest of Peter Sutcliffe, she calmly announced that she wanted him to stop Diana from dying in Paris.

The request took him by surprise, because after their initial conversations when they first met, they rarely spoke about the things they knew were coming. She had never shown any inclination in wanting to change things, other than in the positive way they both believed they were achieving through their charitable foundation. But, recognising how much she admired Diana (and maybe her feelings went way beyond mere admiration, but he did not want to explore that) and how simple the task might seem to prevent her death, it was not all that surprising after all.

He agreed to give it some thought and to try to come up with a plan. Knowing him the way she did, this answer was quite enough.

"I suppose you'll create a spreadsheet for it?" she asked, and he allowed her to gently mock him this way – but he did indeed prepare one and developed it over the next few days. He wondered whether an intervention of this sort had been in Carol's mind when they first met. Was it even a reason why she had responded to his advert in the first place? He decided that even if it was, the way things had evolved had made him so happy, there was nothing to be gained from probing her reasons in any way.

He asked her one evening if she could remind him of the circumstances that led up to Diana's death and was not surprised when she was able to give him a detailed account. For the next half hour she covered Diana's flight to Paris with Dodi Al-Fayed; their brief stay in his suite in The Ritz Hotel; the fateful car journey (which he learned for the first time was supposed to end at Dodi's apartment near the Arc de Triomphe) their pursuit by paparazzi; the driver who was well over the legal blood alcohol level; and the final, fatal crash with a white Fiat Uno car – a car that was never fully identified.

"So, apart from the missing car, it was all pretty straightforward?" he asked.

"Yes, the missing car will always fuel conspiracy theories, but it does seem to be a clear case. A drunken driver trying to avoid pursuers drives too fast and crashes."

He'd taken a few notes as she went through the story – and promised her he would give her a plan a few days later.

A week later, as they were clearing the dishes after their evening meal, he told her that he had a plan that he wanted to show her.

"I try to have both a primary plan and a backup when I do these things. So, my plan is quite straightforward and has two parts to it. Firstly, we need to make sure that whatever his name was that was over the limit is not driving,"

"Henri Paul" she interrupted him

"Yes, Henri – we need to make sure he is not driving the car. Secondly, we need to make sure that there are far fewer photographers pursuing the car."

She nodded in agreement and listened carefully to his plan. Half an hour later he had told her the whole thing and she simply got up from her chair, walked round to his side of the table, and gave him a big kiss.

"I knew there was a reason I shacked up with you," she said. "If that plan of yours doesn't work, then nothing will." She took a tissue from the nearby box to wipe the tears from her eyes which had trickled forth as the pain she had felt at the untimely death of such a beautiful person resurfaced.

The next day, she started her part of the plan and began an online French language course. Graham had told her that they needed one of them to be able to speak with locals and he was going to be busy with the other parts of his plan, so that role fell to her. She was delighted to be involved.

He asked her to contact estate agents in Paris to rent an apartment with at least three bedrooms, as close as possible to l'Etoile (which is how Parisians refer to the Arc de Triomphe), preferably in the Rue Arsene Houssaye.

He rejected the first few properties that she showed him – but eventually, they sent details of a three-bedroomed apartment on the very street he had requested, and he immediately told her to set up a one-year rental agreement.

Little else had to be done until May when the detailed parts of his plans began to take shape. He rented a suite at the Ritz in Paris for the evening of August 31st and hired a car for that day and the following day, stressing that it must be a large, black Mercedes saloon. He booked a private jet to fly from London to Paris on the morning of August 31st, with the return flight scheduled for an unspecified time on the following day.

He also re-established contact with those of his middle eastern contacts whom he thought would have contact with the Al-Fayed family in Egypt. Eventually, he hit the right button and got an introduction to Dodi.

Graham's contact set up a meeting for them at Dodi's office in the west end of London. When they met, there were two aspects of Dodi that he immediately noticed. He was an extremely good-looking young man, but neither this nor his great wealth seemed to have adversely affected his personality. He was an extremely likeable young man, and it was easy to see how a beautiful princess could be so taken with him.

Graham explained the aims and objectives of the charitable work that he had been involved in since his retirement, and Dodi commented on Graham's renown as a financial expert who had helped many of his acquaintances.

"But how can I be of any assistance to you?" Dodi asked.

Graham had read about the Al-Fayed Charitable Foundation, which had spent the previous twenty-five years bettering the lives of impoverished, traumatised, and very sick children, working with major children's charities. He knew that Dodi gave a lot of his time to the foundation.

"I like to help as many charities as possible," Graham explained, "but for personal reasons, I must keep below the parapet, so to speak, and it can be difficult to find charities that we can help. I thought that your organisation might receive applications for help that you're not able to assist with - and wondered if you could pass their details to me so that I can see if we can help."

"I'd be delighted to, that seems an excellent idea. It's always so disappointing when we are not able to assist, and this would give those charities a second chance. I'll make sure we put a programme into place as soon as possible."

They talked for a while, but their business dealings were essentially over in the first few sentences they had exchanged.

Graham left the meeting delighted to have killed two birds with one stone. He had opened a pathway to help more organisations in his charity work and had established a connection with Dodi which would be essential to his plans in a few months. After all, it would be an attempt to save not only Diana's life, Graham realised – but Dodi's as well!

Over the next couple of months, he exchanged a few emails with Dodi as the names of charities were passed over. As the end of August neared, Graham mentioned in one of his emails that he would be at the Ritz hotel on August 31st and, hearing that Dodi planned to be there on the same day, asked if Dodi could spare him a few minutes, to which Dodi agreed.

"Call me on my cellphone in the early evening, I'm sure I can find a few minutes."

Meanwhile, he contacted a modelling agency that specialised in providing look-alike models for promotional purposes. Meeting their managing director in her plush Mayfair office he explained that he wanted to hire the best Princess Diana look-alike for a job that would take place over the last weekend in August. He also explained that he would need a lookalike for Dodi Al Fayed – he even had a few photos in case they were needed. He was impressed with her well-tuned celebrity antenna when she informed him that this would be no problem, she had already lined up a suitable candidate. Lastly, he told her that a generic male model would be needed to fill the role of Diana's bodyguard.

She asked what the nature of the assignment would be – Graham knew that this was not just idle chatter as she would want to ascertain that the purpose was appropriate.

"We're making a film about Princess Diana and Dodi," he said. "There's a huge public appetite for this sort of thing – modern celebrity romance and all that. But we've run into a bit of difficulty with the privacy laws in France. We wanted to shoot some footage of them in Paris – you know walking hand-in-hand, having a coffee together, getting in and out of limousines, that sort of thing. It'll illustrate how they can do that sort of thing in Paris whereas they can't in London."

"So, we want your two people to do just that. Walk down the street together, sit at a pavement café, et cetera. We want to film it on the right day, with the right weather, and the right background – just in case anybody notices, which I don't expect they will. Then we'll mix it in with the real footage of them to complete the film. Should be out sometime in September."

"That won't be a problem," she replied. "I assume you will take care of transport and accommodation?"

"Yes, my partner deals with all that – can she call you tomorrow to sort out convenient flights? We'll have them back in the UK by the end of Sunday."

Graham had one last piece of preparation to do. Despite all the reassurances he had received that the conspiracy theories concerning Diana's death completely lacked merit, he was a cautious man. He made a call to John Bishop and told him that he was planning a weekend in Paris and had heard some strange, unsubstantiated rumours. He asked him to check whether "any of his mob or his close friends" were planning anything in Paris in the next couple of weeks - and was reassured on a return call that they weren't.

The fake versions of Diana, Dodi, and Trevor (the bodyguard) flew into Paris on the afternoon of August 31st and followed their instructions to meet at Mr Henderson's suite at the Ritz. Carol's detailed briefing meant that Graham knew Dodi and Diana would arrive at the Ritz around four pm. Soon after they arrived, he placed a call to Dodi, saying that he had urgent information concerning him and his companion and needed to meet. He was invited to their suite.

He took the private lift to the first floor and was met by a member of the Al-Fayed staff. Dodi appeared from a side room, smiled, and extended a warm handshake. The room was like no other hotel suite Graham had ever seen. After all, not too many suites have twenty-foot ceilings and are lit by chandeliers. 'This is what you can get when your father owns the best hotel in Paris', he thought.

Diana was in the main lounge area of the suite, and, despite having seen so many photographs and so much TV footage of her, he was still taken aback. Here, away from media attention, relaxed and in the company of the man she was so obviously in love with, Diana was even more beautiful than he had imagined. Lounging on the floor, wearing a dark blouse, and pale grey trousers that seemed to exaggerate her long legs, she truly brightened the room, and it took him some effort to tear his look away from her and concentrate on the important matter at hand.

Dodi was accustomed to losing the attention of people when meeting them in her presence and gave him the few seconds he needed.

"Thank you for seeing me, Mr Al-Fayed," he began.

"Call me Dodi, please," came the response.

"I've received some information of an urgent nature concerning the security of you and your colleague – might we discuss it briefly alone?"

He had planned his words carefully - homing in on the security that he knew was a concern (some might say obsession) of the Al-Fayed family. He was relying on the fact that Dodi knew of Graham's extensive work in the middle east to establish his credibility.

Dodi took him into the bar area of the suite, putting a little space between them and the other people in the room.

"As you know, Dodi, there are several members of the press gathered outside the building, interested in you and your companion", he said pointing towards the main area of the suite.

Dodi simply said "Yes", but in a way that expressed his frustration and annoyance surprisingly well.

Graham continued with his rehearsed speech, "I've received reliable information that some members of this group may wish to bring harm to you. They have already executed the first part of their plan - the man you intend to drive you later today has been compromised. He has been coerced into drinking far too much to drive safely and I must ask you to *not* use Mr Paul to drive you tonight."

Dodi did not speak, but Graham knew he had his undivided attention.

"I'd also like to offer you some assistance. I'm accompanied this evening by two people who are working on a film project for one of my companies. One of them is a lady who makes a living by her very close resemblance to your companion." Graham again indicated towards the main area of the suite, "and the other bears a remarkable likeness to yourself."

He paused to let this sink in. "If you give me a few minutes' notice of when you wish to leave this evening, I'd like to offer to take these two people out of the hotel a few minutes before you, and hopefully distract some, or all, of the members of the press."

They discussed the plan a little more, and Dodi accepted his suggestion and agreed that he would summon a different member of staff to drive them home. He thanked Graham for his help, agreed to notify him of his departure, and promised to arrange to meet again soon.

Delighted with the way his suggestions had been accepted, Graham returned to his suite and told his three companions that they were to shoot a little of the film tonight. He explained that it was a subterfuge, but a necessary one to film them being surrounded by paparazzi. He asked them to dress in a way that befitted their roles, describing as best he could the clothes that Diana has been wearing. He knew that this was something the press had likely taken note of and would help their planned deception. He also told them what Dodi was wearing and they enjoyed the joke that this wouldn't matter – he could be stark naked as nobody ever paid attention to anyone else when Diana was around. He apologised that they might be hassled by the press and asked them to stay in their roles as well as they possibly could. He also let them know that regrettably, they would not be staying at the Ritz that night – but promised that they would find the accommodation at the luxury apartment more than acceptable.

Once the costume change had taken place, Graham called for a hotel porter and accompanied him downstairs with the luggage belonging to his three actors. Once downstairs, a taxi was called and asked to deliver the bags to the apartment on Rue Arsene Houssaye. He used his schoolboy French, topped up with some of the vocabulary he'd learned from Carol's newfound language skill, to explain his request to the taxi driver, who was at first suspicious of the strange request from a foreigner but was quickly persuaded with a five hundred franc note to pay for the short journey.

Shortly before six pm, Graham received a call from Dodi. He immediately collected his car from the hotel garage and instructed his companions to descend five minutes later and head to the rear of the hotel, where he would be waiting.

All three of his companions got into the car with him and it seemed that the deception was at least partly successful. As he pulled out of the hotel into the Place Vendome before turning into the Rue de Rivoli, he noticed that almost a dozen motor-scooters and motorbikes were following him.

He drove slowly through the Place Concorde into the Avenue des Champs Elysees. The rear windows of the car were darkened and prevented any paparazzi from getting a clear sight of the car's occupants, so it was not until he turned into the Rue Arsene Houssaye and pulled up outside their apartment that the press got a clear sight of them.

The three passengers had to traverse a short distance to the apartment. Carol had been awaiting their arrival, and immediately held open the door when she saw the car pull up.

There was enough light for the snappers to get a clear sight of their prey, and doubt was sewn amongst the members of the press corps. Some departed immediately, while others remained. But it did not matter, the first part of the plan had been achieved.

Graham congratulated the three models on their excellent performance and Carol showed them to their separate rooms. He explained that they couldn't dine out that evening because of the aggressive press presence, and Carol eased their disappointment, by showing them the full range of food and wine she had bought that day.

"Now you know why you were asked to supply information about your dietary preferences when we hired you," she smiled.

Graham and Carol could not yet fully relax, but when an hour had passed, and no news had been received of any accident, they joined their three guests in a celebratory meal. Graham had wondered whether to ask Dodi to call him when he arrived safely at his apartment but thought that would have pushed things too far.

The following morning was filled with a series of fake activities for the three hired hands. They were asked to stroll down the street holding hands, admire the Arc, window shop in the Champs Elysees, stop for breakfast at a pavement café, and then, when called, make a quick dash to the waiting Mercedes limo. They were told that their every move would be caught on cameras, which for the sake of authenticity would remain hidden.

Once their series of activities had been completed, and they were reunited with their luggage in his limo, Graham drove them to Charles De Gaulle Airport for their return flights. He then returned to the apartment and collected Carol, who had been finding ways to dispose of the uneaten food from the night before. She had cleared it all, and some of the homeless in central Paris ate well that day.

Finally, they arrived at Le Bourget Airport, where their private jet waited. He had chosen this airport as it was the same one that Dodi and Diana had used, and it was part of his backup plan in case plan A had not worked. But it had, and once airborne, he and Carol could begin to celebrate their success.

The events of that weekend, or to be more precise, the results of the events – the saving of the lives of Dodi and Diana - had a marked effect on Carol. It was as if she could fully come out of her shell for the first time. Not only did she seem happier, brighter, and more relaxed, but her tastes seemed to change. She began wearing brighter, more fashionable, and more varied clothing. She began to shop for her underwear and night attire in Victoria's Secret instead of Marks and Spencer. She even said that she enjoyed a meal at Graham's favourite restaurant, Nobu, with its strong connections with Japanese cuisine that she had previously hated because it "didn't serve any real food".

She was more openly affectionate and took a more active part in planning their activities, both business and pleasure. One evening she even walked into the lounge area dressed in a scanty nightdress, carrying a large hairbrush. She lay across Graham's lap, handed him the brush, and said "I've been a naughty girl. You need to spank me." As he obliged with a few playful slaps, she turned to him and in a breathy voice said, "Harder!" He stopped before any bruising could occur, and she got up and said, "Let me show you how grateful I am for my punishment", and promptly did so in no uncertain terms.

On a more mundane level, she asked him to book somewhere special for the upcoming Christmas break. "I want snow. Lots of it. And warm fires and mulled wine. You must know where to go.".

All in all, he was very happy but felt some concern that Carol was overdoing it – like a candle burning too brightly in an atmosphere of pure oxygen or a lightbulb that is being fed with too much current (or too high a voltage, he couldn't be sure of the right analogy). He was a little uncomfortable, but knowing how fond she was of Diana, he trusted that the euphoria would end soon – and hoped against hope that his darling lightbulb would not burn out.

But in early December, the burnout occurred. Leaving Carol in their lounge, Graham went to the kitchen area to refill their wine glasses just as the main news came on the TV. He heard Carol loudly exclaim "Oh no!" and rushed across to see what had caused her outburst.

A black-tied newsreader was breaking the news of Diana's death. The only details available were that an accident had occurred at Dodi Al-Fayed's apartment in central Paris, where the couple had been staying. An ambulance had been called and despite arriving there extremely quickly, Princess Diana had been pronounced dead at the scene. No more details were available.

It later emerged that Diana had been working with a member of Dodi's staff to prepare Christmas decorations for the apartment. A fault in the ancient wiring of the building had caused her to be electrocuted. But this detail was not known at the time and the news could only focus on the reaction from prominent members of the royal family and government, and a general re-hashing of her whole life story.

Graham wondered why it was that once again his attempts at changing history had been thwarted. Was it a coincidence? Was there some way in which time automatically corrected itself so that the differences that might result from any interference would be corrected? Or, even more crazily, was there in truth a real conspiracy to kill Diana that he had thwarted, and which had now been put back in place? But he did not have time to concern himself with these issues.

As the news moved from reporting facts to more mawkish footage, Graham turned to Carol, who had not moved for several minutes. He tried to talk to her, comfort her, and even gently shake her, but when she did not so much as move a muscle, he grew concerned and called an ambulance.

The paramedics, who responded to his call within minutes, were also unable to get a response from her, and she was admitted to hospital later that evening. After many fruitless hours of holding her hand and hearing first a doctor and then a senior doctor state (but not in so many words) that they did not know what was wrong with her, reluctantly Graham left the hospital without any progress having been made. Staff reassured him that he would be called if there was any change in her situation overnight.

He returned after a short and very poor night's sleep and spent much of the following day by Carol's bedside, interrupted by her being seen by several medical staff, and being taken at various times for different tests.

At the end of the day, he was taken aside by a consultant who told him (without actually saying so) that there was nothing wrong with her physically, and that her problem would appear to be psychological. Although he was told that she would see other specialists in the coming days, Graham made the easy decision to move her to a private hospital.

Over the next couple of days, she was again tested repeatedly, and the same conclusion was reached and delivered to Graham by a consultant. The only difference from the first time he had been told was that the office in which he heard the news was larger and better furnished. This time he asked for a recommendation for further action and the consultant recommended a facility he knew in Surrey, where longer-term care was given to trauma sufferers.

Graham had every confidence in the recommendation but made an appointment to visit and took a trip down the A3 into rural Surrey the next day.

Tilehurst Hospital was a converted old Manor House set in spacious grounds. The original owners had the foresight to construct a high wall around the circumference of the grounds, and the ancient iron gates had been replaced by a modern electronically controlled pair, managed by cameras discretely located in the walls of the gatehouse. The original stream still flowed across the front of the property, but the lake had been filled in (for obvious reasons) and the garden landscaped. The modern extensions to the building had mostly been placed to the rear of the building, and those to the front had been heavily screened by trees. The whole place had a restful look to it – but the presence of a play area and goalposts to the right of the main building showed that they catered to younger as well as older patients.

Graham had an appointment with Mr McKenzie, the head of the establishment. Nigel McKenzie was a no-nonsense Scotsman, who, having heard the explanation of Carol's condition and the events that led up to it, was astute enough to remark that he did not believe he was being given all the facts – but was prepared to work with what he was being told.

Graham quickly decided that this was a man he would probably never be able to address by his first name, but felt he could have full confidence in. He was surprised to be told that once she was admitted, his visits, which he had previously been making every day, should be restricted to once per week.

"We need to allow her to ease her way back from this event and to gradually phase her return to the outside world. And while you're with her, I'd like you to try to keep your conversation with her entirely focused on personal events, if that's possible. Let's leave the outside world outside for a while, can we?"

He asked if Carol received any other visitors and Graham explained that he was the only family she had, but her friend Tilly visited almost every week.

"We'll allow her a weekly visit too, so long as you pass on the same directions to her, is that clear?" were the instructions given. Although not warming to McKenzie's personality ('or possible lack thereof,' Graham thought) he was impressed by his efficiency and obvious dedication to getting Carol well again. She was transferred the following day.

Graham had only met Tilly a couple of times during his relationship with Carol - and knew very little about her other than her obvious close friendship with his partner. He found her contact details in Carol's papers, called, and suggested they meet. He guessed that the coffee bar in Worthing where he had first met Carol would be familiar to Tilly and arranged to meet there.

Tilly was a tall, thin, angular woman whose dress sense made even Carol's earlier conservative style seem trendy. She joined him at the table and sipped carefully at a large latte. He discovered that she had shortened the unfortunate name of Matilda that her parents had bestowed on her, lived alone with a cat, worked in a local bookshop, and helped at the women's refuge where she had met Carol. They had met almost every week throughout his relationship with Carol.

She had no problems with the restrictions to visiting frequency and conversation content that Graham passed on to her from Mr McKenzie. She let him know that she was so concerned about her friend that she would continue to visit her once a week.

"As long as Minty lets me," she remarked, and when queried revealed that 'Minty' was the nickname for her car. Graham was introduced to Minty at the end of his chat with Tilly because he asked if she had any papers or letters for Carol. Tilly had left them in the car but was happy to hand them over.

Minty turned out to be an ancient Volkswagen Polo – the P on the registration plate betraying it as one of the first to have been sold in the UK, and its continued service was a tribute to German engineering. It had once been red, he assumed, but twenty years of exposure to the sun and the salty air of the English south coast had turned it to a dull, ugly pink.

'A Polo called Minty', Graham thought, 'Perhaps she does have a sense of humour buried in there somewhere.' He collected the letters for Carol and said he would try to meet Tilly when she next visited –

her visits always being on Mondays as this was her half day at the shop.

Knowing that Tilly would continue to visit Carol come what may, and, considering the possibility of her car breaking down on the journey between Worthing and the hospital, Graham resolved to show his gratitude practically.

On their second meeting, he said he had something he wanted to give her and handed her a large brown envelope. "What's this?" she asked.

The envelope contained the registration and ownership papers for a new VW Polo.

"I've been in touch with a garage in Goring – I believe that's close to you, isn't it?" She nodded a confirmation. "They've got a replacement for Minty ready for you to collect when you're ready. She's brand-new and they'll take care of her. And when you need to fill her up with petrol or have any repairs done – then you take it to the same garage, and they'll send me the bill."

Tilly at first refused his offer. Her old-fashioned attitudes bred a natural suspicion of any unsolicited gift – especially from a man. But once Graham explained the entirely practical reasons for his gift – and how essential he felt it was that she could be relied on to make her visits every week – she relented.

"I don't know how to say thank you, but I am very grateful, and you can be sure I'll keep visiting her as long as I can," were her final words.

"You don't have to say anything – I want you to know I'm very grateful for your friendship with Carol and I want you to be safe and sound – and not out of pocket - when you travel to see her. Oh, and the new Minty is bright red, I hope you'll like her," he said, leaving a slightly flummoxed woman behind.

Graham noticed a slight improvement in Carol's condition on his first visit to her in her new surroundings. She was now sitting upright in a chair and taking solid food when it was fed to her. 'Small victory, but progress,' he thought. And so it continued week by week. Little by little, the woman he knew and loved began to return. He played his part, keeping all conversation to personal memories and updates on some of the people she had dealt with in their charity work. He said nothing about events in the wider world. The months passed through the winter into the spring. Early in the new year she started to say a few words and began walking small distances. He had memories from his first life of the development of small children in their early years and recognised the similarities. He would occasionally meet with McKenzie and discuss the progress, which, although painfully slow, was clearly taking place.

On one visit, he noticed that Carol had made considerable progress in the space of a week. Asking about what she had been doing since they had last met, she was able to tell him that she had met some children and spent some time with them, enjoying it immensely. She was leading the conversation with him for the first time, and he saw the very first signs of the person he knew emerging from the gloom.

It was time to meet with McKenzie to discuss matters.

He learned that they had conducted a small experiment during the week, introducing Carol to a group session being held for some of their younger patients suffering from various mental traumas. The results had been quite remarkable – both for the children and Carol. She seemed able to relate to them in a way that even the most seasoned professionals had not achieved. Maybe the children recognised in some way that she was 'one of them,' or perhaps they had uncovered some innate ability in her, nobody was quite sure. But they planned to capitalise on the benefits of the session and repeat it as often as they thought beneficial over the coming weeks.

And indeed, it did produce results. He had to take as given that the children were benefitting – the staff all told him they certainly were – but the improvements in Carol were manifest. Within a few weeks, she was, to all intents and purposes, fully recovered and Graham knew he had to speak with Mr McKenzie. The next step would have to be taken with great care.

The decision to involve her with the children, which had been taken by Mr McKenzire himself had obviously proved to be a tremendous success. His caution and the interests of the institution both led him to make no changes and to keep the sessions going for as long as possible. But he understood that Graham would want Carol's return to normality to trigger the end of her stay and her release back to the real world.

Their discussion covered a whole range of issues, both wanting the best for her, and neither being sure what it was. Graham came close to telling him the full story of Carol's past to persuade him that he was truly the only man in the world who could relate to her needs. But he decided against it. The situation was complex enough and did not need this to cloud their decision.

Finally, they decided that they should have a meeting with all three of them present. Carol was now fully compos mentis, and the ultimate decision should at least involve her. The meeting took place a week later, and both men were surprised at her input. Once the reason for the meeting had been stated, Mr McKenzie asked what her thoughts were.

"I've really enjoyed these sessions with the children," she began, turning towards the psychiatrist. "I am so grateful to you for coming up with the idea. I've felt happier in my time with them than almost any other time in my life." Turning to Graham, she smiled and said, "Don't worry, I said *almost* any other time."

"I've felt that I'm actually doing some good, and I'd love to keep doing it – as much and as often as possible. And I don't feel any need to get back to the real world. Could I stay here?" she ended abruptly and directed her question to the room, rather than either of the two men.

Graham looked toward McKenzie, inferring that he thought the professional in the room should give the first response to the unexpected question. "Of course, we would love it if you could continue your input to the group, but don't you want to go home?"

"I know that Graham will understand it if I say that I have never really been *at home* while I've been living with him. I've loved it – but it's never been home to me. I've felt more at home here in the last few weeks than I've probably ever felt since I was a child." She looked towards Graham for a response, but he was unable to express all the different feelings he was experiencing. Sadness for her, for their relationship, and himself; but most of all sympathy for someone he had grown to love and who had suffered and survived the major setbacks of her disastrous first marriage, the major upheaval of jump in time that she had been through, and then the final disappointment after investing so much of herself into the Diana situation.

Finally, he gave his answer. "I want what's best for you. If that means you staying here, then there's no question in my mind, that's what we should do."

The discussion went on for almost an hour, but the key point had already been reached. Graham and Mr McKenzie would work out the details. Carol would no longer be classified as a patient – she no longer needed their professional help – but would be enrolled as a helper. She would work with the professional staff to provide care for the children and would be provided with on-site accommodation. They agreed to meet again in a week when Mr McKenzie would come up with a detailed proposal.

The second meeting followed a couple of phone calls between the two men to work on financial matters. On Graham's insistence, Mr McKenzie's proposal included a career development plan for Carol, and when it was put in front of her, she had no hesitation in agreeing to it.

She then dropped her second bombshell. "You don't need to visit me every week, my love. I don't mind if you're not here for a week or two. I enjoy spending time with you and look forward to it every week, but it mustn't be something you see as your duty. If you came here once or twice a month it would be like someone visiting a friend – that's what I'd like it to be. And we could have so much more to talk about when you do come."

And that is what happened. A visit once or twice a month between friends. Very close friends. Friends who shared secrets that were of a size and scope that was probably beyond any that had ever been shared by two people. But only a friendship. He harboured hopes that they might one day return to their former relationship. But as the months turned into years, these hopes diminished.

He had his work – a couple of days each month when he went into his former office and the increasing workload of his charitable endeavours. Then there was his domestic paperwork – ensuring his investments prospered and the small amount of time dealing with Carol's financial affairs. And a slowly growing list of domestic tasks delegated to him by the Prescotts. There were occasional meetings with contacts from the Middle East with whom he kept in touch - and even the occasional visit to the Youseffs with whom he had kept in touch since his time at university.

He kept Carol's Worthing property, employing a property maintenance company to make sure it remained in good order, in the hope that one day she might return. It also allowed him an excuse for the occasional visit to Worthing for coffee with Tilly when they would talk ceaselessly about Carol.

"What I don't understand is how you've been able to discover an entirely new type of radiation that nobody else has ever detected."

"Ah, that is because you suffer from a delusion that sadly is shared by so many scientists and has been for hundreds of years.... Throughout history, scientists have always believed that they completely understood things. But there are many things that have not been discovered, and many more that have been discovered but not understood. My team and I have found a type of radiation that nobody else has yet found. Which means that no-one can detect it. Which is why he (indicating John) is so interested in it."

Chapter Seven - The First Event of its Kind

On December 31^{st,} 1999, Paternosters took the unusual step of holding a party for its employees and their plus ones. It was, after all, the beginning not just of a new year but of a new millennium. After some thought, Graham decided to attend. He had been living a very quiet and unsociable life for the last few years and felt it was not unreasonable to let his hair down for one night.

The morning after the party, he realised that he had probably let it further down than he had planned when he woke up next to Molly. Or to be more precise, woke up to the sight of a dent in the bed next to him and the sound and smell of Molly preparing breakfast in his kitchen. She must have had a more abstemious evening than he had - and was preparing a full English breakfast for herself. He declined the offer of sharing it, breakfasting only on buttered toast and strong black coffee.

It rapidly became apparent that Molly did not regard the previous evening as a one-night stand. She was not unattractive, was several years younger than him and was, he knew, the subject of some speculation by some of his junior work colleagues. He had known her for several months but could not remember any lengthy conversation they had ever had before the previous night. And if they had had any lengthy conversation the previous night, he was unable to remember that either. He could not even remember what must have been a lengthy taxi ride home either. He decided to go along with the current situation, and thus their relationship began.

He sometimes felt that he had been targeted and was a little taken aback by how quickly she was prepared to develop the relationship. He made sure to tell her about the situation with Carol, but this did not seem to deter her. He even felt that he moved up in her estimation by his dedication. He went along with the flow but stopped short of her heavy hints about moving in together. He persuaded her that he worked so hard that he arrived home late several times each week and sometimes travelled on business. Reluctantly she settled for a mid-week date night every week and a regular weekend stay at his house.

But as the new millennium moved into its second year (or for those who insisted that a new millennium began in 2001, its first year) the truth was that he still had time on his hands. That spare time, and the size of the disaster that he knew was approaching, helped him to make up his mind on his course of action. For the first part of his plan, it would be very useful for there to be a girlfriend in his life and in his home.

Thus far in his second life, he had noticed that his attempts to change the course of events, to improve matters for would-be victims, had been largely unsuccessful. He had saved some lives with the early capture of Peter Sutcliffe, but this had been the only intervention that had not had some recoil (as far as he could tell). His prevention of the original Hillsborough disaster had resulted in the coach crash which had almost equalled the size of the original event (albeit the effects were not stretched over almost a quarter of a century as the original had been). And the complex steps that he and Carol had taken to prevent the car crash that had originally ended the life of Princess Diana had only bought her a few months of extra life.

Now, in the early days of the twenty-first century, he had to give some thought to the impending terrorist events in the USA, which would take place on September 11th, 2001.

He decided that the scale of the event – its effect not only on the thousands killed on the day itself, and their immediate families but also the resulting negative impact on every person who travelled anywhere in the world for the foreseeable future – not to mention the negative economic impact and the 'War on Terror' – meant that he would have to try to prevent it.

But he would not take any risks. He had had enough of that. He decided to construct a realistic warning and direct it as well as he could to the right ears. That would be all.

He thought long and hard about how, where, and when to deliver his message. The 'where' was obvious. He had established credibility with John Bishop from years of providing him with reliable information. And John knew that Graham had multiple good contacts in the Middle East. So, if Graham supplied him with information about a possible terrorist attack it would be believed.

And when the warning was passed over to the US Secret Service from their British counterparts, there was every chance that action would be taken. So now he had to decide when it would be best for him to deliver his message. It would have to give the authorities enough time to do something, but it also must contain enough urgency that rapid action would be needed. He decided that six months' notice would be just about right. So, in March 2001, he acted out a brief subterfuge in which Molly would play a vital but unwitting part.

Most Friday evenings she would finish work a little early and take a taxi (charged to his account) to his house, cook a meal for him, and stay the weekend. So, one Friday when he had work commitments in London, he deliberately left his mobile phone at home. Shortly after she arrived at his flat and found he was not yet home she was surprised to hear his phone ring.

(Graham was glad that the security features that would in later years make it impossible for her to answer were not yet standard on mobile phones.) When she answered, he said he would be home in about an hour, apologised for being late, and expressed his relief that the phone was at home and not lost or stolen as he had feared.

She did not know of the full pantomime that he was performing nor its reason. She would have been surprised to know that he travelled from his office to the West End of London just to place the call. He used a pre-paid mobile phone while standing in the street close to the Embassy of the Kingdom of Saudi Arabia and then threw it in a bin and took a taxi home.

Graham had conducted the charade to establish that a short phone call had been made from a burner phone to his mobile – and if the location of the call could be traced, it would further substantiate the story he was soon to tell John Bishop.

On Saturday morning, he used the emergency number John had given him years earlier and requested an urgent meeting. Moreover, he specified that the meeting must take place outdoors in a public place, which he knew would sound a warning. He had long been sure that John was employed by a branch of the secret services.

They met a few days later and Graham delivered a simple message.

"I had a call from one of my contacts in the Middle East. I don't know who it was, and he didn't say his name on the call. But the number he called me on means he's a contact of mine (or one of my contacts has given him a number that I only give to very close contacts). And his tone on the call convinced me that the information he gave me was accurate, or at least he was sure it was. He sounded frightened, and when I tell you why, I'm sure you'll understand. He said there's a terrorist cell targeting the USA. There may be as many as a dozen of them and they're planning to hijack multiple planes on the same day and crash them into high-profile targets on the east coast." He paused for effect. "They're in the USA now. Maybe training as pilots. And they're all backed by someone called Yosama ben Raden. That's it – he told me all that and then hung up."

He'd thought long and hard about this story. He needed to give enough information, such that might have been leaked, but not too much. And crucially omit some information and slightly corrupt part of the remainder.

John asked him a few questions about the call and the caller. He asked if Graham could identify the caller and Graham said he was not sure – and even if he was, he felt he should preserve his contact's anonymity. Accepting this, John asked if he could identify which part of the middle east the call came from. Graham said he thought the caller was probably from Saudi Arabia – he used some words and phrases of Classical Arabic which would infer he was a Saudi national – but he couldn't be one hundred percent sure.

John also asked about the name the caller had given as the instigator. Graham said he had reported it as well as he could, but with the traffic noise in the background, he might not have heard it clearly. (He'd learned about the importance of sometimes giving 'near-accurate' information to help establish the veracity of the overall message.)

Now Graham had to just wait. Worse than that, he had to wait for something *not* to happen. When they had their next dinner together, John informed him that the message had been passed on, but he also confirmed Graham's suspicions. Even if John got to hear from his American counterparts about developments resulting from the information, he would not be able to pass on much if anything. He reiterated his gratitude – and smiled knowingly when Graham intimated that passing such high-grade material cannot have done John's standing any harm. And he allowed Graham to order a very expensive bottle of wine on his tab.

Graham watched his news feed very carefully on September 11th and was never happier to see a boring no-news day pass by.

-

He continued his life: his visits to Carol, his charitable work, his two days a month of work for Paternosters, and occasional dinners with contacts. He pottered around his home and enjoyed a diminishing number of weekends with Molly. He noticed that Mr Prescott was more frequently being assisted in the garden by Mrs Prescott and that he was being asked just slightly more often to 'get someone in' to deal with maintenance issues.

His relationship with Molly did not end – it merely petered out. Her weekend stays had gone from every, to most, and then to some weekends. And their mid-week dates became fewer in like manner. She had met most of his family during the two summers that their relationship had lasted – inevitable as she was often in residence for the weekend when they visited. He had noticed, and occasionally asked why he had met so few of her family, never receiving a clear answer. Although she had never given any indication of wanting to deepen their relationship – which Graham would probably not have agreed to anyway, he eventually blamed his lack of interest for yet another relationship ending.

Otherwise, he had few contacts with the rest of the world. He felt so frustrated at his inability to help the parents of Millie Dowler when she went missing – he simply could not remember the name of the man eventually found guilty of her murder. And when he called the police to anonymously report Ian Huntley (whose name he did remember) when the press reported that two children had gone missing from a school in Soham, it was sadly obvious that it had no effect.

And when England won the Rugby World Cup in 2003, he regretted not being able to fully share in the joy (as he remembered doing over a very alcoholic breakfast in his first life). It was different when you knew the result before the game even started.

He was almost as shocked as the rest of the world in September 2005 when a United Airlines flight from Logan International Airport in Boston Massachusetts crashed into one of the twin towers of the World Trade Centre in New York.

Having lived through an identical situation some fifty years earlier, he was less shocked that such a thing could happen. He had visited the US only once since 2001 in his second life, and airport security had not much changed. Presumably, the terrorist cell had been broken up in 2001, and the warning had not been fully acted upon. Or, as he soon found out, the warning had been acted on in some ways but not in others.

Details coming into the news feeds were confusing. But with the knowledge that Graham had of the original 9-11, it was clear that the US had beefed up their military preparedness for such an event, even if they had not beefed up their civilian security levels. He quickly realised that the reports coming in of other plane crashes could mean only one thing – further terrorist hijacks had been identified, and the military was shooting down the planes before they could reach their targets.

This news emerged over the next few hours and was confirmed over the next couple of days. Three planes had been shot down by USAF fighters, and the impact on the consciousness of the American public was huge. But it was different from how he remembered it the first time around. The targets for the public's anger were split – anti-foreign sentiment got its expected airing, but many organisations with an anti-military axe to grind used this as an opportunity to sow division. Protests – some of them ironically violent – took place outside military establishments throughout the USA and beyond.

Graham wondered if he would become involved in the backlash, as the fallout from this event would produce a witch hunt to end all witch hunts. He was sure it would be common knowledge in the intelligence community that there had been a clear warning of this event some five years earlier, even though it would never be made public.

The way he was involved caught him by surprise. Two days after the attacks, several police vehicles, blue lights flashing, pulled into his driveway. A group of men, armed and in combat dress, emerged from the vehicles and began hammering on his front door. Once he had admitted them to his home, he was arrested, handcuffed, and placed, none too gently, in the back of a police van. As he was driven away, he could see the throng of police entering his house - intending a thorough and untidy search.

His restricted view from the police van did not give him a chance to see where he was taken. The journey took about half an hour, and he did not recognise the police station whose back door he was bundled through. He was summarily 'processed' and placed in a cell; the few contents of his pockets duly removed and recorded. And there he sat for several hours – the provision of one cup of lukewarm tea being the only interruption, and the constable who brought it to him refused any engagement in conversation.

It was thus dark when he was ordered again to stand back from his cell door before two large policemen entered, placed handcuffs on him and escorted him back the way he had come. He noticed that this time the van he was placed in was unmarked, and neither the driver nor his companion wore uniforms. His second journey of the day took over an hour to complete.

What little he could see when the doors were opened told him that he was now in a rural setting, and the building he was being taken into was a nondescript country house. It was too large to be a family home but too small to be used by any major organisation. It looked plain and slightly rundown – and could have been any one of hundreds of similar properties to be found on the periphery of London.

The lack of any type of decoration on the corridor he walked along, and the room in which he was placed told him all he needed to know. The room was about fifteen feet square with plain walls and contained only a table and three cheap office chairs as furniture. This had to be an interview facility – and probably, Graham guessed, some part of Her Majesty's Secret Service.

After a few minutes, two young men entered the room. He presumed that the one on the right, the slightly taller and heavier of the pair, was the junior as he had been delegated the task of carrying a file, a notebook, and a pen. The other was empty-handed and was the first to speak.

"I'm sure you know why you're here, but just to make it totally clear, you are suspected of involvement in a major terrorist event that has threatened the free world. Don't worry about your right to have a solicitor present or anything like that. You're here for as long as we say you're here, and certainly won't be going anywhere until we're sure you've given us all the information we want. Is that clear?"

"That's clear", Graham said. He was worried – but not yet too worried.

"And by the way, you've just sent an email to all your contacts telling them that you are going to be out of contact for a few days and they won't be hearing from you," he was also told.

The initial questioning concerned his contact with John Bishop and the information he had given him five years earlier. He was asked repeatedly about the content of the phone call he had reported and was pressed to reveal the identity of the caller. It was made clear to him that this information was considered a vital lead to uncovering the network that had carried out the atrocity.

After frequently repeating his original words to John, that he did not know the identity of the caller, and after much pressure to speculate he made his position clear.

"Look, if I give you information that leads you to investigate the person who made that call, you'll investigate him. And the terrorists will know. They'll know he leaked information, and very soon after, they'll know to whom he leaked it. There's nothing you can do that frightens me more than the thought of a bunch of terrorists who have just murdered hundreds of innocent people, and intended to murder thousands of innocent people, knowing my name. So, even if I did know, I wouldn't tell you."

And that was pretty much how the first session, which had lasted about two hours, ended. Graham was left alone for another half an hour before two more interviewers – one male and one female – entered the room.

This time the questions were on an entirely different topic - his time at university. He was asked about how he had come to have enough money to buy a house when he was only nineteen. "And don't say you got the money from your family. We've already checked that out and it's a lie," his female interviewer told him.

Graham was beginning to get a little worried at this stage. He could understand – and was quite expecting – a good level of interest in his original statement to John about the US terrorist attack – but this digging deep into his past –signified a more detailed investigation – and one that must have begun more than a couple of days ago.

"I won the money from betting on football," he answered.

"Oh yes," she continued, "always the answer. I put money on a horse or a football team and won a huge amount."

He took the opportunity of filling the silence she left him.

"It wasn't one big bet. It was lots of small bets. I'm sure you found out that I wrote a computer program to predict football results – well, I used that program to tell me where to place lots of small bets and I built up the money over several months. I'm sure that somewhere I've still got a list of all the betting shops that can easily be reached from the Central Line."

He silently congratulated himself on having the backup story of using his computer program as a false justification for his success. He had always thought that this deception might prove useful but had never imagined that it would be in circumstances like these where he would use it.

At this point, the male interviewer leaned over to his female companion and whispered something in her ear. Graham suppressed a smile – it was obvious that they had by now searched his house and found the list somewhere amidst his paperwork. As he turned his head to speak to her, Graham noticed that he had a small plastic device in his ear.

'Either they are more inclusive in their hiring than I thought – employing deaf people – or he is being spoken to by someone outside the room. Probably the latter,' he thought to himself.

There followed a few questions about his relationships at university and his early entry into Paternosters, but they seemed somewhat aimless. He answered them all as completely and as fully as he could, and, after another brief word from the male interviewer into the female interviewer's ear, they departed, and he was alone once more.

He tried to keep a clear head. He had some concerns about the length of his stay and the unfriendliness of his interviewers, and he began to wonder how long this was likely to persist. He was prevented from dwelling on these matters for too long by the return of the original two interviewers.

This time the junior agent had more work to do. He'd taken very few notes, and not even referred to his file once in their first session, but this time was more involved.

"We'd like to show you a few photos." his colleague started. "Let us know if you recognise any of them."

The junior agent then produced photo after photo from his file, placing them one at a time on the table in front of Graham, allowing him to look at them, and, confirmed by gestures, to pick up the photo and look more carefully when needed.

They were a mixture. Some were posed photos showing the subject's head and shoulders – the US habit of college yearbook photos came to mind. Some were more obviously cut from personal or family photos, and yet others showed every sign of being the products of covert surveillance. Almost every one of them was of a young adult male of middle eastern appearance; and Graham sensed that he was being tested, if not tricked. The subjects were a mixture of people he had dealt with when at Paternosters, some known celebrities, politicians, or members of Arab aristocracy, and some that were completely unknown to him. He was also sure that some photoshopping had taken place as every person appeared in western dress, casual or formal – even some who seemed, by their hairstyle or other give-away features to be entirely inappropriately presented.

After a couple of dozen had been passed in front of him, he began to wonder if the same person – a face that he was not able to identify – was being presented to him multiple times, each in different wrapping as it were.

When he thought it happened again – he looked up and spoke to the file holder. "Could I have another look at that photo I couldn't recognise – about eight or ten photos ago?" he asked. The agent confirmed his junior status by looking at his colleague to provide an answer.

Senior turned to junior and said, "If you could keep the ones that Mr Henderson is not able to recognise to one side, we may come back to them later."

The procession of photos resumed, and Graham did his best to respond. After another twenty or so had been passed in front of him, with half a dozen of them being unknown to him, this stage of the task seemed to have been complete. The last photo was an unexpected one, which he took a few minutes to distinguish. It was one of those occasions when you go 'I know that face' but have trouble placing just where and when you saw it.

Suddenly it came to him, "that's Tariq from university – I haven't seen him in years," Graham answered.

"Indeed, it is. Now perhaps you could look again at one or two of the photos you have not been able to identify for us," said the senior interviewer, prompting his junior to start pulling the photos from that section of his file.

Graham looked carefully. "It's Tariq, isn't it?" he asked. His lack of certainty was caused by nearly thirty years of ageing that had occurred between the previous photo (taken either at university or very shortly

172

thereafter) and the one he was looking at now. They looked to have been rough years for Tariq.

The conversation, or more properly, the interrogation, changed direction as he was questioned about his relationship with Tariq.

"You were very close while you were at university," was the opening gambit from his interviewer. "Everyone said you spent a lot of time together," he continued.

Graham had to work hard for the next half an hour to persuade his interviewers that he was not, and never had been, friends with Tariq. He repeated in every way that he could that Tariq had only ever been his Arab language tutor. He reinforced the fact that they had never mixed socially – in fact, he had found Tariq to be unresponsive to any social invitation.

When they had first met, they were both newly starting at university – friendless and alone. He gave his opinion that Tariq was a real loner – who seemed not to have any friends either inside or outside the community of Arab students, many of whom Graham had got to know from the Arab Society. He gave his opinion that Tariq was probably as friendless after their three years at university as he had been at the start. He was a loner, and it was no surprise to Graham that he had shown no interest in keeping in contact after they left university.

His interviewers asked him about several of his contacts while at university, but it was obvious that Tariq was the one they were interested in. Graham told them that anything he said about Tariq would be speculative because he had learned so little about him. Even after spending probably more than a hundred hours in his company as he honed his language skills.

He thought that Tariq was estranged from his family. He never spoke of parents, brothers, or sisters, was always short of money (which was unusual in that community, Graham remarked), and seemed to think himself superior to many of his fellow Arab students. He had been critical of the way they had picked up western habits and deserted many of the traditions of their heritage. Graham repeated Tariq's jibe about them all being 'bounties' – but this drew no reaction.

Eventually, even his interviewers felt that they were now going over the same ground multiple times and ended the session.

He suddenly realised how tired and hungry he was. He'd had nothing but a glass of water since the lukewarm tea in the police cell, and he began to wonder if his mental and physical stamina would prevail. But they were not put to a further test as a few minutes later the two junior interviewers (as he thought of them) returned and asked him to accompany them. This time without handcuffs – a distinct sign of progress, he thought.

He was escorted to a room containing a bed, an upright chair, a small table, and nothing else. "It makes Premier Inn look positively luxurious," he quipped to his two escorts.

"There's a bathroom behind that door," one of them replied, indicating a door in the far corner of the room, "and the light switch is here," he said pointing to the only other feature of the room, next to the door through which they had entered. "You can sleep for a few hours."

As soon as they left, Graham followed their instructions, collapsed on the bed, and fell asleep immediately. He didn't even use either the light switch or the bathroom.

He was not sure whether he was watched by a secret camera, and had been woken by some means, or whether it was a coincidence that the door rattled, and an agent walked through minutes after he woke. A plate containing two bacon rolls and a small carton of orange juice – complete with a plastic straw – was placed on the table. He was also given a small bag containing a few items of clothing and a toilet bag. He was sure the clothing would fit him and had no problems using the toiletries supplied since all the items had come from his home.

"You can freshen up and eat – we'll expect you to be ready to answer some more questions in an hour," he was told.

He welcomed the chance to shower and change, and to have the chance for the first time to reflect on the events since his arrival at wherever he now was.

It was plain that he had been investigated – and it was probable that the investigation had begun before the events of the last few days. He guessed that his long-term role as an informer to whomever John Bishop worked for had made that a necessity. But it looked like the only real in-depth investigation had covered his time at university before he met John. Or else surely there would have been some questions relating to his visit to Sheffield or to Paris, both of which might have been uncovered with the access that was no doubt available to his questioners. And it seemed that a significant focus was being placed on Tariq – even though he had had no contact with him for almost thirty years. The fact that they had a recent photo of him must mean that Tariq was of some interest to them.

He realised that he would face more questions – but was content in the knowledge that what was being sought – the name of his 'terrorist informer' would elude them – for the simple reason that he did not exist. His only worry was that if he was pressed to a point where he had to say something, he could not take refuge in the truth. 'I know all this because I've travelled back in time and am living my life for the second time,' was just not going to sound good as an answer under pressure!

True to their word, his door was unlocked sixty minutes later. Refreshed by his food, drink, shower, and change of clothing, but still carrying a day's stubble (they'd forgotten to include a razor in his guest pack), he was returned to the interview room.

The pair interviewing him now was comprised of the senior one of the first pair of the previous evening and the junior from the second pair. They covered no new ground, but instead reiterated and confirmed what he had been asked and answered the previous day. After about an hour, the junior partner turned to the senior and spoke into her ear. It seemed obvious to Graham that he had received words in his ear – a fact that he felt was confirmed when the interview was brought to an abrupt end and the pair left the room.

He was once more left alone for another half an hour before the door opened and a familiar face entered.

"I'm so sorry for this misunderstanding," were the first words that John Bishop said as he entered and shook Graham's hand. He gestured for him to sit down and took one of the other chairs.

"I knew these guys were interested in you – obviously we share information – but I had no idea they'd go this far. I guess they're under a lot of pressure from across the pond, and in my way of thinking they spend far too much time with those guys and pick up some very bad habits. We'll have you out of here as soon as I can make it happen. They haven't been too rough on you, I hope."

Graham reassured his friend that nothing had been damaged ('although that doesn't include our relationship' he thought to himself.)

175

"I told them that you had no contact with that guy, but they had to make sure for themselves," John continued.

"It's Tariq they're interested in, then?" Graham asked.

"Well let's just say we don't have all of those photos of him because we admire his rugged good looks, shall we?" John replied with the obvious intention of closing the discussion. After a brief amount of small talk, John left the room with a promise of sending in some coffee and having him out of there 'in a trice'.

Graham drank the first cup of a pot of surprisingly good coffee and considered this most recent development. John's performance was convincing – but it still felt like it had been a performance. This had to have been an elaborate 'Good Cop Bad Cop' routine – at least that was what he thought. He would need an awful lot of convincing that it wasn't.

Nonetheless, he was soon reunited with his possessions and politely asked to take the back seat in a car outside the building a few minutes later. Wearing his change of clothing – and his watch and belt once more - and carrying his dirty laundry and toiletries in his bag, he was delivered back home that afternoon. He began the task of cleaning up after the search party. And he continued the task over the next few days, accompanied by Mrs Prescott while doing his best to reassure her that his brief time with the police had all been the result of mistaken identity. He hoped that she would convey this to the local community, who by now had no doubt heard of the raid and his summary departure.

But he knew that the locals would never see him in quite the same way ever again.

-

Graham adjusted once again to the quiet life. He continued to spend a couple of days each month working for Paternosters. He visited Carol at least once a month and had a monthly dinner with Tilly. He was able to increase his charitable work, and his occasional meetings with clients from the middle east, and infrequent meetings with John Bishop all helped to pass the time. He noticed that both Mr and Mrs Prescott were more often calling on his help as they found some tasks too physically challenging.

He occasionally passed information to Pat Threlfall. He made anonymous calls to Suffolk police to inform them that the serial killer on the loose in

Ipswich was Steven Wright – and was confident that this action saved a couple of lives.

As soon as the tragic news of the disappearance of Madeleine McCann broke in May 2007, he gave a tip-off to John Bishop that the Portuguese police should look for a well-known German criminal who had been seen in the Praia da Luz area in the previous few days. Sadly, it transpired that this had no effect on the investigation – and he had to carry the frustration of knowing information but being unable to successfully impart it.

He let his life slip by for some five years, always with the knowledge that October 2012 – the date of Carol's 'jump' - was approaching. This date loomed like a growing cloud on the horizon. He never mentioned it during his visits to her, but in August of that year, she mentioned it to him for the first time.

They talked for a while about it, both unsure if anything would happen on the date, and if so, what it might be. Knowing that whatever it was, it was unlikely to be good, and sure that they were powerless to affect it anyway, he felt sure that Carol had reached a quiet acceptance of whatever fate had in store for her.

As a distraction, he decided to tell her about the visit to City Road which he had recently made when it had first struck him that the date of her 'jump' was almost upon them. The building they both remembered had now been built, and he had visited the solicitors that she had been dealing with all those years ago. He had never got round to making a will, and so he pretended that a friend of his had recommended them. His meeting had been with a Ms Grenfell and when he gave a brief description of her to Carol, she thought this might have been the person she had met. But since the meeting had taken place some forty years ago – quite literally in another life – she could not be sure.

He told her that they had met in what he presumed to be the same office as Carol's meeting. After outlining his straightforward wishes for his will and setting a date for his second visit, he had taken the opportunity to have a good nose around both the solicitor's office and as much of the rest of the building as he could.

He reported that the financial company that he had met in 2022 when his jump had occurred (which was of course both forty years ago and ten years into the future) had not yet moved into the building. He'd been able to look at the floor they were going to occupy as there were some empty offices. He had blagged his way into a tour from the management company on the basis that he was looking to open an office for his own company.

He also told her that the floor between the offices of the solicitors and that of the financial advisors was occupied by the Department of Work and Pensions. He had deliberately got out of the lift on the wrong floor and spoken to the receptionist. It seemed to be a perfectly normal government office that was full of civil servants busily doing whatever it was that civil servants do.

But his visit to the solicitor, the tour of the offices on the empty floor, and his mistaken visit to the DWP had not revealed anything useful. They agreed that they just had to accept this as a mystery they would never crack.

As October neared, he arranged a meeting with Mr McKenzie, who was still in charge of the institution where Carol had once been a patient and was now a 'special employee.'

"You've always known that there is part of Carol's story that I can't tell you – and I'm afraid that will always remain so," he told him. "But I need you to know that the date of October 8th has always been a special day for her. This year that date marks a very significant anniversary. I need you to arrange a special watch over her for forty-eight hours. And to have all emergency services available on standby."

Mr McKenzie pushed him to reveal more, but Graham was adamant that this was not possible. He also made sure that he understood that any expenses would be fully reimbursed. If it was not possible for the security measure that he'd asked for to be implemented, he would have to make separate arrangements, which he was sure was not what was wanted by either party. He also made sure that under no circumstances were these measures to be made known to Carol.

Unhappy to be kept in the dark as he knew he was being, Mr McKenzie nonetheless agreed to keep a careful eye on her.

But, once again, Graham's carefully laid plans went awry.

In the early hours of October 8th, he received an urgent call from the institution to tell him that Carol had died without any warning. She had been checked every half hour as instructed, but at three am she had proved to be unresponsive. A crash team was with her in minutes but was unable to resuscitate her.

Even though he had known that this was one of the possible occurrences on this specific date – he had so hoped that the measures he had put in place would have prevented it. But a part of him knew that it was unstoppable. In the way that the close relatives of someone with a terminal disease, who know that death is just around the corner, still react with shock and all the stages of grief when it happens, so did Graham.

Her cause of death was confirmed as heart failure.

For the last fifteen years, Carol had been no more than a friend that he had visited once a month. But he still had the memories of their time together – and the unique and truly incredible bond that they shared. Her death seemed so needless and weighed heavily upon him.

Only when some three months had passed, the funeral had taken place, and most of the administrative procedures had been dealt with, was he able to respond to Tilly. She had sent him several requests to discuss something important concerning Carol. He knew that he had to sell Carol's house and had postponed this task for as long as he could. But this now needed to be faced and a visit to Worthing would make the ideal opportunity. He called Tilly and arranged when and where they should meet.

Returning to Worthing, to the very coffee bar where he and Carol had first met was difficult. Tilly was quick to suggest an alternative meeting venue, but he told her he wanted to confront all his ghosts - so they met there once again. Their conversation dealt with some of the minor touchpoints – messages received from her ex-colleagues at school, and letters from her colleagues at the institute were passed between them until Tilly told him the reason that she had asked him to come down to the coast.

"It's easiest if I show you what it is. We'll need to visit her house," she said, and when he realised that he was not going to get any more explanation, he agreed to accompany her. He was still waiting for the probate of Carol's will, but at some time the house would have to be sold, and it would be sensible for him to look at the place. It was many years since his last visit, and he had never seen the whole house.

Tilly opened the door and showed him in. He knew that she had been visiting the house every month – they had agreed to keep it while Carol was alive, in the faint hope that one day she might want to see it. She had insisted on keeping it, even when living with Graham, and back then he had no need or wish for it to be sold.

"I need to show you the back bedroom," Tilly said, and when they reached the top of the stairs, he was surprised to see her take the set of keys from her pocket and unlock the door.

Once inside the room though, the reason was obvious. This was not a back bedroom – it was a shrine. A shrine to the late Diana, Princess of Wales. The walls bore several pictures - reproductions of her official portraits, all properly, and probably expensively, framed. Two display cabinets housed various commemorative items – not the cheap tacky kind, but the official and (slightly) more tasteful varieties of plates, cups, mugs, and so forth, bearing the names of manufacturers such as Wedgwood and Royal Doulton. The overflow of these items covered the surface of a large coffee table. Looking at a small bookcase, Graham saw the spines of various books on the life of Diana, and on the bottom shelf a set of large books whose spines were too narrow to house any lettering. They seemed out of place, but it was one of these books that Tilly removed and opened in front of him.

It was a beautifully prepared scrapbook. As she turned the pages, he could see the press cuttings neatly secured, and the occasional small piece of paper with Carol's neat writing upon it pasted to the page.

"She kept every cutting from The Times and meticulously put them in. Some days she had to go and buy an extra copy of the paper if there was something about Diana on both sides of a page. And she even ordered a special reproduction of an earlier edition where Diana's birth was announced. She used to update these books when she came down to Worthing from your place, and she made me swear to keep them up to date - ever since she could no longer do it herself."

Tilly made her little speech in a sad, rueful voice, and Graham felt so moved that he found it very difficult to reply.

Eventually, he spoke his thoughts aloud. "This is beautiful. And it deserves to be seen by as many people as possible. Maybe the Spencer family would be interested."

He promised Tilly he would do everything he could to see that the contents – especially the scrapbooks - were properly looked after. He asked if she would like any of the mementoes for herself. She chose a beautiful, engraved glass bowl and promised to keep it on display in her own house as a permanent reminder of Carol.

Feeling like they were closing a secret chamber, they left the room and parted company on the doorstep.

Sadly, they saw each other less and less as the years passed. Graham did establish contact with the Spencer family – but was not able to arouse any interest from them. There was an exhibition of items commemorating Diana's life, but they were unable to incorporate any part of the collection as it was due to close the following year. He took everything from the room and housed it in a dedicated room in his own house – which sadly saw too few visitors.

However, he did manage to persuade one important visitor to visit the collection. It was his only meeting with Dodi after Diana's funeral, and he was able to show him the room and tell him the story of his partner. He was pleased that Dodi – now with very little time on his hands as he was largely running his father's empire – took the time to visit. He was happy to comply with Dodi's request that Graham would pass the contents of the room to Dodi if he was ever unable to maintain them.

-

At the age of sixty, he thought the time had now come to retire from Paternoster's – it was becoming more and more difficult to raise the enthusiasm to make yet more money – even though there was never any shortage of charitable projects in which to place it.

The Prescotts eventually retired, and the upkeep of his house, gardens, and boat took up more of his time. He continued to work on his charitable projects, both alone and jointly with the Paternoster Charitable Foundation - and prepared himself for what he believed would be one last challenge.

Chapter Eight - The First Retelling

Once again Graham reviewed his history of interventions. None had been spectacularly successful, he had to admit. Each action seemed to have been met – to paraphrase Isaac Newton – with an (almost) equal and opposite reaction. Only when the effect of his interference seemed minor did there appear to be no pushback. But one last event was approaching – an event that was so far-reaching in its consequences that he could not possibly refuse to attempt to change it. And maybe the fact that the event he was thinking about was so close to the point at which time was recalculated (or October 2022 to put it another way) would mean that there was less time for the pushback to occur.

He was thinking, of course, about the Covid pandemic. The start had been recognised as occurring late in 2019, and the general agreement was that the virus had escaped from a laboratory in the Wuhan region of China. Although the alternative source of a fish and livestock market was still considered to be a possibility. And, in addition to the death toll, there were massive economic and socially negative consequences.

He had to at least try to do something. But what and how? One thing was certain – he would need time, and he would need help. The only possible assistance he could think of calling upon would have to originate with John Bishop. And it would probably have to start years before the event.

One sunny afternoon in August 2016, he finally decided that he would start the process. He assumed that there might be some delay in getting hold of John, and he wanted to allow two full years to see if they could implement any plan so that the pandemic could be avoided.

But he was no longer in contact with John. There had been no formal end to their relationship – just a gradual fading as Graham no longer had anything to report, and they had not spoken for years. Realising that John was probably at least five years older than him, it was almost certain that he had retired – which would make contacting him even more difficult.

He began the process by calling the number he had always used. There was, as usual, a delay in making contact, but this time the delay between asking to speak to John and a connection with either a human being or a voice-mail system was even longer than normal. He assumed that the person answering the call had to look up John Bishop and find an extension to connect him with (he never thought for one moment that was his real name) and this could take several seconds. Eventually, he was told that his call could not be connected, and he was asked to leave a message.

But it was not John who returned the call.

"I'm afraid John no longer works for the department. He retired a few years ago. Can you perhaps let me know the nature of your call?" an anonymous male voice asked him.

"My name is Graham Henderson and I have some important information to pass on to him. I need to speak to him personally."

"I understand – but as I explained, he has retired. Could you possibly pass the information to me so that I can decide how to deal with the matter?"

"No, I need to speak directly to John," Graham stated firmly. He knew that what little hope he had of implementing a plan would rest on his improbable story being believed. And only John had the direct involvement that meant this was even possible.

He gave the caller his telephone number. "In case he no longer has my number can you please pass this on to him and ask him to contact me."

He decided to cut the conversation and see what happened. He could only hope that his years of providing good information would warrant his call being forwarded, and the good relationship he had with John (despite one small blemish) would be sufficient to get him to return the call.

A few days later he received another call. This time the caller announced himself as Alan Poe and declared that he was head of the section in which John used to work. Graham first double-checked his name, he wondered initially if the last name was Pope (as this would be a much more fitting name for the boss of a bishop) but rapidly understood that it was, indeed Poe.

They danced the same dance, Alan asking Graham to explain what it was he wanted to speak about, and Graham reiterating that it was essential that he spoke to John in person, as only he would be able to connect what he wanted to tell him with all that had gone before.

He eventually received a call back from John a few days later. After a brief catch-up and the normal pleasantries, he asked Graham if the information could be delivered in a phone call.

"Afraid not. I've got a long story to tell you – and I can only do it face to face," was the response.

"If you insist. But I'm buggered if I'm coming to London to hear it. I'm out of that rat race now. If you insist on it, you'll have to come here."

Graham assured him that he would have no problem travelling to meet him and that he was sure that he would find the information to be of interest.

'Here' turned out to be the village of Llangennith on the Gower peninsula in South Wales. As John said he would not be available for a couple of weeks, Graham finally set out on October 8th, taking a train from Reading to Swansea followed by a seemingly endless taxi ride, culminating in a drive up a narrow, bumpy, unsurfaced road to an isolated cottage.

He had no problem making the journey on his birthday, as this was a date that forever invoked mixed emotions in him – especially since Carol had died. It was not only the anniversary of her death but also the anniversary of the most jarring experience of his own life. He was also reasonably sure it was the day on which he too was destined to die in six years' time. So, any distraction that enabled him to forget about the date – especially a significant distraction like this, was always welcome.

John was waiting for him on the doorstep. Graham suspected that his choice of retirement home deliberately incorporated a private road so that he could hear if he had visitors, minutes before they arrived.

The cottage was old and moderately sized but showed signs of refurbishment, and the grass and flower beds were well-tended. Graham paid the driver, taking note of his number for the return journey, and entered the cottage.

The refurbishment had been more substantial and more transformative on the inside than on the outside. The whole ground floor had been divided into two areas. On the right was a modern kitchen and dining area, separated from the lounge/study area on the left by a substantial brick wall and a central staircase.

John led him to the left and he was immediately struck by the fabulous view to the rear of the property. The whole rear of the study was glass, giving a view of what he learned was Oxwich Bay. A sweeping sandy beach with the Worm's Head peninsula to the left, and green fields in the foreground. Even on a grey October day, it was something that you could easily waste several minutes admiring.

"Nice view," he said and smiled at the obvious understatement.

"Well, I reckoned that I'm going to spend a lot of my time looking out the window, so better make the view as good as it can be."

Graham noticed for the first time the accent that John had been disguising all these years. His return to his native land had rekindled his Welsh lilt.

"And it looks like a very comfortable retirement pad you have here – but aren't the neighbours a little intrusive?" Graham asked, seeing a second cottage, located just to the left of where they were."

"No – I own that one as well – it's useful for my sister and her family for weekends. She's a nurse in Swansea hospital and it's the only way she and her kids get to have a holiday."

"Good to retire on a nice government pension," Graham smiled again.

"And I had a friend who used to recommend some good investments for me from time to time - so I'm very comfortable, thanks."

Their friendship duly rekindled, John made a pot of coffee, and they sat down in the armchairs. Graham had mentally rehearsed the story several times, but even now found it difficult to get going.

"John," he began, "you'd better make yourself comfortable because I'm going to tell you a story. A long story. One that you'll find hard to believe – but you'll know it's true because you've been part of it. And then you and I are going to decide how to write the last chapters."

He paused for effect. "You see, I'm living my life for the second time. I went to sleep on the evening before my seventieth birthday - and woke up to find that I was eighteen again. Fifty-two years earlier to the day. I got the chance to experience every man's wish. To have my time again. Everything else I've done flowed from that."

And so, Graham related his story – his deliberate decision to learn Arabic because he knew the fuel crisis of the nineteen seventies was coming; his betting on football matches whose results he knew, to raise the capital to buy his first house; the smokescreen of his computer program to hide this fact, and so on. He omitted the trivial pre-writing of a hit song.

When he got to the point in the story where he met John, he had to establish that this was something he could not have planned – it was a lucky by-product of his dealings with the Arab guests. He linked this to the connection he had made to Pat Threlfall and his first attempt to change history by identifying the Yorkshire Ripper to the police and press.

"I knew his name, but also knew some of the facts that came out after he was originally caught. In my original life, I think Sutcliffe killed thirteen women, so I believe I saved the lives of half a dozen – and made a connection with Pat Threlfall as a by-product. Ever since Pat moved on to the national Sunday press, I've been able to drop him the occasional hint about some of the stories he's worked on, and in return, he's been able to get some information for me on odd occasions too."

John interrupted very seldom as the story unfolded, clarifying the occasional point, and seemingly confirming to himself the answers to some points that had maybe caused him some questions in the past.

Graham covered the Hillsborough story – both as it had originally occurred and how it had changed because of his interference.

"I was always puzzled why you wanted that meeting with that northern gangster – but we put it down to you resolving some private issue and didn't follow up on it. You took a lot of risks with that. Was it worth it?"

Graham silently noted the use of 'we' rather than 'I' in John's comment. It told him that John had talked to his colleagues. He explained that he was pleased with the results of his intervention, even though the outcome was mixed. To do this he had to explain to John something of the agonies of the twenty years of delay for justice that the families had originally suffered. He was not fully getting his point across – but continued.

"There are different theories about time travel," he explained. "The most popular one is called the butterfly effect – which states that when you change one small thing you alter everything in the future of the universe for all time. If that's true, then there's nothing I can do about it. The very fact that I'm reliving my life differently will change everything anyway. The wife and kids I had the first time around aren't with me the second time. And that affects every generation to come. But there's also a different theory about time travel that says that time resets itself in some quantum way. I don't understand it, but it seems to fit my experiences. So, when I change something, the river of time resets its course so that it ends up in the same place. That's about the best way I can begin to explain it. But faced with known disasters, it's very difficult not to intervene if you think you might do some good."

By now they had been talking for over two hours and it seemed sensible to take a break. John offered some Welsh cheese and locally baked bread as a possible teatime menu, washed down with a bottle of local beer and Graham was delighted to accept. They walked around the garden to stretch their legs briefly before continuing.

During the break, John asked the obvious question, "Have you found anyone else who's had this experience - this time travelling?"

This gave Graham the ideal opening to tell the story of Carol, her own 'jump', and its tragic consequences. He knew that John was completely accepting it as true when he commented "She had a much bumpier landing than you did, obviously." They even spoke briefly about how difficult it was to adjust to such a jump, and how much easier it had been for Graham.

He didn't link her to Diana, her obsession with the Princess, her suggestion that they take action, and the fact that Diana's death had triggered her admission to hospital. He felt that this connection was not essential to the story and would only complicate matters. He merely said that she had suffered a mental breakdown.

He could not prevent himself from saying, "It was four years ago this very day that she died."

John asked him several questions at this point, which Graham had expected. He would want to cling to the logical threads in the story, trying to find the connections between their two experiences and engage his mind in trying to solve the mystery. There were a lot of questions about the connection between their two different experiences – the date and the location where the last days of the two of them overlapped seemed to give John considerable food for thought. He even made a couple of notes on a pad by the side of him which had so far lain untouched. Eventually, he ran out of questions, and they paused again for a refresh of the coffee pot.

"You may remember me once asking you an oblique question about Paris," was how Graham began the next part of the tale.

"Er, yes," John said hesitantly. "Didn't you ask me if we had got any activities planned over a weekend or something like that?"

This gave him the chance to tell the Diana and Dodi story – again giving both the original (first life) version as well as the results of his interference. He had thought long and hard as to whether to include this whole episode – but once John remembered the odd question that Graham had asked him, it proved a vital part of the web of evidence. Before he began, he had been concerned that the story might seem just too outlandish to be believed by a hard-nosed veteran such as John. But the more he continued, the more engaged his listener became, although his explanation of the conspiracy theories surrounding the original car crash was given very short shrift.

"It seems that your interference has not had much to recommend it. She died, what, six months later?" John commented.

"It was nearer three months," Graham replied. "More proof of that theory of the world somehow correcting itself. I couldn't find any evidence of anything happening after Peter Sutcliffe was arrested. I can only assume that this was because the number of people whose lives I saved was small, and they probably wouldn't have gone on to have much influence anyway. Whereas Diana would have altered history if she had lived."

"Not to mention the possible influence of young Mr Al-Fayed, whose life you presumably also saved."

"Yes, if only he knew it," Graham said and smiled. "As a matter of fact, we've become friends in a way – we're involved in some charity work together."

Further confirmation that John was now appearing to fully believe the story came as he blurted out, "So, all those great stock picks you gave me were all based on stuff you knew was sure to happen. In fact, your entire career and all the money you've made was pretty easy, wasn't it?"

"Yes – but there were some difficult moments along the way. There's the matter of the terrorist plot for one thing."

"I did apologise for that."

"Yes, no harm done. And I won't embarrass you by asking you how much you knew about my detention and when. But I never did receive a tip-off. That's why I could never reveal whom it came from. I just knew what they were planning."

"Because you'd experienced it the first time around." John completed his sentence for him.

"Yes. The first time around it was always referred to as nine-eleven. It happened on September 11th, 2001. Two planes hit the World Trade Center, one hit the Pentagon and the other was brought down, somewhere in Pennsylvania I think, by the passengers storming the flight deck."

"And I assume that the consequences were pretty much the same afterwards."

"Yep. There was a whole lot more disruption to air travel because the terrorists had actually succeeded – but all the rest was the same. The mighty army of the United States of America, backed by some of its NATO allies discovered in the twenty-first century what the army of Russia discovered in the twentieth century and the army of Great Britain discovered in the nineteenth century – Afghanistan is a very difficult country to conquer. Only this time around it all happened a few years later."

John got up to answer a call of nature. Returning to the room he clicked a button that closed the curtains across the glass wall. It was already getting dark.

"I don't know how much more there is to your story, but we're going to need to decide what to do with you tonight – there are no trains to London that you can catch. Have you got a change of clothing in there?" he asked pointing to the bag that Graham had brought with him.

Graham confirmed he had, and accepted John's invitation to sleep in the guest cottage.

"How much more is there to the story?"

"Nothing much. I need to move on and let you know what is going to happen soon and why I feel the need to let you know about it."

"Why do I get the feeling that this is not going to be good? You've stopped a major disaster and the death of a Princess without any help –

what on earth is it that you need me for? You know what? I think it might be a whole lot easier for you to tell me the story tomorrow in the cold light of day. In the meantime, we could do worse than walking down to the local pub and grabbing something to eat. What do you say?" John asked.

When Graham signified his agreement, John continued "I've also got a little tale to tell you. It's not something I would normally have thought of relating to you – but as soon as you mentioned October 8th, I knew I would have to let you know. It'll answer some of your questions, and probably raise a whole lot more. But I'm sure it's relevant to your situation. Besides, I'm done with listening – it's time I did some talking."

John showed Graham around the guest cottage and left him to unpack and freshen up.

"We can walk to the pub – it's less than a mile. The fresh air will do us good, and it'll help us work up an appetite. The food's simple, but it's all locally grown and properly cooked."

They walked and small-talked their way to the pub. John was greeted by the landlord with the familiarity reserved for regulars – but Graham noticed that he called him Tom. He decided not to comment – he always knew that John Bishop was not his real name – and guessed that Tom probably wasn't either.

Following their host's recommendation, they ordered roast lamb and took their pints of local IPA to their table – a window seat as far away as possible from the bar.

"Like I said," John began, "I've got a story of my own – but you have to understand that once I've told you, this mustn't go anywhere. I mean anywhere," he said with quiet emphasis.

"You can trust me," replied Graham, "I think I've shown I can keep a secret."

"Well, this story is about a government employee who has worked for a good few years in the service of the people ..."

"That would be in the secret service of the people," Graham interrupted with a smile.

"Alright, alright, you know what I mean. Anyway – he's worked his time and is getting ready to retire. He has been fortunate enough to have a friend who has helped him make the most of his retirement funds," (a nod to Graham) "and he's ready for the quiet life. So, he tells his boss he'd like to give notice and his boss says, 'you've got quite a lot of information in your head, can you stay on for six months so we can make sure everything's handed over nice and neatly,' and, being a good employee, he agrees. Then his boss says, 'you won't want to be kicking your heels for the next six months – can you give them a hand in special projects?' and he says it in a way that doesn't really allow the offer to be turned down.

So, our man goes to work in the special projects department. It's a department that deals with all the odds and ends of this type of work. Things that involve secrecy, some strange projects, people seeking government funding for odd ideas, and so on. A bit like that awful American program X Files, but without a glamorous assistant like Gillian Anderson.

And our man is put on a project with the archetypal mad professor. Well, he's not mad, of course, just a little unusual. He has been working for years on a project at Moorfields Hospital where he's based. It's a project so revolutionary that even after working with him for several months, I still can't explain it fully,"

John noticed his slip from third person to first person but said nothing.

"This professor's been working on the optic nerve – you know, the thing that carries messages from the eye to the brain. Working with patients who've suffered damage to this nerve, and despite having perfectly good eyes, still can't see anything. He's been trying to replicate the communication between the eye and the brain by artificial means and discovered (according to him) a completely new method of communicating.

So, he comes to the government for some additional funding. The way he explains it is it's a bit like the internet – he was very good at explaining complex things to mere mortals by the way. He says that when you first started using the internet, you had to have your computer physically connected to the router. But nowadays, nobody does this – we connect wirelessly. And that's what he's done. He's created a method of transmitting the message from the eye to the brain without a wire, or in his case, an optic nerve."

191

The story had to be paused as their meals were delivered. Graham had found it very interesting as far as it went – but could not see how it related to his own story. He knew John would get there sooner or later.

He continued over mouthfuls of a delicious crown of lamb and fresh local vegetables, cooked to perfection.

"Anyway, as part of the procedure for claiming his funding, his project is reviewed by a panel of government scientists, and one of these scientists has a brainwave of his own. If this method of communicating from someone's eye to their brain is completely new, maybe it could have other uses. You know we all have these satellites up in the air watching everything down below – but one of the problems is that when they send their signal down to earth, if other people can intercept and understand that signal, then they can see what we see – and a lot of the advantage goes away. If we could find a new way of communicating – like this professor says he's discovered – then maybe we can use this to prevent other people from understanding our satellite transmissions."

They ordered dessert to allow the story to continue to a conclusion.

"So, our loyal government agent goes over to Moorfields Hospital and starts work on improving security. There was a lot to do. Physical security had to be improved so nobody could just walk into the lab. It was relocated to the top floor just to make it a bit more secure. All the people who worked on the project had to be security vetted, and then all the data and communications had to be made watertight – you can imagine it all took a bit of effort. And then the prof gives us a demonstration. He has the room screened into two separate sections. Two guys wearing headsets are shown images in one area, and two other guys wearing different headsets in the other area write down what they see. It's very impressive. They draw pictures and the guys write a description; they display some text, and the guys write it down word for word, even when it's in a language they can't understand. Very impressive.

But now he needs to make the communication work over a distance, which is where he needs more help. So, we rent a floor in an office block across the street and set it up for him to try. We made it look like a government pensions office I seem to remember. The people in the pensions department were delighted because we paid all the rent and only used the two rooms at the front of the building."

Suddenly John's attention was grabbed. He had, until this point no idea where the story was going – but immediately grasped that the main street that ran past Moorfields Eye Hospital was City Road, and on the other side of that street stood the building where he had met his financial advisor, and Carol had met her solicitor. He felt the hairs on his arms stand on end.

John was sensitive to the effects his words were having and made eye contact. The next part of the story was delivered more slowly and with a complete lack of the jocularity that had been present in the early part of the story.

"I think you've guessed where this is going. October 8th, 2012. Four years ago, to this day. You're not the only one who's happy to be distracted today." John paused his narration - he seemed to want to strengthen himself before tackling a difficult task.

"To be entirely accurate," he continued, "the test was conducted on the previous day, October 7th. The guys doing the reading of the information were still in the original lab above the hospital, and the prof had rigged up some form of communication device pointing between his lab and the offices in the City Road building, where the two guys who were to receive the images and transcribe them were located. Actually, there was one man and one woman because we wanted to test if there was any difference in the male and female ability to receive the messages. There were also a few other people in the room with them - a technician monitoring the apparatus to test signal strength and a couple of government scientists observing the proceedings. I was in the room next door with a security guy.

The first test was run at about nine thirty and produced no results at all. They just couldn't see anything. There was a phone conference between the two buildings, and they made a few adjustments and ran the test again at about ten-fifteen. They got some results – but they were very poor. So, the prof says he can increase the power and run the test one more time. Thinking back, I wondered why he hadn't run it at full power the first time – and I was going to find out later. Anyway, this third test ran at about eleven o'clock and produced a perfect set of results. And everyone was delighted. Champagne all round. The prof could carry on his work for his patients, and the government scientists could go back to wherever they came from and start planning how this could be used for satellite transmissions."

The story was building to a climax – and it seemed appropriate for an order of two large cognacs to be made. John took a swig before continuing carefully.

"The alarm was raised the next day when neither the man nor the woman who had been on the receiving end of the signals showed up for work. We got called in and found they had both died at home in their sleep. And soon we found that the two government scientists and the other technician – everyone who had been in that receiving room – had suffered the same fate.

There were autopsies of course, and we were able to get a deeper investigation done on the bodies of the two government scientists, but all that showed were the symptoms of heart failure. No explanation. And then there was a footnote to the additional government autopsy report on the two scientists that stated, 'Unusual amounts of low-level electrical activity were observed in the brains of both of the deceased.' I asked what the hell this meant, but they gave me a whole lot of guff that meant they didn't know. It was just as they had reported, 'Unusual amounts of low-level electrical activity in the brain'. I asked them to clarify that they were actually dead, and they confirmed that by every known measurement, both were dead. But that phrase really spooked me."

"So, what you're telling me is that there are two or three, or maybe more, bodies buried, or maybe cremated, with – what was that phrase you used? – oh yes, low-level electrical activity in their brains, is that right?"

"Yes. That's what has kept me awake at night these last five years."

"Do you know what keeps me awake at night? A family. A son, a daughter, a daughter-in-law, a son-in-law, and four grandchildren. They were there when I went to sleep, but when I woke up, they were all gone. Completely wiped out. No longer in existence. That's what has kept me awake for the last fifty years! Did you even consider whether anyone else in the building had been affected?" Graham asked.

For a moment, the anger he had felt at his original situation, aggravated by the recently acquired knowledge that it might have been caused by a government-sponsored experiment that had not been properly supervised, threatened to get the better of him. He knew he needed to calm down.

"It may have crossed someone's mind, I can't say. We had enough of a problem keeping the story under wraps. If we had gone around asking

194

questions, we might not have liked the answers we received. And anyway, there was nothing we could do about it."

There were a few moments of silence between them. The brandies were finished, the bill was presented and paid, and they walked back to the cottage. Graham had a lot of thinking to do and some questions he needed answering, but the revelations he had just received were so significant and so unexpected that he remained silent.

"I've got a bottle of Remy back at the cottage – would you care to join me in a glass or three?" John said to break the tension.

They sat in the same armchairs they had occupied earlier, nursing very large measures.

"I think I can piece some of it together," Graham said. "But I can't make any sense out of it. Carol was by the window in her solicitor's office one floor below where your receiving room was. At the very moment that your professor sends the full-strength signal, she is talking about her wedding day. That evening she feels exceptionally tired – I know that because we discussed having the same symptoms. She goes to sleep, and then when she wakes up, she is back on the day she was thinking about when she got zapped."

John nodded and sipped his Remy but did not comment.

"But what I can't understand is if this is all known about, how on earth does it get to happen all over again to me in 2022? Even for the government, this seems pretty damned reckless. And anyway – why should it work like that? I can understand the causing heart failure bit – but time shifting?"

"I don't know. And like I said, I'd never have told you the story if it hadn't been for you mentioning the date and the place where it happened to you both."

They speculated a little more, drank too much, and agreed to get around to the purpose of their meeting – the things that Graham was going to tell John about the future – the following morning.

"One last thing," was Graham's final remark. "You need to arrange for me to meet this professor."

Veterans of many a night of excess consumption of alcohol as they both were, they managed their hangovers adroitly the next morning. The final part of the storytelling took part in the kitchen of the cottage, accompanied by strong coffee.

"I guess the first part of the last chapter of this story – background I suppose – is that Donald Trump is going to win the American election next month," Graham began and paused for the expected expletive or two in reply, which was duly given by John. "You'll see why that's relevant in a minute or two. Our government is going to continue to get its knickers in a twist over Brexit – and in 2019 Theresa May is going to have to resign – to be replaced by Boris Johnson."

"Boris as Prime Minister, you have to be joking!"

"It gets better. In late 2019 there will be an outbreak of a new disease in China. It's a respiratory disease that can be fatal to anyone who's not in the best of health – mainly the elderly, people with breathing problems or compromised immunity. But it kills young healthy people too. It has something around a one percent fatality rate. And it's very easily transmitted. It turns into a global pandemic in early 2020, and to give you an idea of scale, by the time I left the scene in 2022 it had killed some two hundred thousand people in the UK, over a million in the US, and official estimates of global fatalities placed the number at anywhere between five and twenty million."

As expected, John continued to show his mastery of the expletives of the English language.

Graham completed his explanation by telling John that even after the event, nobody was exactly sure where the disease had originated. There was a lot of finger-pointing about a research facility in Wuhan, but the Chinese insisted it started in a seafood and wildlife market.

"So, you're saying that the world faces a global pandemic, nobody knows how it started, and we've got Brexit icing on the top, while Boris is in number ten and Trump's in the White House. Shit!"

"And it's not just that – most of the world's economies shut down for several months to try to prevent the spread of the disease, and this produces lingering economic and social problems, shortages of goods, inflation, massive delays for medical care… it's the gift that keeps on giving."

There was a pause. Graham thought it only fair to allow John a few minutes to digest what he had just learned. Briefly, he thought to himself, 'If I continue with the replacement of the PM, the death of the Queen, a forty-four-day premiership, economic and energy crises, and a war in Europe he'll either reach overload or kick me out.'

"Okay – I've got a million and one questions – but I'm guessing that the reason you're telling me all this is that you want to try to stop it. Am I right?"

"Yep. I'm hoping that since we are so close to dealing with this in real-time, there's a better chance that we can achieve something without there being too much pushback as I've called it. And if we can't stop it, then maybe we can take some actions that minimise its effect."

John got up and began to walk up and down the kitchen – he was a man who found physical activity helped stimulate his thought process.

"Now I don't want to throw too much of a dampener on this. It's a fine objective – but I do see a couple of problems. First of all, only you and I know about this – unless there are a few others out there who've been bending the laws of nature like you and your partner. And I think that is going to pose a major problem. Even if I could inform a few people – they would have to believe your story, a story by the way which I believe not only because I've known you for so long, but also because I had a few points to corroborate it over the years. I think it will be damned difficult to convince anyone else to believe you."

"I agree. Probably pointless to even try. The only hope you've given me is that if your story about the professor and his weird transmitter does turn out to be the reason for my jump in time, there may be a couple of other people who were there at the re-run in 2022 and that the same thing has happened to them. But that's unlikely. I think our only chance is to contact your ex-colleagues and tell them that there is a very dangerous set of experiments going on at a place called Wuhan – somewhere in China – and see if they can put a stop to it."

John went and fetched his notepad and pen from the lounge area, brewed another pot of coffee, and began to note down the answers to the questions he fired at Graham.

By lunchtime, they had the outline of a plan. It had two objectives, and both relied heavily on John. First, he agreed to get in touch with the professor – whose name turned out to be Zubin Karbajanovic (no wonder he's known as 'prof', thought Graham) – to arrange a meeting. Secondly, he would contact a couple of his previous colleagues and try to get some information on the research facility in Wuhan. Both tasks were important, one for the future of mankind and one for a possible major leap in scientific knowledge (not to mention the understanding and possible resolution of Graham's situation).

John knew that he would need to get personally involved in both - and confirmed he would progress both, but not to expect anything for weeks, possibly months. If he was going to have to face the hated journey back to London, he would want to deal with as many issues as possible on the one visit. They made their plans, and Graham took a taxi back to Swansea Station for his return journey.

Graham returned from his visit to Wales with much on his mind. The fact that there was some sort of explanation for his unique situation gave him a feeling of reassurance. As did the feeling that John was going to be doing something to try to prevent the Covid outbreak. But his patience was being tried as he knew he would just have to wait for a call.

The call came in early January. John was abrupt, even for him, merely stating that he would need collecting from Paddington Station at quarter past eleven on the following Monday. Graham appreciated that it might not make sense to discuss anything over the phone and was at the gate to the platform when the Swansea train arrived punctually at 11:12. They walked together and joined the taxi queue.

Once ensconced in a black cab, John informed him, "We're having lunch with the prof, I managed to speak to him just before Christmas and gave him enough information about you to intrigue him. We're guests at his club, and he's agreed to keep his diary free for the afternoon, so we'll have plenty of time to talk."

John gave the driver the address and indicated to Graham that they would talk later – he was not willing to talk in front of a taxi driver. He passed over a file with a brief resume of the professor typed on a single sheet of paper, which he quickly read – seeing nothing that he had not already found out himself. The phrase 'Developer of the Moorfields Regression Analysis Algorithm' was one he remembered. He had no idea what it meant, but it was important enough to appear in the professor's biography and he wondered if he would have the chance to find out what on earth it meant.

Half an hour later they pulled up outside one of the huge Georgian terraced houses in Cavendish Square, paid the fare, and entered the premises.

Giving the name of the professor to the receptionist, she asked them to wait a moment before they were escorted down a corridor, lined with portraits of famous medical personnel of the past, into a private dining room. Professor Karbajanovic joined them shortly afterwards and introductions were made. Even an auspicious meeting like this had to begin with small talk about the weather, Brexit, and the previous week's tube strike. But they were soon seated, food and wine ordered, with instructions that they would want to conduct their discussions for the next hour before the food should be delivered. The talk began in earnest.

After John's introduction, Graham gave a brief outline of what had happened to Carol when she had made her jump through time, and what had happened or was yet to happen (depending on your point of view) to him when he experienced the same. He let the professor know that his objective was to try to reach a greater understanding of what had happened. He was willing to provide any information that would help further scientific understanding of the phenomenon. But his current situation was best expressed as total bafflement.

The professor then took over the conversation, letting them know that he knew that John always referred to him as 'prof' and was quite comfortable with them using that when addressing him.

"The communication between the eye and the brain is amazing – even to someone who has been studying it for years," he began. Somewhat incongruously, he stood up and walked towards a sideboard at the far end of the room and picked an apple from a bowl of fruit, talking all the time.

"The amount of information that is conveyed, the speed at which this information travels, and how it is processed is truly remarkable," he continued, and without pausing, lobbed the apple towards Graham, who had no alternative but to catch it.

The prof smiled and continued, "in a fraction of a second, your eye conveyed to your brain that it had observed a change in the size of an image of an apple. Based upon years of processing such information, your brain was able to realise that the apple was travelling. Not only this but also the brain was able to prepare an accurate prediction of its path and move the necessary muscles in your body to place your hands in the correct location to catch it. Even the smartest computers yet developed by man are barely able to duplicate this. And of course, at the same time, your brain has gathered information about the room, the fruit, the bowl, the characteristics of the apple, and much, much more."

He resumed his seat, no doubt pleased with his attention-gathering introduction, which Graham thought was highly likely to have often been given before.

"So, this is what I have studied, and until the unfortunate incident some four years ago, this is what I was experimenting on. But now I am restricted to research only. Maybe one day we will make some progress, and my aims to improve the sight of so many people in the world will be realised - and others," he paused to look meaningfully at John, "will be able to progress other matters which result from this knowledge."

He paused, whether for effect or because this train of thought had reached its destination, Graham was not sure. He recollected John's remark and agreed that the prof had suitably demonstrated his ability to convey complex matters straightforwardly. He decided to try and steer the conversation his way.

"Have you been able to put your mind to what the link may be between your experiment and what happened to Carol and me?"

"Ah, yes. The questions of what the brain sees – the things which are there but not there. This too is intriguing," he began.

"Let me explain to you. One hot day you looked at the road in front of you and you have seen a mirage of water, yes? "

Momentarily thrown by the apparent change of direction in the conversation, Graham paused before answering "Yes," as he believed he was expected to.

"And you are a learned man – you have studied mathematics at university, I understand. So, you must have learned the explanation for this phenomenon. Was it not part of the syllabus for GCSE Physics?"

"I learned it so long ago it was called O Level Physics back then – but yes, it's caused by light refracting through hot air."

"That is correct. The light bends and you see something blue on the road, maybe it is rippling slightly in the heat, and your brain says to you 'I know what this is. I recognise it. It's water. And so, you 'see' water. Yes?"

Again, Graham confirmed.

"Let me take it a little further. Now that I am restricted to theoretical research, I have been looking into other occasions when the brain sees something which is not there. Have you ever seen a ghost? Or do you know anyone who has ever seen one?"

Graham was once again, not surprisingly, a little puzzled by the direction in which the prof was now heading but thought for a few seconds and then remembered.

"Yes. In my first life, my mother-in-law saw one."

"What did she see? A woman in white? A headless horseman? What?"

"She saw a naval Petty Officer."

"And how did she know he was a Petty Officer?"

"It was not long after the war. She had been in the army – and she could identify a man's military rank by the stripes on his sleeve."

"Yes, I can see that this would have been a very useful skill for a young woman back then. And where did she see him – this Petty Officer?"

"She saw him one afternoon in the bedroom of the flat where she was living at the time."

"And when was this?"

"In the early nineteen fifties?"

"And was he known to her - this Petty Officer?"

"No – but later she was shown a photograph and recognised him. He used to live in the flat before she and her husband moved in."

"And when did he die - this Petty Officer?"

"Sometime during the war, I believe."

"So, when she saw him – he had been dead for what – ten years?"

201

"Yes, that seems about right."

"And when your mother-in-law saw him – did she see a rotting corpse that had been lying underground – or underwater – for ten years?"

"No – she thought he was alive."

"Exactly – you will shortly see my point. This entity, this ghost of a Petty Officer, communicates with your mother-in-law. It sends a message to her brain. And her brain interprets this message and sees an image and says I know what that is – it is a Petty Officer standing in my bedroom. Just like the mirage of the water on the road, your brain receives a message and interprets it for you. Now maybe this image is very clear. Or maybe it is not – it depends on how well the entity is transmitting and how well your mother-in-law is receiving. Did she see a clear image?"

"I think so. She said she had seen a petty officer, not the ghost of one. So, I assume she saw him quite clearly".

"Well maybe the entity is a strong transmitter, or your mother-in-law is a good receiver. But when this happens, many people do not see a clear image. It is perhaps transparent, shimmering, ghostly. Do you understand?"

This time it only needed a nod for the prof to continue.

"Your mother-in-law. Was she good at seeing things?"

Graham believed he understood the direction of the professor's question. He was not asking about her eyesight - he was asking about other senses.

"I think so. She used to read peoples' tea leaves and tell their fortunes."

"Excellent. Just what I thought. She can receive signals very clearly – signals that other people find difficult to receive or maybe do not receive at all. So, she sees a clear image – not a ghostly one. You see the theory goes like this – the entity (that is normally referred to as the ghost) wishes to communicate, and so it sends a message. The brain of the recipient receives the communication and reconstitutes a figure and 'sees a ghost.' I believe that this communication is happening across a wavelength we cannot detect – so we cannot measure it.

It is also the same with the images which I have been transmitting. We have found that some people receive a strong image, but others do not see so well. So, when we started the transmission from one building to another, we made sure to use only good receivers. Even then, we had to increase the power of the transmission more than I had originally planned."

Graham nodded – he felt he had to show some agreement, so strong was the fervour with which the idea was being explained to him.

"But I return to your Petty Officer, or rather your mother-in-law's. The image he transmitted was sent across a wavelength we do not understand. One which we cannot detect, but I believe it may be akin to the wavelength we are transmitting in our experiment. But – and this is the crucial part of my theory - the message that he transmitted crossed over time. What was seen – by your mother-in-law - was not the image of him in his current state – it was the image of him some ten years earlier. And this occurs in almost all the thousands of cases where people have seen ghosts. The image received is of a dead person, but the image of the person is almost always seen in a state where they are still alive."

Graham was struggling to take in all this – delivered as it was at a rapid rate and coloured with an East European accent.

"So," the professor continued, "when you tell me that the effect that these rays had upon you and your unfortunate lady friend caused a shift in time, I cannot explain it to you – but I am not completely surprised. There is so much that we do not know.

Let us return to the date on which your partner journeyed. You said it was her wedding day, yes?"

"That's correct."

"And when she was in the office, she was thinking about her wedding day?"

"I think that's what she said. She was meeting her solicitor to discuss her divorce, and I seem to remember her saying that she had spoken about the wedding. I suppose it's quite natural in those circumstances."

"And when you were in these offices, you were thinking about your eighteenth birthday, is that true?"

"Yes. I've replayed that conversation so many times, I'm sure I can recall it. My financial advisor knew that the next day was my birthday and he first asked me what plans I'd got, and then asked me what my best birthday had been. I told him I couldn't immediately recall any particular birthday as being the best, but I could remember one that was probably my worst, and that was my eighteenth. I described how I'd recently arrived at college, hadn't made any friends, and the only person I shared it with was my neighbour. And he hadn't received his grant cheque, so I ended up buying all the drinks!"

"Interesting. There must be a connection. You are thinking strongly about your eighteenth birthday – presumably at the exact moment that the transmission from my device hits you. Then you re-boot your brain when you go to sleep, and it resets to the time you were thinking about. And we must presume the same happened to your friend, Carol."

Just then there was a knock at the door. Graham had never been so relieved at the arrival of a meal. His brain was beginning to ache as he processed so much new information. There was something that had bothered him since he first heard the story from John, and he decided to raise it with the prof. as soon as the waiter left them alone.

"What I don't understand is how you've been able to discover an entirely new type of radiation that nobody else has ever detected."

"Ah, that is because you suffer from a delusion that sadly is shared by so many scientists and has been for hundreds of years." The prof launched into another stream of consciousness. "Throughout history, scientists have always believed that they completely understood things. Let me illustrate. First, they discovered light as a type of radiation and supposed that this explained everything. Then, when they first split white light into the colours of the rainbow, they assumed that solved everything. And then they found infrared and ultraviolet, and they believed that solved everything. And then they found gamma rays and X-Rays and a whole lot of other stuff.

Right up until we embraced Quantum theory, and discovered that everything is actually uncertain, at every point in history scientists thought they knew everything. Not only did they think this way, but they convinced everyone else to share their delusion. And it is not true. Many things have not been discovered and many more have been discovered but not understood. My team and I have discovered a type of radiation that no one else has found yet. This means that no one else can detect it, which is why he (indicating John) and his colleagues are so interested in it."

"But this radiation also has some effects that you do not understand," Graham ventured.

"In medicine, we know that everything has side effects," was the only response the prof could give.

The conversation subsided and they concentrated on enjoying the food in front of them. Graham refused dessert – and pondered what he had heard, sipping a strong coffee while John and the prof enjoyed an Eton mess.

"So, what is the next step?" he asked, directing his question at both his colleagues, neither of whom seemed in any hurry to answer.

After a few minutes of thought, the prof scratched his jaw and held forth. "I will have to give some serious consideration to what I have learned today. I have some significant imponderables – and I am not sure that the answers are within my grasp at this moment. I need to consider the effect that you and your colleague experienced and see if I can find any rational explanation. I also need to consider how it is that you received this effect in 2022, six years from now when my experimentation has been completely turned off at the request of the government."

"You can hardly blame them," John interrupted. "We know that a few people died. And we never investigated the rest of the occupants of the building – it could be more."

"Hmm. Maybe they did not die – but that is another issue. They may have experienced a new life like our friend here," the prof countered, somewhat petulantly.

"I've been thinking about my date," Graham interjected. "It's always possible that my jump occurred on a different plane of time, isn't it? One where you started your experiments several years later."

"Possible. But unlikely, I think. There is an uncanny coincidence of the dates being the same. I can imagine that if I was allowed to conduct the experiment again, and it was close to the date of the original experiment, I might choose the anniversary. But for it to have been an entirely random coincidence seems unlikely. However, we may only have to wait six years and we will find out."

"So, if I may repeat my question, what is the next step?" Graham asked again, not wanting to be side-tracked.

"I'll see if we can do some discrete exploration of the other tenants in the building," said John. "Maybe we can come up with something."

"But from my side, I can sadly only say that I will get back to you when I have anything to report," was as far as the prof seemed willing to be drawn.

"Can we at least agree to have a conference in three months' time?" Graham responded, and the other two somewhat unwillingly agreed.

As they bid farewell to the prof and left the club, he asked John if he had anything else to talk about, but he had nothing to report.

"What about that other subject – the one relating to China?" Graham asked.

"I'm only at the start of that – I need to find out quite a lot – and I don't have full access to the files now. You'll need to be patient," was all he would say.

Graham's parting shot was that he hoped to hear something on both topics when they spoke in three months.

Chapter Nine - The First Pandemic of the Twenty-First Century

The three of them held several conference calls throughout 2017 and 2018. Although the prof spoke at length on a couple of occasions, Graham rapidly recognised that he was exercising the defensive mechanism of an expert who has been caught out. He brought forward plenty of technical data and scientific language – but it was no more than technobabble; both John and Graham realised that he was making no progress in understanding the cause of Graham and Carol's experience. And without the ability to repeat the experiment, there seemed to be no likelihood of any progress in the immediate future.

John was not faring any better in putting together a strategy to mitigate the forthcoming pandemic. "After all," he repeatedly said, "you don't even know if the pandemic started in a virology study centre or a fish and livestock market!"

Several times they discussed the possibility of bringing someone else into their secret. But even though Graham slowly warmed to the idea, as it seemed to be the only way to make progress, it always collapsed when they tried to choose someone. It would need to be a person who was powerful enough to impact events, and yet open-minded enough to believe their seemingly incredible story. If there was such a person, they were unable to identify him or her.

As they passed the midpoint of 2018 with next to no progress, he decided to ask John to change tack. "If we're not going to be able to do anything to prevent it," he said during one of their calls, "then maybe we should concentrate on making sure the UK is as well prepared as possible. We might be able to save a few hundred, maybe even a few thousand lives."

"Yes, and a few million quid of public money too, if your stories of what happened are to be believed," John replied. "I'll see what I can find out about our preparedness for a pandemic and how we might set about improving it."

And so it was that while sitting at home one afternoon a couple of weeks later, Graham's doorbell sounded, and he signed for a package from a courier. Strangely it was one whom he had never seen delivering locally before and was devoid of any company logos on his apparel or motorbike. He took the package into his study and opened it. There were two large folders and a covering note:

"Graham - These are the findings of Operation Alice and Operation Cygnus. Two reports on Britain's preparedness for a SARS-type pandemic and a flu pandemic. They are, of course, highly confidential, so don't go discussing them down the pub with your mates!

They don't make for easy reading, but I think you'll find the sections on Personal Protective Equipment to be an area where significant improvements might be made, to say the least. Naturally, if you are ever asked, you did not receive this from me."

There was no signature on the note.

Graham vaguely remembered hearing about these reports during the pandemic. He thought that they might be interesting, and once he began reading them, was not disappointed. Particularly so since he had been given a copy that had been notated by unknown hands with some very unflattering comments. He concentrated on the section on stocks of PPE – that acronym that nobody had ever heard of before the pandemic but was soon to become universally known.

There was even an addendum that detailed the various types of PPE, the likely volumes to be needed, and the (considerably smaller) current stock levels. It showed a massive shortfall.

Yes, of course, he remembered – those early days of the Covid outbreak when there were reports of front-line medical and care staff unable to use proper protective equipment and having to make do with inferior and home-made substitutes. The scramble to source items all over the world, the Heath-Robinson, and homemade substitutes. The vast amount of public funds squandered.

The report detailed shortages, based on estimates of consumption in the first three months, that were huge – running into millions of items. Here was something he could help with. All he had to do was figure out how. He knew he could have relatively little impact on the enormous amounts that were to be spent on this whole area in the next two years. But he wanted desperately to have stocks available in the early days to try to reduce the risks being run by frontline workers. And if, beyond that, he could make profits which he could redistribute to good causes, all the better.

He read the report, and then re-read the section on PPE. His plans for the next few days were now set. He would research the various items and find out all about their manufacture and the supply chains of the constituent parts that fed them.

By the end of the week, he was a lot better informed, but still unsure of what to do. He had become quite an expert on PPE, focussing on those items that could be made relatively easily. They appeared to be made from plastic, rubber, paper, or fabric. All would be needed in their millions in the next few years.

He was reading his notes and putting them into some sense of order when he was interrupted by a phone call from his brother. He very rarely received a call from Andrew and so his first reaction was to worry that it must concern some bad news about some family member. Both their parents had died years before, so Graham naturally worried that it was going to be about one of the younger members of the family. But it wasn't.

Andrew must have known that by making the call he would cause some consternation, so, after the briefest exchange of pleasantries, he established the reason.

"Can I pick your brain about a problem with the family firm?" his brother asked.

Andrew had taken over the small engineering company that their dad had started and had run for almost his whole life. It was a small business with about fifty employees, dealing with all aspects of compressors. They sold, installed, and repaired them in every type of industrial situation imaginable, and were well-known and respected throughout the UK.

Graham had never had any interest in the company and lacked any sort of practical skill to assist in its day-to-day operation. So, it was natural that his brother, having joined after completing a technical diploma, should take it over when their father retired some years earlier. And it looked possible that the third generation of Hendersons might one day continue the trend as Andrew's son, Callum, had joined straight from school a couple of years ago.

"Is it something we can deal with on the phone, or is this an excuse for the family to get together?" Graham asked.

"Probably needs a bit more than a phone call," Andrew replied.

"Well, why don't you come down to my place this weekend?" Graham suggested, and within minutes they made the arrangements for Andrew and his wife to spend Saturday and part of Sunday at his place.

He was pleased to tackle what he hoped would be a much smaller problem than the one he had in front of him right now. He had a dim and distant memory of a management training course he had attended in his first life where they had taught a technique whereby you solve a small problem to help you tackle a larger one. 'Let's see if this strategy works,' he thought to himself.

Over lunch at a riverside pub, Andrew outlined the challenge that their son, Callum was causing them. In many ways, it was a good problem, but it was a problem, nonetheless.

Andrew summed up the situation, "For the first two years Callum stayed in the workshop, and by then he could fix just about anything that crossed our path. So, we let him go on customer visits. At first, he went with an experienced colleague, but for the last two years, he's been going on his own. He seems to have a unique knack for understanding customers' businesses and their requirements. In fact, he's often made suggestions that have proved highly beneficial to some of our customer's businesses as well as bringing us more revenue."

"So, what's the problem?" Graham asked.

"He's too good," his brother replied. "I can't keep him occupied and challenged enough for much longer in our little outfit. But if he goes out on the open market, he'll have trouble because he doesn't have any qualifications – and the bigger companies that he deserves to get an opportunity in will never take him on."

Graham understood. There had been some family concern when Callum had had a few challenges at school and left with minimal qualifications. He was not unintelligent, as his success with the family firm had demonstrated, but he was one of those people who 'learn by doing.' He just wasn't suited to a classroom environment.

"Have you thought about expanding the business?" Graham asked, referring to the family firm.

"Yes, but I don't think we could grow enough to give him enough challenges. He needs a bigger stage."

"And no thoughts of retiring and handing the business over to him?"

Graham's question was not serious, and he felt Andrew bite back a comment about the difference in the bank balance of the two brothers as he answered, "No, there's no chance of that."

They chatted over the situation while enjoying a leisurely lunch watching the traffic on the Thames - and returned to it when sharing sandwiches and a few bottles of wine later that evening. Several ideas were kicked around, but no answer seemed to be forthcoming. When Andrew and his wife left on Sunday morning – late enough to allow the hangovers to have dissipated, Graham promised them he would think about it for a couple of days and see what he could come up with.

A crazy idea came to him on Monday morning as he followed his usual practice of tackling a business problem by writing the key issues on a sheet of A4 paper. He wrote by hand – it was a practice he had never computerized – and then temporarily placed the sheet next to his much larger set of notes on his PPE issues. He called his brother immediately.

"Can you spare Callum for a day? I'd like to talk to him."

Andrew was delighted to hear that his brother was getting involved with the problem – but not so happy when Graham said he couldn't tell him yet what he wanted to talk to Callum about. At his brother's request, he brought Callum to the phone.

"Your dad says you've got a good knack for understanding businesses," Graham said.

Callum hesitated to confirm – he was probably not sure what was going on – not surprisingly.

"I've got some documents here about a business opportunity – but I need someone who has some practical understanding of making stuff. Could you come down to my place and have a look at the problem with me? It's quite confidential, so I need to do it here - if that's all right with you."

Callum agreed. His curiosity was raised, and he wondered why his rich uncle – whose house he had often visited when a child, but whom he had not seen since except at rare family gatherings – wanted to talk to him.

The following morning, having ridden his motorbike down the A12 and around the M25, he was drinking a coffee in Graham's study and listening carefully. Graham explained that he had a list of items that would be needed when the government took the threat of a pandemic seriously – and that this was getting more and more likely every year. What he needed to know was how to find the companies that could make the various items without much change to their existing business practices.

Graham had already prepared for the session. He had racked his brains for his own limited experience of manufacturing – which had all come in his first life when he installed computerised project management systems and hence was over fifty years back in his memory.

He remembered some of it – like the time he had discovered that the bright yellow rubber gloves that both his mother and his wife always wore when doing the dishes were made by the same process and in the same factory as ninety percent of the condoms in the UK. He even remembered one of the production managers telling him that if you saw a lorry with an advert on its side containing a large yellow glove, the contents of that lorry were almost certainly thousands of condoms.

Most of his manufacturing knowledge was likewise comprised of half-remembered snippets.

But he had successfully divided the PPE items into groups, each of which he thought might be made by one factory, or at worst by one company. But he needed input from someone like Callum who could confirm his groupings and suggest what other items might currently be manufactured by such a company and what level of change would be needed to switch production.

He showed him a few examples: diagrams of the items, specifications of materials that the item must be made from, tests or certifications that might be needed, and so on.

At first, Callum seemed to struggle, and Graham was worried that his idea was not proving so good after all. But after a few items, it began to click, and he was able to give feedback, modifying the groupings only slightly.

Then, for each group, Graham asked him if he was looking for a company to manufacture the products in that group, what items might that company currently be making? Callum made some suggestions, and for each, Graham then asked what scale of change would be needed to make the switch.

As Callum began to understand the task, he was able to input more and more. He would suggest two or three product ranges to look for, elaborate on the type of manufacturing changes needed, and suggest which original product line would be the easiest to switch from. He was also able to give ballpark figures for the cost of the changes to production methods.

When they broke for lunch. Graham was delighted to find that Callum was keen to return to the task after a quick sandwich – he was warming to the task.

By mid-afternoon, they had examined every item on the list, put it into the appropriate group, identified a target product from which to switch the manufacturer, and the likely production upheaval and cost involved.

Graham now moved on to the next question. Could Callum think of any companies that he had personally visited that fell into any of the categories they had named?

"How will you persuade them to make the changes, Uncle Gray?" Callum asked - whether out of genuine interest or as a stalling tactic while he tried to think of some names, Graham was not sure.

"Good point. I'll have to offer them a big order, and if that doesn't work, I may buy their company." Graham was not being entirely honest with his answer. His strategy would not involve the placing of any orders, he intended to buy companies, not PPE.

Callum was impressed, and slowly began to come up with some names. For each one, Graham asked what he could remember – did it look prosperous or run down, what was the atmosphere amongst the employees, what could he remember about the managers and owners? Every comment was noted.

Callum spoke about machine types and manufacturing rates in a way that confirmed his father's opinion that he had a unique knack for understanding customers' businesses. He wrongly assumed that his older, more experienced, and much richer uncle would understand everything he said, but Graham did not interrupt to disabuse him of this assumption. He simply waited until he concluded.

His observations on people were less detailed than his thoughts on machinery and manufacturing, but often his anecdotes revealed more than he suspected, and Graham built up a picture of some of the potential targets.

It was getting dark by the time they had finished, so Graham asked his young nephew if he wanted to go out to dinner or order a takeaway. The Domino's delivery arrived twenty minutes later.

During this time, and whilst enjoying the pizza - Graham's accompanied by a glass of Cabernet from his wine cellar and Callum's by a bottle of Peroni from the fridge – Graham took the opportunity to ask his nephew about his job and how he felt he was getting on. He was pleased to hear the enthusiasm that the young man had for his work, his enjoyment of each day bringing a new challenge, but also sensed the beginnings of frustration as Callum betrayed the fact that he was beginning to 'know everything' when what he wanted was 'to learn something new every day.'

Shortly after their makeshift meal, Callum left on his motorbike for his return journey and Graham decided to have a couple more glasses of red before turning in for the night. He had a lot of data to collate.

The following day he called his brother and gave him his feedback on the previous day.

"I think I might be able to offer him an interesting project," he said. "If you'll give me a few days to pull together the things we went through yesterday, I should be able to let you know more then. Have you asked him what he thought of the day?"

"He certainly said he found it very interesting – but he wouldn't want a job with you if it was all about reading bits of paper and making notes."

Graham laughed. "No, I'd never offer him a job that was all about reading bits of paper and making notes, that's for sure. I'll call you in a few days."

It took him a week to get everything together. For some of the companies which Callum had spoken of, his details were limited to just a company name and a town and there was more digging to be done. But the following weekend Graham had got everything together. He wanted to discuss it with his brother, and when he heard that Callum was away for the weekend, he invited himself to his brother's place for Sunday lunch – one of the meals he always believed was best served in a house rather than a restaurant – after which he outlined his plans to his brother and sister-in-law.

"I don't know how much Callum told you, but I'm planning to buy a few small companies and convert them to manufacturing medical Personal Protective Equipment or PPE. We'll sell it to the NHS, private medical companies in the UK, and maybe some overseas. But we'll also build up a stockpile because one day soon the government will wake up to the fact that there is not enough to meet the needs when the next SARS or bird-flu scare comes, and we'll make a lot of money."

He paused to make sure they were still with him and not in some post-prandial doze. They seemed to be following.

"I'd like to offer Callum a job – even a minor partnership – because I'll need him for all the manufacturing stuff."

"I guess you don't want to get your hands dirty," Andrew interjected, not totally in jest.

"I know my stuff when it comes to the financials, but you're right – I'm not up to speed on what's involved in making things – and I think that Callum already knows a lot of what's needed and what he doesn't already know, he'll pick up damn quickly. Do you think he'll be interested in joining me?"

"Why wouldn't he? Working for his rich uncle, a partnership, what's not to like? But how do you know it won't go wrong?"

"The simple answer is I don't know. But I can keep it going for quite a while from my existing funds – long enough for it to be a real extension to his CV, so even if it does go wrong, it should help him get a better job next time around."

"And when do you want him to start?"

"It'll take me a month or two to do the first acquisition – but I'd like him on board in a month if that's OK with you. I'll explain to him that he'll have to be looking at quite a few bits of paper for the first couple of weeks – but after that, he'll need to roll his sleeves up and get his hands dirty."

Callum was due back that evening and so Graham hung around – having a second meal in the house on the same day for the first time - and was there to give Callum the news when he returned.

As predicted, Callum was very interested in what was on offer, and Graham promised to send him a proper offer in writing within the week – and Andrew accepted his son's verbal notice to quit.

It took Graham a few days to get back up to speed. He'd set himself a whole list of things to do and set about doing them. He approached the companies on the list he had compiled with Callum's help and made offers to purchase them. Most were accepted quickly, but some took a little more protracted negotiation. Hand in hand with this process, he liquidated many of his shareholdings to free the cash.

He kept each company's name intact (this would form a vital part of his strategy later) but made sure that each of them was re-labelled as 'Part of the Graycal Group of Companies.' Callum was delighted to be made a 25 percent shareholder in the company, whose name was formed from the two owners' first names, and to have his salary increased.

His uncle also informed him that he might want to think about buying a car for himself from company funds. He could choose anything within reason, but some of the places he needed to visit would be a bit too far away for him to travel by bike. But he also reminded him that he was now one of the bosses, so if he wanted to go by motorbike, that was up to him.

Graham accompanied him on the first couple of visits. Negotiations with the owners had to take place to see how involved they wanted to be after the takeover (Graham hoped and aimed for zero involvement but would tolerate some handover period). Then there was the explanation of his plans for the new products they would be manufacturing, the phasing out of their old products, and the changes that needed to be made. And finally, Graham had to make it very clear that from now on Callum was the boss on all things concerning manufacturing, and they should refer to him. Their salespeople were tasked with clearing the inventory of their old products, to try to establish customers for their new products, but reassured that any unsold stock of their new production would be purchased by the holding company.

There were some interesting moments in one or two of their acquisitions as hoary old timers had to take orders from such a young whippersnapper – but nothing that could not be overcome. Callum travelled many a mile in his new BMW and a few on his motorbike. And gradually the inventories of PPE held by Graycal grew.

One of the many tasks Graham set himself was to note the name of the Member of Parliament responsible for the location of each of the companies in his new group. Their contact details were listed on a special spreadsheet alongside those of his MP and the one whose constituency included Callum's home address. He gave it the file name COVID.

Lastly, he took every step possible to secure his source of materials for every company. He knew that once COVID arrived and the dam broke, his manufacturing capacity was not worth much unless he had cast-iron contracts to obtain his raw materials. He made sure to guarantee supply at many multiples of his current levels – to the surprise of many of his suppliers.

As soon as he felt things were ticking over satisfactorily, Graham took a three-week luxury holiday. It was the summer of 2019, and it was to be the last holiday he would take for a long time.

The spreadsheet came into use shortly after the pandemic broke. Graham contacted every MP on the list and let him know that a company in his constituency (or one owned by one of his constituents) was manufacturing medical PPE and had stock available. The MP was requested to put them in touch with officials at the Department of Health. Within days, Graham was contacted by more than one official – sometimes by phone, sometimes by email. It was obvious that the response was poorly managed and somewhat chaotic as it took several days for the civil servants to realise that efforts were being duplicated. But once they understood that one source existed for many of the items they desperately needed – and that there was manufacturing capacity to create more – he was rapidly escalated to contact with senior government personnel.

He was not surprised that they wanted to meet face-to-face. He asked for the initial meeting to take place using a video conference – which they reluctantly accepted. But when it came to the meeting to finalise the contracts, they insisted on meeting face to face. Graham could not help but notice that there was such a belief that the task they were undertaking was so important, and hence they were so important, that meetings must take place in the way they always did. New-fangled video conference rules did not apply to them. This was an attitude that would be the undoing of many of them in the months to come.

In arranging the meeting, Graham let them know that two people from his company would be at the meeting – the two partners in the business. They would require safe parking for two vehicles – a motorbike for the junior partner, and a motorboat for himself, the senior partner. He explained that a boat was the most logical form of transport between his home and their offices close to the River Thames in Westminster, as well as being the most risk-averse method of travel during a pandemic.

He knew that this would present him as an eccentric figure, which he had no problem with. He actively cultivated the image. It would help avoid questions about how he came to be so well prepared for a situation when nobody else was. He also let Callum know that he would receive an official invite to a conference with a Health Minister – so he could probably present this to any policeman asking why he was hurrying down the A12 on his bike during lockdown.

Official invitation letters were sent to him and Callum, and a parking place for one motorbike and a secure mooring for a boat at Westminster Pier were both duly arranged.

They met a group of civil servants in a meeting overseen by a government minister. Terms were agreed upon, and contracts were signed within days. Before the final signatures were inked on, Graham was asked by the senior minister present, off the record of course, if there were going to be any last-minute requests before agreeing. He assumed this was the time when one might ask for a knighthood, membership of the MCC, or something similar. All that he insisted on was that the contracts would run for a minimum of five years and that all invoices were paid within seven days. When this last request elicited some expressions of difficulty, he reminded them that there was a desperate shortage of this equipment throughout Europe. He would have no problem finding alternative customers.

He wanted security of employment for his nephew and the complete elimination of any cash flow difficulties from his business - and was confident that he had secured both.

During the pandemic, Graham was glad he had decided to get involved in producing PPE. He had forgotten just how boring lockdown had been, once the novelty had worn off. Now he had something that not only helped him pass the time but was doing some good.

He helped Callum to ramp up production in every one of the companies, moving them from a 40-hour week to split shifts, twenty-four-hour, seven-day working. Together they overcame all the problems that were caused by this increased load. But they were good problems to have. Doing business was highly profitable, they were doing good, and creating well-paid employment for hundreds of people.

But as the pandemic continued, and 2020 moved into 2021, Graham realised that his time was running out and he needed to spend more of it putting his affairs in order. He had a few conversations with John, even passing a couple of weekends together. But neither of them heard anything from the prof.

So, in August 2022 it was with some surprise that he received a letter from Moorfields Eye Hospital confirming his routine follow-up appointment with Professor Karbajanovic. He telephoned the hospital and spoke to the administrative assistant whose name appeared on the form letter, to be told that it was a routine follow-up to his earlier procedure. It had been requested by the professor himself.

Having never had the original appointment that this letter purported to be the follow-up to, he reckoned that the prof must be shortcutting the system to meet him. There had to be a good reason, so, a few days later he attended at the time indicated and was shown into the professor's consulting room.

"Please accept my apologies for the subterfuge," the professor said before Graham could even say anything. "These days they are keeping such a close watch on me I am sure that if I telephoned you or contacted you in any way, they would intercept it and we would both face significant difficulties."

He was talking with such unnatural haste that Graham found it difficult to follow and impossible to interrupt. He focused on listening.

"They contacted me recently. It seems that the unfortunate results of my earlier experiment have reached new ears and have been interpreted differently. Certain parties have shown interest that by transmitting this signal we can create a situation where someone appears to die of natural causes some hours later.

I have been asked – and I am not sure that 'asked' is the correct word because I do not think that I would be permitted to refuse the request. I have been asked to conduct the experiment once more. This time the two people who will receive the signal will be selected by this government department – which is well aware of the consequences. And I have been reassured that the government department will assume all responsibility for the outcome and will deal with all the consequences.

They tell me only that I should set things up as soon as possible, and that some of the material that I transmit should be in the Russian language, but this will be provided by them."

He paused, and Graham noticed for the first time that the prof was showing concern and deep unhappiness in his expression.

"What have you told them?" he asked.

"I have said that it will take me a few weeks to make all the arrangements – after all, I had to close down everything before. They told me that if I need any assistance, I should let them know. They are confident that they have the resources to overcome any issues. They give me the impression that there is a new boss, and everyone is trying very hard to impress him – or should I say her?"

"Mister Henderson I can only spare you about fifteen minutes – or my assistant will suspect something – and by the way, my assistant was recently changed without my knowledge, so I am being very careful. But I thought you would want to know."

"So, you are going ahead with the experiment?"

"I appear to have little choice in the matter."

"And when do you expect it to take place?"

"It will genuinely take me three or four weeks to make all the preparations, then I will go ahead."

"Can I ask you to do one thing, please? Make sure that it takes place on October 7th."

The Prof looked puzzled for a few seconds and then appreciated why he was asking for this date.

"Ah, yes of course. This is your original date, isn't it? Yes, I will tell them that this is the date the experiment should occur. I am superstitious, so it must take place at exactly eleven o clock in the morning on that day – an exact anniversary of the previous occurrence. It will be conducted in honour and remembrance of those involved. That should work. I can be a crazy Professor sometimes." He finished with a weak smile, but Graham knew that he was a troubled man.

Graham thought for a few seconds and then said, "You understand that I must speak with John about this – I believe he should know – and he may help me to understand what is truly going on. Do you want me to pass the information back to you?"

The prof deliberated for a few seconds and then decided, "No – I believe it is better that I do not know. I will go ahead with the experiment and if I discover anything that helps explain your situation, I will try to contact you afterwards."

"Thank you for that, prof, but I fear that I might not be around to receive your contact," Graham replied, smiling at his 'gallows humour.'

The prof nodded in understanding, and they shook hands. The door was opened, and the prof changed his tone immediately, "Thank you for coming Mister Henderson, it's so good to see you are getting on so well – and sadly we will not need to meet again. Goodbye."

The assistant, for whose benefit the previous speech had surely been made, showed Graham out of the reception room.

Immediately after leaving the hospital, he called John from a nearby phone box. No doubt John was puzzled to hear him say how pleased he was to have received the invitation, that he'd be delighted to come down for the weekend and to expect him on Friday afternoon. John correctly guessed that Graham wanted to pass on some information but did not trust that the phone line was completely secure.

Sitting once more in his Welsh cottage, John was surprised to hear Graham's news about the prof. The fact that there were to be two attendees at the experiment – neither of whom would survive beyond twenty-four hours - and the vital snippet that the prof would need to transfer some material in Russian script gave John enough to build a likely explanation.

"I guess that somebody has thought about using the prof's little transmitter as a weapon. And they want the Russians to know it exists. They'll have found two known double agents," John began.

Seeing the puzzled look on Graham's face, he changed the direction of his discourse slightly and continued, "There's always a few double agents kicking around. We know who they are, but they don't know that we know. So, we feed them duff information and let them carry on. If there are two, then they won't know each other, and this will make a perfect communication method. They'll be fed enough information a few days before this secret experiment. Enough time for them to let their bosses know about it. Then they'll both mysteriously meet their end. Russia will know we've got something that can kill remotely and leave the impression of death by natural causes. All part of the new hard-line we've been taking with the Russian aggressor, ever since they invaded Ukraine."

He noticed that Graham was showing some distaste for the whole matter.

"It's never been the boy scouts, you know," John continued, and then after a brief pause, "I'll try to get confirmation from a few sources next week – but I doubt that I'm very wide of the mark. More importantly, what are you going to do?"

"I've been thinking about that. Seems to me that I've got no choice. I must be in that office one floor up from the experiment, looking out the window at eleven o clock in the morning on the day it takes place."

"Yes, I thought you would say something like that. I can't advise you in any way – nobody knows what the fuck this thing does or how it does it – but it just seems right for you to be there as you say."

And that was pretty much the end of it. They chatted some more, reminisced a little, ate a pleasant meal at the local pub, and drank a lot. They both knew this would probably be their farewell meeting. Graham asked John to call him in the morning after the experiment and to come to his house in the event of not receiving an answer. He told him there would be a sealed envelope with instructions on what to do if he was found to be dead, as he expected to be. He also reassured John that he did not want to take any precautions – he was sure they would be worthless, as they had been for Carol, and after all, having now lived a hundred and twenty years, he could not complain.

Graham found himself remembering the words of a book he had read a long time ago. In the Lord of the Rings, he remembered that Bilbo had lived beyond a hundred and thirty years and had complained of feeling stretched, 'like butter that has been spread over too much bread.' He was beginning to understand the feeling.

Now he needed to make his arrangements. The letter, addressed to John Bishop was prepared and left in a prominent position on his desk. His shares in Graycal were to be split between his family members, but in such proportions that Callum would end up with fifty-one percent and could run the business as he saw fit. The rest of his investments – of which little was left after the purchase of the PPE companies – and the proceeds of the sale of his house were to be split between the two charity foundations he had worked with - Al-Fayed and Paternosters. Graham requested a church service, a burial (not a cremation), and a headstone.

Now he needed to set up a meeting with the financial advice company, and this gave him a small problem. He couldn't tell them anything about his true situation. In the event of his continuing to live, his money was almost all tied up in Graycal – and in the unlikely (or not so unlikely) event of his death, his will was unambiguous. There was very little they could financially advise him on. He would have to invent a different scenario to justify and prolong a meeting with them.

The answer came in a flash. He could recreate the situation of his visit in his first life. He would be sixty-five years old, retiring with three different pension pots – one from his original employer, a self-funded private one from his time with the US company, and a third resulting from his employment with the company that had bought out his US-based employers. He would need these to be merged and managed to give him an income for the rest of his days. Add in a few shares and his state pension, and it would make a typical case for them to handle.

He could remember most of the details and the rest he could make up. He would not have any documentation with him – that could all be passed over subsequently at a meeting that would never happen.

He made his appointment with the financial advisers for 10:30 am, October 7th.

Chapter Ten – A Second Chance

Graham woke with a feeling of confusion. For several seconds he could not understand where he was. But looking around the room in the early morning light, he recognised his bedroom. That was when the uneasiness began. It was not his bedroom in his riverside property (complete with a swimming pool and bordered by the River Thames). It was his bedroom in the suburban Kent house where he had spent thirty years and, accompanied for almost all that time by his wife, had raised his family. It was a bedroom he had not seen for exactly fifty-two years.

He decided to try to mentally process a few things before leaving his bed.

Reaching out to his bedside table he found his smartphone and was quickly able to establish that this was October 8th, 2022, his seventieth birthday.

The only assumption that made any kind of sense was that he had returned to the original plane of time he had left over fifty years ago. He pulled back the bedclothes, stood, and looked at himself in the wardrobe mirror. There was more paunch there than there had been the previous day – after all, in this version of his life, he had not been so easily able to take a daily swim.

He sat back down on the bed and ran through matters in his head.

This must be a world where he was not a multi-millionaire part owner of a string of PPE businesses. He was a retired ex-technical software guy and part-time charity worker.

This was a world in which Peter Sutcliffe had murdered thirteen women in his killing spree, where ninety-seven people had died in the Hillsborough stadium, and where Princess Diana had met her end alongside Dodi Al-Fayed in a riverside road tunnel in Paris. He had never met Carol or John Bishop and had never communicated with Pat Threlfall.

He puzzled briefly over the matter of the prof. Had he and the prof met? After thinking it through for a few minutes, he decided that they could not have met. In both planes of time, the prof conducted his first set of experiments ten years ago, but he would not have been made aware of the impact it had had on Carol. And he also would have conducted his experiment yesterday, under duress. He would be well aware of the effect on the two government-selected human guinea pigs, but the impact on Graham would be unknown to him.

'It will be difficult getting in touch with him,' Graham thought, 'but I must try - both for his sake and mine.'

He thought briefly about how to go about doing this but realised there was no urgency. There were several things he needed to do first.

He took a quick shower, dressed, and went downstairs. He made himself a cup of coffee in the coffee machine and took it and a couple of slices of toast into the dining room and opened his laptop. A few minutes with Google and Wikipedia helped him confirm his earlier assumptions about the state of the world. 'Now, what to do?' he thought, and it suddenly hit him. He was no longer alone. It was his birthday and in a couple of hours, his family would begin to arrive – children, children-in-law, and grandchildren.

It would be a complete reversal of normality. To him, it was much longer since he had seen his grandchildren than it would seem to them. Normally they would think it had been a long time since the previous meeting and he would know it was but a few weeks. He even said it out loud, even though there was nobody there to hear him, "I'm going to see them for the first time in over fifty years!"

And then the tears came. Not being a man who cried easily he shocked himself and was inconsolable for several minutes before drying his eyes and putting his mind to the plans for the day ahead. He had to think for a few minutes to make sure he remembered his children's ages. And he had to find the list he had prepared shortly after his wife's death to double-check the ages of his grandchildren and to see if there were any birthdays soon.

Finally, he said aloud, "Pull yourself together, you silly old bugger" and got his act together.

He returned to the bedroom, dressed, checked the house to make sure it was tidy and tried to relax while waiting.

The day passed without any major incidents. He was hesitant several times when talking to his children and grandchildren, and caught sight of his children exchanging glances once or twice. Glances that he was not supposed to see and that signified they were worrying about his state of mind. But he didn't care – he had his family back together, and his hesitancy was to be expected – even though he could never begin to explain its cause to his children.

He was close to tears on a second occasion during the day when his children presented him with a birthday present that they had clubbed together to buy. Having inherited his father's collection of Giles annuals when he died a few years previously, he had every one that had been published from 1951 (when his parents had married) until the cartoonist died in 1995. His collection was missing the first five published books in the series, and that was what his children had bought him. He knew that these editions seldom came on the market and would have needed some diligent tracing as well as a not inconsiderable sum of money.

He was alright looking at them until he saw the cover of the 1946 edition, holding it for the first time since Carol gave it to him twenty-something years ago. Again, he was reminded that each jump brought pain as well as pleasure.

All in all, it was a thoroughly exhausting day. Grandchildren can be tiring at the best of times, and when added to his mental stress, he was quite pleased when they all left, and he could collapse into bed and enjoy a solid night's sleep.

Sunday was spent doing not very much – mostly catching up by reading the newspaper, the internet, and browsing TV stations – readjusting to the world he had just re-joined.

His mind was clear by Monday morning and his thoughts turned to the question of how to contact the prof. He drafted a letter:

Professor

On Friday, October 7th you conducted an experiment in remote communication from your hospital laboratory to a building on the opposite side of City Road.

I was in an office on the 6th floor of that building at the time of the experiment and was affected by it.

I also know that you conducted a similar experiment exactly ten years previously and I know what resulted from that experiment and why there was a ten-year gap between the experiments.

The reason I know this information will assist you in understanding the effects of your communication – it will also confirm some of your suspicions concerning the parallels between your method and the method used by entities that are often referred to as paranormal.

I would like to discuss this with you, and I fully understand the importance of secrecy. Might I suggest that you access my medical records and invite me for a follow-up appointment to ensure we meet in private? Alternatively, we could meet at your club in Tavistock Square or at any venue and in any other way you request.

I look forward to hearing from you.

He gave his full name and address details and sat back to think how he could get this to the prof. Then it came to him – the old salesman's trick of how to get a message to a prospective customer and bypass any 'gatekeeper' who might open the target's mail.

He found an envelope, put the letter into it, and hand-wrote Professor Karbajanovic's name on it. On Tuesday morning he took a taxi to Moorfields Hospital. Dressed in his smartest suit and wearing a white shirt and what looked like an old school tie, (he wanted to look like a senior doctor, and this was his best guess at the correct attire) he presented himself at the reception desk. He had taken a roundabout route between the main hospital entrance and the reception desk so it appeared to the receptionist that he might have been leaving the hospital rather than entering it.

"Could you pop this in the internal mail for Professor Karbajanovic, please? I forgot to drop it off at his office," he said with a smile and a show of confidence.

"Certainly," the busy receptionist replied.

He was confident that this would circumvent the Prof's security minders, and he looked forward to an interesting discussion with him soon. He doubted whether the information that he provided him with would change much about the prof's research, but he knew that contacting him was the right thing to do. If the letter was intercepted by one of the minders, then he might well be facing an even more interesting discussion with government officials.

'Whatever!' he thought.

Meanwhile, he would now reassess his situation and decide what to do with the rest of his life after its fifty-two-year interruption. He would need to become accustomed to being comfortably off instead of wealthy. He might well go on a cruise, or even two. He certainly would not go anywhere near a certain riverside property in Berkshire and would never visit Worthing. He would do his very best to stay close to his family. All in all, he planned to maximise this second chance at life.

He did not know whether to expect a call from the professor, a call or a visit from the professor's minders, or no contact at all. And he did not really care. He realised that for the first time in a very long while he did not know what was going to happen tomorrow, next week, or next year. This was how it was supposed to be. He had, at last, re-joined the rest of humanity and was very pleased to have done so. He might even be able to find a partner for the rest of his life. After all, he was now as ignorant about what would be happening on a day-to-day basis as everyone else on the planet was.

It was a good way to be.

Acknowledgements

Thanks first, as always to my wife for leaving me alone to get on with it. Then to my helpful proof-readers Cliff Antill, Barbara Primrose, and Alec Cameron; the Bee Primrose Company for help with publicity; the members of the Facebook Worthing Local History Group for the information on their fine town; Zaheer Kadri for his help on the Arabic language (and my daughter, Lorien Kelly, for putting us in touch with each other). Also, to my mother-in-law, Meg Avery, for her REAL ghost story and Katrina Paulson for an interesting article on time travel that helped me structure the story. Finally, and most importantly, to you, my reader – thanks for buying the book (and even more thanks if you post a review on the Amazon website).

As with my previous books, half the proceeds will go to homeless charities – there's more information on these over the page and on my author page on Amazon:

https://www.amazon.co.uk/Ian-Cummins/e/B08LSRKY1Z

You can read more of my thoughts on my blog:

https://iancumminsauthor.wordpress.com/updates/

Also, reach me on:

Twitter @Accidental_Ian

Other books by Ian Cummins:

An Accidental Salesman: Stories from 40 years in International IT Sales

There was the time my car ran into a river in rural Suffolk; the time I had the FA Cup in my possession for a whole day; or when I was billeted to stay with a dead woman in Germany; and, of course, the incident with the flight attendant, the elderly hippy, and the gallon of olive oil on the flight from Athens. There's also my thoughts on how Brits can best deal with Americans, and how to sell successfully to customers who don't have English as a first language.

But it's mostly about the stories.

The Wrong Briefcase

What would you do if you suddenly found a large amount of money?

Mark Reynolds is facing the uncomfortable changes of middle-age when he mistakenly picks up a briefcase containing a very large amount of cash. Unable to trace its owner, and having received no contact, he decides to keep the vast sum, and discretely invest it - a decision which leads him into an unfamiliar world populated by interesting people.

Printed in Great Britain
by Amazon

33374511R00130